THE BRITLINGS
BOOK I

WILDCAT GLEN

THE BRITLINGS
BOOK I

WILDCAT GLEN

SUSAN PALMER-JONES

Printed and bound by CPI Group (UK) Ltd, Croydon, CR0 4YY

Grateful thanks to:

Marion Gardner for re-awakening my creativity with her Journey Therapy;

Sarah Morris for her years of support and enthusiasm while I wrote *The Britlings* saga;

Muriel Young and other members of the St Ninian's book group, for their encouragement and helpful criticism;

Carol Godridge and the late Harlee Watson for enjoying *Wildcat Glen* so much;

Alistair Moffat for his help and praise;

last but not least, the historical re-enactors who apply real-life tests to the statements of dead politicians and have discovered, for example, that woad (while great for dyeing wool) does not work as either a body-paint or a tattoo ink! Another myth exploded.

Translated names

I have translated the names of some of the people and places:

Land of Plenty = *Hibernia* (Ireland)
Hunters = *Selgovae* (Dumfriesshire & Kirkcudbrightshire)
Livelies = *Novantae* (Wigtownshire)
Honey Isle = Anglesey
White Island = Mainland Britain
Queen Victory = Boudicca
Boar Islands = Orkneys
Queen Trimfilly = Cartimandua, Queen of the Brigantes
Hightops = *Brigantes* (West Yorkshire & Lancashire)
Shapers = East Yorkshire
Deerings = Cumbria
Sky's-Eyes = *Silures* (South Wales)
Seagod's Island = Isle of Man

PREFACE

Britlings

'Britlings' is my translation of the word 'Brittunculi,' a racial put-down used by Roman soldiers based in northern Britain.

Timeframe

The story starts in the winter of 69 CE – by our calendar, which was not introduced until 1532. The Romans had their own dating system. I had to invent a way for my characters to measure time.

In 1130 BC or thereabouts, a volcano in Iceland erupted, sending a cloud of poisonous gas and acid rain over Scotland. People and animals died, crops were poisoned. A cloud of volcanic dust lay between Scotland and the sun for several years, causing a drop in temperature that rendered acres of farmland unusable. An event of this magnitude would have entered the historical legends of an oral culture. I've called it 'The Great Darkness'.

Lullaby

My baby's coat is speckled, speckled,
It was made from the pelts of martens.
When your father went out to hunt –
A spear on his shoulder, a club in his hand –
 He called on his lively dogs,
'Take, take! Fetch, fetch!'
When your father went to the mountains
He would bring back a roebuck, a boar, a stag,
A speckled grouse from the mountain,
And a fish from the falls.
At whatever your father aimed his spear -
Be it a boar, a wild cat, or a fox –
 None would escape but that had strong wings.

(Excerpt from an ancient Welsh poem)

Chapter titles

Chapter 1. The journey begins

It was one of those rare fine days at the beginning of winter, clear and sunny with a hint of frost, when Lady Brightleaves left her husband.

She did not discuss it with him beforehand. She had waited for her chance and now it had come. He was going to visit the king. In summer he would have gone by sea, the quickest way to travel. At this time of year the sea would be too dangerous. He took the slower route, overland.

She stood at the door of the house waving farewell as he rode away. Then she ran to supervise her packing, which must be finished before low tide. She was going to take the short cut across the bay.

She could not travel with a cart whose wheels might sink into the mud. She was using pack-horses. She had lain awake at night beside her husband, calculating how many horses to take. Two to pull her little chariot – because she was keeping *that*! Five to carry her travelling companions. One to carry the shields and the linen. One to carry the swords, the spearheads, and the bags of salt. One to carry the hides, the goblets, and her quern – a wedding present from her mother; it had come all the way from Quernstone Hill by the Swan River in the Land of Plenty and she was not going to leave it for a second wife to use; nor would she leave behind the collection of dyed wools she had built up over the years. One to carry her clothes and those of her travelling companions. One to carry the cowherd; and four to carry hay to feed the horses on the way.

Sixteen horses altogether.

What worried Brightleaves was not whether they would make it, across the estuary, along the coast, over the border, through the hills, across the marshes – a journey of nearly four days. What worried her was the social awkwardness of arriving at the home of a person whom one had met perhaps once or twice and asking for hospitality – which would never be refused – when one was travelling with sixteen horses.

Not to mention the herd of cattle.

While her packing was being done, Brightleaves went to leave a message for her husband, to show him that she was divorcing him. She took her sewing shears and began cutting their bedspread in half. Snip snip went the iron shears through the woven wool of the bedspread. It was double-layered, like a winter cloak, the weave tight and tough to cut. Brightleaves' hand began to ache. But she persisted.

What could she say if any of her hostesses asked the reason for her journey?

She could lie. She could say, 'I'm taking all these things as offerings to the High Priestess in Wildcat Glen.'

And her hostess would say, 'The High Priestess must have done you a remarkable service!'

And Brightleaves would say, 'She has.'

That was true. The first time Brightleaves had done this journey was in the summer, when travelling was easy. She had not taken a herd of cattle and a line of pack horses with her. She had travelled light, with only two warriors as bodyguards and a single slavegirl as her maid and hairdresser. So she had travelled fast. That journey had taken less than three days. She had brought gold armbands

2

to offer to the High Priestess. And she had gone to ask a single question:

Why can't I have children?

When she had asked her friends this, they just looked pitying or said things like, Well, there's still time, don't give up hope! She could almost hear them thinking: the poor girl is barren.

What they didn't know, what only her local healer knew, was that Brightleaves already had a child. Years ago, before she was married. A baby boy. Her married sister had adopted him, but he had died. She still grieved for him.

Had she become barren since? Was the Goddess punishing her?

Her healer, the priestess Skylark, had suggested various herbs and combinations of herbs, but they hadn't worked. Eventually Skylark said, 'Perhaps you should go to the land of the Hunters and see the High Priestess.'

The High Priestess turned out to be a very down-to-earth woman who looked at Brightleaves as if she was looking through her and said,

'If you want another child, you will have to get yourself another husband.'

All that way, and the gold bangles, and the answer was so simple!

That night, in honour of her visit, the chief of Wildcat Glen held a feast. His name was Chief Hardy and his young wife had died in childbirth.

Hardy was not as dynamic as Brightleaves' husband, Sparky. But he was solid. There was something immensely reassuring about him. They sat next to each other beside the fire under the stars. There were plenty of other people there; the whole glen was gathered around the fire for the

3

feast. Yet for a moment Hardy and Brightleaves saw only each other.

'More mead?' he asked her.

The strength of her sudden desire for him made Brightleaves gasp.

'Yes please.'

He held up a finger and a slave came with a jug of mead, to refill her cup.

They talked while the stars moved across the night sky. They didn't talk only to each other, of course; there were many guests at the feast. Brightleaves kept telling herself that her feeling had been a passing fancy, meant nothing, she had imagined it. But every time he looked her straight in the eyes, it rose within her again. The guests left, in pairs or groups, until there were only Hardy and Brightleaves sitting by the fire, with her bodyguards and his warriors watching them from a respectful distance, and the dogs snoozing with their noses on their paws.

When winter came, Brightleaves had been married to Sparky Roughrock Lively for seven years and therefore was allowed, by law, to leave him and take her share of their wealth with her.

Yet the law was not as certain as it had been when she was younger. The druids made the laws, and made sure they were obeyed; but the druids lost more than their lives after the Romans invaded their sacred Honey Isle. They lost their credibility. They were not all killed; some kings and chiefs still had their own resident druid as counsellor and judge. On Honey Isle, however, was the druid college, with all its teachers – and its students too, many of them the sons of chiefs and kings. So in attacking the druids, the Romans killed several princes, which did not endear them to the peoples of White Island. Many White Islanders rejoiced in the triumphs of Queen Victory; her massacres of the Romans were sung by bards as far north as the Boar Islands.

After the slaying of the druid teachers and their students, druids in countries occupied by the Romans fled to Brightleaves' homeland, the Land of Plenty. In the north of White Island, in countries the Romans had not invaded, the resident druids stayed put. But people began to ask, If the druids are such powerful magicians, how did they let Honey Isle be invaded? How did they let themselves be killed?

A druid's word now carried less weight than it used to. And when the older druids began to die, there were few young ones to replace them. Kings and chiefs were beginning to make their own laws.

That was one reason Brightleaves did not tell Sparky she was leaving. He might turn round and say, 'Never mind the druids, I'll find out if the king thinks you're allowed to divorce me!' Also, Sparky would make a fuss. He would sulk, complain, fume, argue. He would interfere with the packing, scattering the contents of barrels and panniers on the ground. He would be a nuisance.

She had waited until a convenient royal summons called him away.

Now, with a triumphant final snip, she cut through the end of the bedspread. She bundled up the half from her side of the bed, quietly said a regretful farewell to the other half, then carried her half outside and ordered it to be used for wrapping her quern.

She wished she could have taken her mead with her. But she would have needed so many horses to carry it all. The bags of salt were a good substitute – highly valued inland, while the coast-dwellers thought nothing of salt because they could collect all their cooking water from the sea.

The pack-horses were loaded, the riding horses saddled and bridled, her own white horses harnessed to her chariot. The tide was nearly out. Brightleaves climbed into her chariot, sat down, took one last look around the place she had called home for the last seven years, then clicked her tongue and shook the reins.

The procession set off. The herd of black cattle went first, followed by the cowherd; their awareness of all the horses and people behind them would keep the cattle trotting along. After the cowherd, at a little distance from him to mark their superiority, came two handsome young black-haired warriors riding black horses. Their red and yellow cloaks were thrown back over their shoulders, even on this cold day, to show off the finely wrought bracelets and gleaming armbands on their muscular arms. Next came Lady Brightleaves, wearing an otter-fur cloak whose hood fell back to reveal her hair, red as the gean leaves in autumn for which her mother had named her. She drove a red and yellow chariot drawn by two white horses. Behind her rode two dark-haired girls in pink cloaks, each with a line of four pack-horses tied to her saddle. Last in the procession was a mature blond warrior wearing a green cloak and riding a chestnut stallion.

The horses held their heads proudly and their harness-pieces gleamed, glinted and jingled. The gold torc around Brightleaves' neck shone like woven sunlight. The warriors' fiercely polished spearheads and shield-bosses reflected the sun in points of light that danced over rocks and tree trunks as they rode past.

After they had left the small, sheltered bay guarded by Chief Roughrock's fort, they rode along the coast for a while. On their left were gently rolling fields, green with patches of brown leaves lying between the tufts the sheep were munching, and woodlands where some of the trees were bare while others still wore skeins of flame-coloured leaves. On their right, the wet sand gleamed in the bay. The hills across the estuary were dark shapes against the eastern sky. Brightleaves felt a thrill of excitement. That was where they were going!

They rode down to the beach and started out over the mud towards the far side of the estuary. Some of the travellers began to feel nervous. The cow-herd, Fadge, did not often ride. He preferred to walk while he was herding cattle and, frankly, he thought that cattle which had been running ahead of horses for five days would not give milk or be fit to eat. But her ladyship would not let him walk. The horse he was riding could tell he was nervous and acted accordingly, tossing its head, snorting, shrugging its shoulders as if trying to shrug him off. He expected that at any moment, as they crossed the estuary, one of the cows would bolt sideways, either inland or out towards the retreating tide, then other cows would follow, there would be cows running all over the place – and it would all be her ladyship's fault for making him ride this stupid horse.

The warriors, Hooky and Badger, were not nervous, of course. But they felt the sense of awe that any right-minded person would feel in one of the in-between places where two worlds met – in this case the world of the earth goddess and the world of the sea god – and met in such a way that you were not quite certain which was which. Sometimes, as they rode, their reflections rode beside them on the water;

then these images were gone and there was nothing beside them but mud or wet sand; then their reflections were back again. The estuary was not exactly the same depth all the way across. They knew that. But this explanation did not make the experience any less magical. It was as if the sea god and the earth goddess were claiming them in turn – 'They're mine!' 'No, they're mine!' or perhaps playing with them, tossing them to and fro, 'You have them!' 'No, they're yours!'

Brightleaves, at the core of the group, was longing to get to the other side and continue her journey. Sitting in her chariot, she could feel every part of it through her body: the movements of the axle; the wheels rolling over sand or mud. When the wheels seemed to hesitate for a moment she clicked her tongue, her gallant white ponies pulled a little harder, and the chariot rolled on. It was not a heavy chariot, more like a basket on wheels.

The pink-cloaked girls, Willow and Cherry, were riding in that blank but vaguely hopeful frame of mind that arises after some turbulence has forever altered your life-course but then things turn out to be not as bad as you expected and might still get better. They were the daughters of a chief and had planned to grow up and marry chiefs as their mother had done. Then there was a civil war in their country. Their father was killed in battle. They were captured, sold as slaves, and bought by Chief Sparky as a present for his wife, along with the pretty little chariot that used to belong to their mother. It still gave them pangs of mother-loss and home-sickness to see Lady Brightleaves driving it.

The chariot was quite unsuitable for this hilly landscape, of course. Their home country was flat for miles and miles;

their people held chariot races there. But they would never tell Lady Brightleaves that. She was kind to them, so being a slave was not as bad as they had expected. Other slaves in their cage at the market had told them, 'It depends entirely on your owner, what sort of life you lead.' Their work was not hard. They served drinks at feasts. They looked after Lady Brightleaves' clothes, fetched her washing water, arranged her hair. They helped to make soap with her, just as they had helped their mother; and sometimes they entertained her with songs and music, for they were both talented musicians. When she heard that they used to play for their parents at home, she bought them musical instruments; a lyre, a deer-horn pipe and a tambourine. They might play these later in the journey, perhaps, to entertain the travellers.

For now they were in charge of the pack-horses. As they rode across the bay they had to concentrate on all these horses, which carried her ladyship's wealth. Sometimes a horse stumbled and a girl squealed.

Willow, the older of the two sisters, looked about at the beauty of the landscape in the winter light: the mud gleaming silver, the blue hills away to the south. On the shore they had left, there was a large tribe of black-and-white geese feeding in the grass, chattering between mouthfuls. Something startled them and they rose up, yapping and swirling, to settle down again further along the coast.

Bringing up the rear of the procession was the blond warrior, whose name was Stern. He had travelled with Lady Brightleaves from her parents' house in the Land of Plenty when she first married, and he was devoted to her. He had vowed never to leave her. This was a promise made to a dying comrade long ago.

Such was the group of people and animals crossing the estuary that day.

They were halfway across when there was a distant purring sound and a slim line of white foam started moving up the estuary.

'Hurry!' Brightleaves shouted.

It was a known fact that the tide came in faster than a galloping horse. They urged their horses to a gallop. 'You two ride either side of the cows to stop them veering off!' Brightleaves ordered the two young warriors, while Stern rode forward unbidden to help Fadge whose horse, bored with his indecisive riding, had finally shrugged him off. He was floundering in the water and mud, trying to stand up.

The purr of the tide had become a roar, the line of white foam thicker and more threatening. Willow hesitated for a moment, watching it. She had seen the tide rush up the estuary often enough since she'd been living here but she had never stood directly in its path before.

Her pack-horses were not in the mood for poetic rapture. They turned and fled, pulling Willow's horse with them – not across the bay but straight up it, away from the threatening tide.

'Willow!' Cherry yelled.

Brightleaves sent the warrior Hooky to chase the fleeing pack-horses. Some of the cows veered off, running towards the incoming tide, then changed their minds and ran back again; the rest of the herd saw them coming and started to run away from them.

Only a few miles out of Roughrocks, and Brightleaves' well-organized procession had collapsed into chaos!

Ignoring the roar of the inrushing tide, she rode her little chariot to and fro behind the cattle until they were once again moving as a single unit. Fadge, now on foot – his wish granted just when he didn't want it! – walked behind them, as fast as he could, his feet slipping on the mud or sinking into it. Stern rode up to him and hoisted him on to his chestnut horse; there was no room for him on the saddle, so he sat awkwardly on the horse's rump, clinging to Stern's waist and vowing to the gods that if he survived this, he would make all kinds of offerings to them and would never, never, never ride a horse again. Hooky managed to catch Willow's pack-horses and led them to the shore, a firm shingled beach.

'Willow, what were you thinking?' Cherry chided her sister as they sat on their horses watching the cattle come ashore. 'Lady Brightleaves is very kind to us but she's not our mother, she's our owner! Mother would forgive you for letting those horses get out of control – but Lady Brightleaves could sell you!'

Brightleaves drove her chariot up on to the shingle, jumped out, stroked her horses and praised them, then turned and beckoned Fadge. He ran across the shingle and stood before her, head bowed.

'Did we lose any cows, Fadge?'

'One, milady.'

'It wasn't your fault.'

As soon as he heard this, Fadge began to praise the qualities of that cow: a beautiful animal, a good milker, a sad loss to the herd.

'Well, we shall just have to regard it as a sacrifice to the gods for our journey,' said Brightleaves. 'Thank you, Fadge.' She looked at Willow and beckoned. 'Come here!'

Willow began to swing a leg over her horse, ready to

dismount, but Lady Brightleaves called to her,

'No, stay on your horse.'

Willow rode across the shingle to Lady Brightleaves.

'You did not follow my instructions,' said Brightleaves. 'You did not focus on what I told you to do.'

'I'm sorry, my lady, it was just so amazing, I–'

'Yes, yes, you wanted to look at it in a bardic way and never mind the horses! Being bardic is all very well in your leisure time. I do give you leisure time, don't I?'

Willow sat with her head hanging.

'Well, don't I?' said Brightleaves.

'Yes, my lady.'

'Perhaps that will change in future,' said Brightleaves. 'Perhaps I shouldn't have encouraged the bardic side of your nature. Your musings have cost me a cow – a beautiful animal, a good milker, a sad loss to the herd.'

Fadge, standing nearby, looked smug.

'I am sorry, milady!' said Willow.

'No you're not. You're just frightened in case I'm going to punish you. Well, let me set your mind at rest. I don't want you to be in any doubt. I am going to punish you. Then you will be genuinely sorry. Hooky, bring Willow's pack-horses, please.'

Hooky rode across the shingle leading Willow's four pack-horses. Brightleaves held out her hand for the leading-rope.

'It's very muddy, my lady,' said Hooky as he held it towards her.

'Yes, it was in the care of a very sloppy maidservant,' said Brightleaves. She took the muddy rope-end.

'Take this,' she said. 'I won't tie it around your wrist because that might pull you off your horse. You'll have to keep hold of it. For the rest of the journey. And that means no day-dreaming. You'll have to manage your own mount with your right hand and these four horses with your left.'

Willow held out her hand and Brightleaves slapped the muddy rope-end into her palm.

'Hold tight now!' she said.

Willow's fingers closed around the rope. Grey mud squidged between them.

Brightleaves crouched to wash her muddy hand in a pool. 'By losing that cow,' she said as she stood up, 'you have lost one-third of your own worth. Think about that while we ride to our next destination.'

But Willow was wondering when she would be able to wash the mud off her own hand.

'Think of it as like a mud-pack,' whispered Cherry.

The tide was now lapping at the edge of the shingle. The procession reformed and set off along a track that ran eastwards along the coast. Fadge herded the cattle on foot until they were off the shingle and on the track. He was just starting to stroll along behind them, in his normal way except that he was leading a horse by its rein, when Lady Brightleaves called, 'Fadge! Get on your horse!'

'I can't, milady. I made a vow to the gods, when the tide was coming in, that if I survived, I would never ride a horse again!'

'Tell the gods that what you meant was, if you survive this entire journey. The journey is not over yet – and you're not walking while my chariot's behind you.'

Fadge looked around, up at the sky, out at the sea, over at the hills, in any direction where a god might be found, and shrugged as if to say, what's a man to do? Then he climbed up on to his horse's back.

The horse slumped and hung its head.

'You and me both, mate,' Fadge told it quietly.

The procession moved on, with the hills on one side and the sea on the other. This was not unfamiliar territory. The warriors had travelled along this track several times and although Fadge and the slavegirls had not been here before, they had seen these hills from a distance. It was well known, however, that on these hills there were all kinds of sacred places, cairns and stone monuments built before time began. So they travelled quietly, with respect, not wishing to offend any ancient gods.

* * *

Towards sunset, which came earlier every day now, they left the main track and walked up a steep hill. Brightleaves got out of her chariot and walked beside it, to make it easier for her horses. All the riders walked. The cows were left at the bottom of the hill, beside a stream, in the care of Fadge.

There was a warrior on guard outside the house.

'Please tell Lady Steephill that Lady Roughrock is here,' Stern told him.

The warrior knocked on the door. A slavegirl came out, was given the message, went inside.

Lady Pearlywaves Steephill came out to greet Brightleaves. She was a plump, lively, woman with green eyes and pale wavy hair.

'My dear,' she said, hugging Brightleaves, 'how wonderful to see you! Fearless has gone to see the king – goodness knows why the king has to call a meeting at this time of year!'

'I hope you don't mind, I have rather a lot of horses with

me,' said Brightleaves. 'But we have brought hay for them.'

Pearlywaves stood back and looked at the pack-horses, and the maids and the warriors.

'You're not exactly travelling light, are you? Where are you off to?'

'There's a herd of cattle at the bottom of the hill, too. By that stream. Will it be all right to leave them there or would you rather I had them moved somewhere else?'

'Oh, leave them, leave them! Girls, you come into the house with us. Men, Quickspear will take you to the warriors' house, and if you want to do some fighting practice, he can show you where.' Pearlywaves said this to all visiting warriors. So near to sunset, however, the warriors were unlikely to want to do anything except sit and drink beer. 'Thistledown!' The slavegirl re-appeared. 'Get a man or boy to unload these horses and take them to the guest-stables, then come back to serve our drinks.'

She led Brightleaves towards the house.

'I need to go to the latrine first,' said Brightleaves.

As at most houses, the latrine was round at the back, with a rain-butt outside it for washing one's hands, and a bucket of moss inside.

Moss! thought Brightleaves. She knew where all the moss was near Roughrock, knew the best places to gather it, had known for years. Now she was going to a new home and would have to find out where the best moss-places were, all over again.

'Tell me what's going on!' Pearlywaves demanded when Brightleaves had come into the house and the two women were sitting by the fire drinking mead.

At the rain-butt outside the women's house, Cherry was wiping the dried mud off Willow's palm, which had been chafed by the harsh rope.

'I used to think she was really nice!' said Willow in the quivering tones of someone about to burst into tears.

'You've never killed one of her cows before,' said Cherry.

'I didn't kill it!'

'It was your pack-horses running away that panicked the cattle. So your day-dreaming killed it.'

Willow began to cry.

'That's right, cry. Just like you always do. You're pathetic. I wish we'd been sold into different households.'

Cherry walked away. Willow put her hands over her eyes and sobbed.

At home, she would have flung herself down weeping – on her bed, on a bale of straw, on the grass – and someone would have found her and comforted her, her mother or her father. It's all right, Cherry can be a bit sharp sometimes but she loves you really.

But home was gone. Her mother and father were gone. They would never comfort her again. She carried on crying.

Someone tapped her on the shoulder and a boy's voice said, 'Scuse me!'

She opened her eyes. A slave-boy stood before her.

'We're unloading the horses. We need to know which bags are to go in the house and which in the store.'

'Ask my sister,' said Willow. 'She's the one who's good at organizing things.'

She ran down the hill. By the time she reached the stream where the cows were grazing, she felt better. She knelt on the bank and scooped up water to wash her face.

When she lifted her dripping, refreshed face and looked around, she saw Fadge sitting with his back against a tree, his cloak wrapped around him.

'Are you going to stay here all night?' she asked him, wondering if Lady Brightleaves had ordered him to do so.

'No,' said Fadge. 'I was waiting in case someone sent word that I had to move the cattle. When you came down the hill, I thought you might have a message.'

Willow remembered the conversation between their hostess and Lady Brightleaves.

'Lady Steephill says it's all right to leave the cows here.'

'I suppose they'll be safe enough,' said Fadge. 'But I'd rather sleep nearer to them than away on the hill-top. There might be wolves, this time of year.'

'But you can't sleep out in winter! Her ladyship can't expect that!'

'Oh no, she doesn't expect it. It's just for my own peace of mind. There's a house along there.' He pointed downstream. 'I'm going to ask them if I can stay the night. Near enough to the cattle but in the warm.' He ran off.

Willow waited. Before today, she would have chosen the company of Lady Brightleaves over that of a cowherd. Now it was the other way round.

He came back, smiling. Hospitality had been offered, and the family who lived in that house had invited him to share their meal.

'I'll tell her ladyship,' said Willow.

'Thanks!'

Fadge went back to his tree and sat down to watch his grazing cattle, gilded by the low winter light. Willow walked back up the hill.

In the stables, Cherry supervised the unloading of the pack-horses. She made sure everything was handled carefully and stacked in piles that would be easy to repack tomorrow. She picked up the cloth bag containing things that would be needed overnight or next morning and carried it into the house. The light coming in through the open door was pink now, and a slavegirl was setting rushlights into their metal holders here and there. Cherry was going to ask their hostess where Lady Brightleaves would be sleeping; but seeing the two women sitting talking by the fire and sipping their mead, she remembered that she was a slave – easy to forget in a strange house – so she asked the girl with the rushlights.

'She'll be in that one,' said the girl, pointing a lighted rush at one of the bedspaces. 'I've already put a light in there.'

The girl lit a new rushlight from the lighted one, which she then stuck into a holder on the wall. She carried her bunch of rushlights to the next pool of shadow. With her went the smell of burning mutton fat – the best fat for rushlights.

'Thank you,' said Cherry. 'What's your name?'

'Reed,' said the girl. She shrugged. 'They had to call me something, I s'pose!'

This remark implied a whole life story, which Cherry felt unable to cope with. Heart-to-heart talks were more Willow's kind of thing.

'I'm Cherry.'

'Nice to meet you. I've got to get on now – we'll chat later.'

All evening, now, until everyone went to bed, someone would have to go round the house as the rushlights burned down, pulling them up another inch or two out of their holders, and then replacing them when they were used up. It was a task impossible to combine with weaving or spinning, because you got grease all over your fingers.

Willow arrived at the door in the last pink rays of sunset, to find the dim interior of the house dotted with rushlights like little stars, each creating a pool of whiteness around it. The fire glowed red in the centre. Lady Brightleaves and Lady Steephill were sitting beside the fire, their features and the folds of their dresses highlit by the flames, the torcs around their necks gleaming gold. One of the hounds lying at Lady Steephill's feet raised its head and growled as she came in; Lady Steephill silenced it with a word of command.

Willow stood at the edge of the circle of firelight.

'Yes, Willow, what is it?' Lady Brightleaves asked.

'I've seen Fadge, my lady, and he's going to stay in a house at the bottom of the hill, to be near the cows.'

'Thank you for letting me know.'

'What about his meal?' Lady Steephill asked.

'He's going to share their meal, my lady.'

'That's kind of them,' said Lady Steephill. 'I'll make sure they get some food from our store.'

Willow hovered, knowing she should fade into the background, but not knowing where to go. Lady Brightleaves said,

'I think you'll find Cherry preparing my bedspace, over there.'

She gestured toward the other side of the house and smiled at Willow. She had a wonderful smile. You could forgive someone almost anything if they smiled at you like that.

Willow found the bedspace and Cherry in it, working by rushlight, laying out the beads and ribbons Lady Brightleaves might want to wear in her hair in the morning. The cloth bag lay on the bed. Willow felt inside it, to find out if there was anything left for her to do, and pulled out a linen night-tunic, soft with many washings. She held it up, trying to shake out the creases of the journey, then spread it flat on the bed. The sisters looked at each other.

As chief's daughters, they had worn linen night-tunics. Now they slept in the same tunics that they wore under their dresses all day. They were getting used to it; but every time they laid out Lady Brightleaves' night-tunic, they remembered the comfort of the lives that had been taken from them.

'So, why has the King summoned all the chiefs, at this time of year?' Brightleaves asked Pearlywaves. 'Sparky couldn't tell me.'

'Ah, well,' said Pearlywaves, 'Fearless thinks it's something to do with Queen Trimfilly!'

The girls in the bedspace stood still, listening. Queen Trimfilly had been their queen, ruling a union of three countries, of which theirs was one. It was in the war between Queen Trimfilly and her ex-husband that they had been captured and sold.

'You see, when she was in charge,' Pearlywaves continued, 'her country acted as a sort of barrier between them and us. Fearless explained it to me. There was Trimfilly and her Hightops – and the Shapers in the east, and the Deerings in the west, both allied to the Hightops – so their lands stretched all the way across the middle of White Island, between us and the lands to the south. The Romans saw them as a finishing point. The Hightops were friendly to the Romans, so the Romans didn't need to go any further. The Hightops' country was a sort of convenient edge to their empire. But that's changed now.'

'Has it? Why?'

'Because Trimfilly's ex-husband, Champion, rebelled against her and won. And he doesn't like the Romans!'

'So?'

'When people don't like the Romans, the Romans invade them. So the Romans will invade the Hightops' country, and Champion will fight them, and the Romans will probably win, because they usually do – and then what's to stop them coming here? You know how they like conquering people! They can't seem to help it.'

'So the King is trying to make a plan?'

'Yes. That's why he's summoned all the chiefs. The Romans won't come until the spring, but it's as well to be prepared.'

'All this because Queen Trimfilly divorced her husband!'

'Ex-husbands can be dangerous people, Brightleaves!'

The listening girls thought about their uncle, who was supposed to protect them but instead had allowed them to be captured while he took over their parents' home. They hoped the Romans would kill him. Or better still, enslave him.

In the pale white light from the burning rush, they glanced at each other, sensing that they were both thinking the same thing. That happened sometimes.

The women by the fire had stopped talking. Pearlywaves was making ear-flapping signals to Brightleaves, who nodded.

'Girls!' she called.

Willow and Cherry came out of the bedspace.

'You can go now,' they were told.

As they left the house, they heard Lady Steephill saying, 'We can't have a proper feast, of course, without the chief here, but the warriors will eat with us.'

So all the handsome young men would be eating with the two married women, and Willow and Cherry would be eating with the female slaves. It was so unfair!

It may not have been a feast, but it was a fine meal of roast goose, or rather roast geese, for it took several of the birds to feed the household. They were cooked over the fire in the women's house, which was extra hot as a result, lovely and cosy on a winter evening, so that nobody minded the roasting smells.

The food was carried out, first to the main house, then to the men-servants' house, on trays woven from the local rushes. Each diner was given a slice of bread to serve as a platter. The diners carved hunks of meat off the goose with the little knives they carried at their belts. The scent of the roast meat rose towards the rafters like an offering to the gods.

Then a message came from the main house that perhaps Willow and Cherry would like to entertain the diners. They ran to the store to unpack their instruments. After the goose, they went into the main house to play and sing for Lady Steephill, her warriors and her guests. Cherry blew on her deerbone pipe while Willow played her lyre, now plucking the strings, now stopping them. When they sang, Cherry exchanged her pipe for a goatskin tambourine with bronze rattles, so that she could sing too.

The warriors would have enjoyed any songs these pretty girls sang; but to please their audience, the singers chose old favourites. As they had been travelling for most of the day, journeys were on their mind, and they worked their way through several popular wayfaring ditties including 'It's a long way to Rayfort market', 'My old da said follow the cart', and one beginning 'Is this the way to…?' that could be applied to any destination, provided the singer could think of suitable rhymes for the place-name. The warriors joined in, adding their deep male voices to the songs and slapping their thighs in rhythm.

'Thankyou, Willow and Cherry,' said their hostess as a signal that the performance was over.

They left the house, to applause from the warriors.

'Perhaps our music will pull us out of slavery,' said Willow as they went back to the women's house.

'D'you think so?' said Cherry. 'Could it? I'm sure that when our mother and father taught us to play, they never imagined us becoming bards!'

Everyone was full of goose, but Lady Steephill handed round sweets, little squares of crab-apple cheese made with honey. Most of the warrior didn't want these; the mead had all the sweetness they required.

'Couldn't those girls come in and play for us again?' one of the warriors asked another, in a murmer loud enough for Lady Steephill to hear. Now they would start to get drunk, if she let them, and there would be drunken warriors lying on the floor of the house all night.

'Thank you for your company, gentlemen,' she said. 'I'd like you to leave us now and go back to your own house.'

They could get as drunk as they liked there. They stood up, thanking her for the meal, and went out into the starlight, some of them staggering slightly.

'Why can't we get those girls to come and sing to us?' one warrior demanded loudly as they made their way to their house.

'They're probably asleep now,' said another.

'Nice girls. Wake them up!'

'No, leave it, come on, this way.'

In the women's house, Willow and Cherry lay wrapped in their cloaks, listening, flattered but glad they had not gone back.

Brightleaves was discussing her route with Pearlywaves.

'I'm planning to stay in the hostel near Rushglen Ford tomorrow night.'

'You need to be careful there. The hosteller tends to overcharge; and I've heard that if you take food for your horses with you – as you are doing – he gets his boys to steal it and feeds your horses with mouldy rubbish. He keeps the good hay to sell. So you'll need to have someone guarding your horses all night.'

'Oh dear!'

'You'd be better off staying with a chief.'

'But I don't want to impose on people. I'll be staying with chiefs all the rest of the journey! I thought the hostel would be my one opportunity not to bother people!'

'Don't talk of "bothering", Brightleaves! Why d'you think we have this law of hospitality? People love having guests because it means meeting new people, hearing new stories. Guests are entertaining! So people are delighted to welcome you.'

'Me, perhaps – but all these horses and a herd of cattle too? At this time of year, when the grass is poor enough for people's own animals?'

'Look at it this way: if you stay the night with Chief Rushglen, that will be your last night in the land of the Livelies. The day after, you'll be crossing into the land of the Hunters and your horses and cattle will eat Hunter grass after that. So they'll only be eating Lively grass for one more night.'

'But Chief Rushglen will have gone to the King's

meeting, won't he?'

'No, he's a border guard. He has to stay at Rushglen all the time. And the hosteller has to tell him who spends the night at the hostel, too.'

'Are the Hunters especially keen on raiding, then?'

'No more so than the Livelies. The Hunters have two forts on their side of the ford, you know – which suggests that, historically, we're more prone to raiding than they are!'

Brightleaves was persuaded. The next morning, she spent some time with Willow and Cherry, trying to decide what colour ribbons and beads to wear in her hair, so that she would look her best for Chief Rushglen.

But they had to ride with their hoods up, because it rained, a continuous fine drizzle that soaked through everything. The horses trotted along unconcerned. They were tough little beasts whose winter coats had already grown, the long greasy outer hair keeping the warming inner fluff dry. The people, however, rode with their heads down. The tightly woven tweed of their hooded cloaks was almost as good as a horse-pelt for keeping the rain off, but not quite. Brightleaves shook herself like a dog to shake the rain off her heavy fur cloak. Willow tried to maintain continual awareness of the pack-horses roped to her saddle. She was determined that today, she would not have a single bardic moment.

They rode upstream along the Swift River until they reached the ford, then urged the cattle and ponies across. This added to the general wetness. They clambered out on the other side and carried on. For a short time they were in woods, where the trees, despite their bare branches, bore the brunt of the rain. But then the track came out among open fields. They rode on. Raindrops hung at the edge of their hoods and dripped on to their faces if they looked up.

The mud of the track was getting wetter and wetter. The riders didn't want to urge the horses to go at any speed in case they slipped. The procession slowed down.

Might as well walk at this rate, Fadge thought – but when he turned to ask her ladyship if he could walk instead of ride, he saw that she was in no mood to grant favours.

The rain become stronger, pattering on the ground like the fingers of many tiny drummers, hissing into the soil like spears. It was cold.

This was why people didn't travel in the winter, if they could avoid it.

The entire company lapsed into dull acceptance, plodding onwards, soaked and shivering. This went on for a long time, or a time that seemed long. Suddenly the rain stopped, the sun came out and in the distance they saw a rainbow, arching out from the dark grey clouds and down into the east, to where they were going.

Well, if that wasn't a good omen!...

They all smiled at each other. Brightleaves shook her head, so that her dank hood fell back. The raindrops on the edge of her hair sparkled like jewels. They rode on in better spirits.

But the rain couldn't stay away, that would be too much to hope for. There were plenty of grey clouds piling across the sky, waiting to pour down on the land of the Livelies and on anyone who might be travelling across it.

They decided to make the best of it and sang a hymn of praise to the goddess whose bounty filled the streams, giving them fresh water to drink, and green grass for the cattle to eat, and the horses, and the sheep, and the goats.

They arrived at Chief Rushglen's house while it was still daylight. The sun was out of sight behind the clouds but it had not set; there was still time for them to travel to the hostel if need be. Not that Chief Rushglen would refuse Lady Brightleaves Roughrock his hospitality. No chief of the Lively people would ever do such a thing. But if she detected any hesitation about hosting a herd of cattle for the night, there was still time for her to move on to the hostel.

She had Willow and Cherry attend to her hair while she sent Badger to the door of the chief's house. He came back to say that she was more than welcome. She rode to up to the house, dismounted, and leaving her horse unattended with the casual air of one who is used to having slaves milling about to look after practical matters, she went to the door. She was met in the porch by a slavegirl who started to take her cloak. Brightleaves stopped her.

'Has the Chief been told that I have a herd of cattle with me?'

'Oh, don't worry about that, my lady!' said the girl, almost pulling Brightleaves' wet cloak off. 'He won't care a bit! Not at the moment! Please come in, please!'

From within the house came the unmistakeable cries of a woman in labour.

Chapter 2. A birth

Leaving her cloak in the slave's arms, Brightleaves walked into the house, into a scene of chaos.

The fire was blazing, making the whole house hot, which was just as well because the mother-to-be was wearing only a night-tunic. She was lying on the floor with a girl crouched beside her, trying ineffectually to wipe her brow with a damp cloth while the woman rolled her head and screamed.

Slavegirls ran to and fro with buckets and bundles of cloth. Over by the loom stood a wiry man with grey hair – the chief, judging by his colourful clothes. He looked scared out of his wits. Next to him stood two hounds, heads drooping, whining.

Brightleaves clapped her hands and shouted, 'Silence!'

Everything stopped. The slavegirls stopped running about, the hounds stopped whining and lifted their heads, the chief looked hopeful, even the woman on the floor stopped screaming and took a deep breath.

'Where is the healer?' Brightleaves asked in the silence.

The slaves all started talking at once. Brightleaves held up her hand to stop them and looked at the man.

'It seems she had to go over to Crooked Hill,' he said. 'That's many miles away.'

The woman on the floor groaned.

'I'm sorry you find us in such chaos,' the man babbled desperately. 'I'm Chief Firebrand Rushglen–'

'No time for politeness!' said Brightleaves. 'You and the

dogs, out! Out, out, off you go! Is there a birthing chair in the store? One of you answer! Come on!'

A slavegirl nodded. 'Yes, Ma'am, but–'

'Go and get it.'

Willow and Cherry came into the house, Cherry with Brightleaves' travelling bag.

'Thank the Goddess you two are here,' said Brightleaves. 'Cherry, I want you to organize these women, find out who's carrying stuff that should be taken out and who's carrying stuff that might be useful here. Willow, come and help me with this lady.'

They knelt down beside the groaning woman, one on each side of her. The brow-wiping girl moved aside to make room for Brightleaves. The sound of Cherry organizing people in the background was quite soothing, Willow thought.

'We're going to stand you up,' Brightleaves told the birthing mother. 'It's no use you lying on the floor like this. You need to be able to push. Come on, Willow! At the count of three – one-two-three!'

They hauled the woman to her feet and held her there. Her hair was plastered to her head with sweat; dark curls stuck to her flushed face.

'Just walk forward very slowly,' said Brightleaves. 'Little tiny steps, that's right. Cherry, have someone spread a towel in our path. Have your waters broken? Have her waters broken?' she asked the slavegirls. There was general assent; they nodded and mumbled. Brightleaves wondered briefly if they were ill treated, for they seemed afraid to speak.

'Lay another towel,' she told Cherry. 'We'll just keep on gently walking about. What's your name, dear?' she asked the mother-to-be; but a contraction blocked the answer. 'What is her name?' Brightleaves asked the slaves.

'Lady Rushglen, Ma'am,' said one in a quavering voice.

'Idiot!' said Brightleaves. 'I am Lady Roughrock but my name is Brightleaves. What is this lady's name?'

There was a pause. Each slave seemed to be waiting for another to speak.

'Cherry, find out what her name is and if this is her first child,' said Brightleaves. She and Willow walked the woman along the towels, then turned her round and walked her back again. She was clinging tightly to their arms. Whenever she had a contraction, her fingertips dug into their flesh.

'It's a pity we can't play music to soothe you,' Brightleaves told her patient, 'but one of my musicians is holding you up and the other is talking to your slavegirls.'

My musicians! thought Willow. It seems we've had a rise in status!

'Her name is Dainty,' Cherry told Brightleaves; then the birthing chair was carried into the house and Lady Dainty screamed at the sight of it.

'Her first baby was born dead in this chair,' Cherry explained.

'But that's not the chair's fault!' Brightleaves told Dainty. 'Perhaps the little spirit decided not to incarnate after all.' She thought of her own baby, who had decided not to incarnate after all because she had given him away. He would have been eight years old now. Tears came to her eyes, her throat choked and she could not speak. She signalled to the slaves to put the chair in position.

Willow started to hum, a gentle, rhythmic, soothing tune which gradually shaped itself into a familiar lullaby.

As if under a spell, but in fact yielding to firm pressure from Brightleaves, Lady Dainty sat down in the birthing chair, Brightleaves pushing her with one hand and pulling up her tunic with the other. Willow began to sing the words of the lullaby. Cherry joined in, and the slavegirls too, after a while, tentatively at first and then with growing confidence, while Brightleaves said 'Push!' every so often.

At one point, with Dainty pushing and everyone else singing, Brightleaves beckoned Cherry aside and whispered, 'Try to find out why they're all so frightened of her.'

Dainty grew more frantic as her contractions came faster and faster. The singing stopped. Brightleaves crouched on the floor now, in front of the birthing chair. Suddenly Dainty flung herself forward off the chair – Brightleaves ducked away – Dainty knelt on all fours and with a great roar pushed out her baby.

The slavegirls stopped being useless and became competent and helpful. One brought a sharp iron knife for cutting the cord. One brought a cloth and a bowl of warm water to clean the newborn. One brought a soft nettle-cloth wrap.

Dainty had collapsed on the floor. When she heard the baby cry, she pushed herself into a sitting position. Willow knelt behind her, to support her. Dainty held out her arms and received the clean, wrapped baby.

'It's a little boy,' said Brightleaves.

She sent Cherry out to bring in Chief Rushglen while the new mother gazed at her child.

The chief ordered flagons of mead, beer, and berry wine to be opened. Lady Dainty was carried to her bed, where she sat holding her baby and receiving congratulations from members of the household. The new father sent messengers out into the twilight to all the people of Rushglen, to tell them the good news. Farmers and craftsmen and their wives came from all over the glen, through the dusk and the drizzle, bringing their congratulations and offerings – but when they reached the chief's house, they hesitated, all trying to cram into the porch out of the rain but not going into the house until the chief himself came out and asked them to come in.

Brightleaves took Cherry aside. 'Did you find out why they act so strangely around her?'

'She's a bit touched,' Cherry whispered.

'Touched?'

'You know, not right in the head. She's been like it ever since her first baby was born dead. The healer treats her with herbs, to keep it under control.'

'Under control?'

'She can get quite wild. They're all hoping this baby will put her right.'

A heavy task for a newborn, Brightleaves thought.

She sent Cherry and Willow out to make sure that the warriors, pack-horses, cattle and Fadge all had their needs met. Chief Firebrand brought everyone in for a drink. The mead was excellent; Brightleaves sipped and praised it.

'My mother makes it,' said Firebrand. 'She lives here normally but she's gone to visit my brother in Loudwood. We weren't expecting the baby to arrive quite yet.'

'I've been admiring your shirt and trousers,' said Brightleaves. 'Beautifully woven!'

'Yes, my mother made these. My wife doesn't care for weaving, she gets – impatient.'

If I lived with a mother-in-law who was a perfect mead-maker and a perfect weaver, I might get a bit impatient,

Brightleaves thought. Possibly even a bit touched. She wondered that her friend Pearlywaves hadn't warned her about this household. Perhaps she didn't know! Brightleaves began to look forward to having a good gossip with Pearlywaves. Then she remembered. She wouldn't be going back past Pearlywaves' house. She wouldn't be going back at all. Pearlywaves had squealed with delight when she heard that Brightleaves had fallen in love with a Hunter chief and was going to live with him. But they had not talked about when they might see each other again.

Brightleaves concentrated on being agreeable to her host. The baby was brought out for all the locals to admire, then taken back to his mother. Brightleaves followed the maid who was carrying the baby. The curtain was drawn across Lady Dainty's bedspace; the slavegirl pulled it back just enough to pass the baby through, then let it fall and went away.

Brightleaves peeked around the curtain.

'Hello! Are you receiving visitors?'

Dainty's dark hair had been combed and her face was no longer flushed. She looked quite pretty, sitting up in bed holding her child. At that moment she also looked startled.

'Are you real?' she asked.

'Yes,' said Brightleaves. 'I arrived seeking shelter for the night while you were giving birth.'

'I thought you were a dream.'

'No.' Brightleaves held out her arm. 'Pinch it and see.'

'I thought one was supposed to pinch one's own arm, to test if one was dreaming,' said Dainty, doing so. 'Not much point in testing the arm of a dream image. It might turn into a wing, or a tentacle.'

Brightleaves laughed. 'Well, mine won't,' she said. But

then a dream-monster might say the same. She looked down at the sleeping child. 'Isn't he lovely?'

'Yes,' said the young mother, and smiled. She nodded at the edge of the bed. 'Sit down!'

Brightleaves sat. 'Your mother-in-law will be delighted, won't she? She'll be so pleased to have a grandson.'

Dainty sighed. 'Yes, she will.' She looked down at the baby in her arms. 'And we won't let her take you away from us, will we?' she said to him.

'Is that likely?'

'Oh yes. As soon as she hears the news, she'll come rushing back, march in and take over. She's already got a wet-nurse lined up for him. I heard her talking about it with one of the women.'

Outside the bedspace was the chatter of people partying. Then came the sound of pipe and lyre; Willow and Cherry were entertaining the party.

Dainty beckoned Brightleaves to lean closer and whispered, 'She thinks I'm touched. And sometimes I think I am. Sometimes I feel very strange. I hear myself saying really odd things. But I never did that or felt like that before I came to live in this house.'

'Has your mother-in-law always lived here?'

'Yes, she was here when I arrived.'

'Perhaps she's putting something in your food – but surely your healer would know that?'

'Our healer's very young and this is her first practice. The old healer would have known. But she died and this young one came.' Dainty paused for a moment. 'Come to think of it,' she said, 'my trouble only started after the old healer had gone.'

'Why don't you go and see the High Priestess? If your

local healer can't help you, it's the obvious next step.'

'They won't let me.'

'Won't let you?' Brightleaves was appalled. 'Surely that's against the law?'

'We hardly ever see a druid these days. Firebrand makes the law in Rushglen now – which means his mother makes it, of course.'

'Come with me! We'll be leaving first thing tomorrow. I don't think Firebrand on his own would stop you, would he? Not if I was there to persuade him.'

'But I can't ride a horse just now!'

'You won't have to. You can sit in my chariot. You'll just need to bring a pack-horse for your luggage – and the baby's luggage. And you might want to bring your own slavegirl.'

Dainty looked doubtful.

'We've already got twelve horses with us,' said Brightleaves, 'so another two or three aren't going to make that much difference.'

'How would I get back?'

'The High Priestess has a guest house, I expect she would let you stay there until you're fit to ride home. And two of my warriors are coming back after they've escorted me, so they could wait and ride home with you.'

'It's all happening so fast!'

'You've got all night to think about it. We'll be leaving at sunrise.'

Then, at last, the meal was served. Firebrand's mother, before setting out for Loudwood, had given directions for a bullock to be baked in a firepit. It was the time of year when bullocks began to be slaughtered so that they wouldn't have to be fed through the winter. There was an ample supply of beef throughout the country.

Now the pit was opened and menservants used long metal claws to lift out chunks of meat. The scent of the cooked beef rose from the pit in the steam, mingling with the smells of wet grass, hot stone, burned wood. Servants ran to and fro from the house to the pit with trays to collect platters of meat for the chief, the new mother, the guests and the well-wishers.

For the sweet there was bread and butter spread with honey. The butter was not fresh; Brightleaves saw the butter-barrel on a table outside in the winter coolness, doubtless lifted from its bog that day. Butter-bogs! When she reached Hardy's house, away in the land of the Hunters, she would have to find out where the nearest butter-bog was. A woman needs to know these things.

During the feast, as the guest of honour, she sat next to Firebrand.

'Did I tell you that I'm on my way to see the High Priestess?'

'Er – you may have done,' he said. 'I do apologize if you did and I've forgotten! There's been rather a lot happening today.'

'I only mention it,' she said, 'because I think your wife should come with me.'

'Oh, she can't do that.'

'Why not?'

'Well – surely she can't ride, having just given birth?'

'No need. I have my chariot with me.'

'Have you really?'

'Yes, would you like to come and see it?'

'I'd love to!'

The chariot delighted him and put him in a good mood.

'You see, she can sit in this and hold the baby.'

'Oh no, she can't take the baby with her.'

'But she must! She's feeding him, and he's bonding with her.'

'My mother arranged a wet-nurse so that Dainty wouldn't have to feed him.'

'It's very painful for a woman whose breasts are full of milk not to be able to feed her baby. You wouldn't want to hurt her, would you?'

'No, of course not! I just thought that a wet-nurse would save her the trouble. Also – well, between you and me, we didn't want her passing on her madness with her milk.'

'Well of course she can't carry on taking those herbs while she's feeding the baby.'

'Can't she?' he looked alarmed. 'But the herbs are the only thing that are keeping her half-way normal!'

'I think they're making her worse. Your local healer is clearly not coping with her.'

'My mother didn't think it would be a good idea for Dainty to go and see the High Priestess.'

'Of course not, if she had to travel alone with only a couple of body-guards! But my being here changes the story entirely. I'm going to see the High Priestess. If your wife comes with me, she'll be travelling in comfort, well guarded, and with a woman of her own class for company. It's a perfect opportunity. If your mother were here I'm sure she'd agree!'

Firebrand gave in. He was used to obeying a bossy woman.

She restored his sense of male superiority by asking his advice about her route. 'In the summer, after I'd forded the Blackwater, I went directly north, past Freshloch.'

'Oh, you can't do that at this time of year!' he said.

'Remember that wooden causeway that runs across the bog?'

'Oh yes. That was a bit scary!'

'Think what it would be like at this time of year, with all this rain, and you travelling with so many animals! You couldn't help but lose a few. The goddess would take them as her tribute.'

'You're right. And my salt would be ruined! So what would be my best route, do you think?'

'I think you should travel north along Head Loch, then turn east at White Ford.'

'Thank you. That's what I'll do.' She smiled at him. 'I'm so glad I asked your advice.'

Next morning, when they were all dressed, and packed, with most of them mounted and ready to go, Fadge ran up to her and threw himself on the ground beside the chariot.

'Mercy, mercy!' he said.

'What on earth is the matter with you, Fadge? Are you drunk?'

'No, milady, I wish I was drunk! I can't do it! I can't!'

'Can't do what?'

'I can't cross that river.'

'But you've crossed rivers before. That one's not unusually dangerous, is it?'

'It's not the river, milady. It's what's on the other side!'

'Do get up, Fadge! I can't talk to you when your face is in the mud.'

Fadge stood up and stood, muddy-faced, hanging his head.

'Now, what's wrong with the other side of the river?' Brightleaves asked him.

'It's the land of the Hunters, milady!'

'And what's wrong with that?'

'It's a foreign country, milady! I've never been abroad before!'

'It's not so very different from here. Willow and Cherry come from another country, and you get on all right with them, don't you?'

'Yes, milady, very nice girls. But the thing is–' he glanced at Willow and Cherry to judge whether they were within hearing distance, then whispered, 'the thing is, milady, they're living here. So they can't do any funny foreign customs, can they?'

'I'm sure their customs are not so different from ours. They have the same gods and goddesses, the same festivals.'

Fadge shook his head. 'Aye, but you hear things…'

'We hear all sorts of nonsense. I can't waste time like this, Fadge. Get on your horse.'

Fadge fell to his knees. 'I can't, milady, I can't! They're not like ordinary foreigners over there. They're the Hunters! If we take the cows there, they'll hunt them!'

'I'm getting cross, Fadge.'

'Kill me if you like!' said Fadge. 'But don't make me go to the land of the Hunters!'

'May I make a suggestion?' said Chief Firebrand. 'Let this man stay behind – I'll buy him from you, if you like; and I'll lend you someone to take the cows across the river. Once they're across, you can buy another cowherd, at Greenslope or Rockridge, or somewhere on your route, and send mine back.'

'You are an excellent peacemaker,' said Brightleaves. 'I can see why you make a good border guard.' She gave Firebrand a dazzling smile, then scowled at Fadge. 'You have turned my journey into a shopping trip!' she told him.

'And I am not best pleased. But it's your choice. You can come with me and find out that the Hunters are people like everyone else. Or you can stay here, where you'll still be in the land of the Livelies, but you'll be in Rushglen instead of Roughrock.'

'I'll stay here!' said Fadge. She could tell, by the cunning twinkle in his eyes, that he was already working out a ruse to get himself back to Roughrock. He liked what he was used to.

'Would you like livestock, jewellery or coin for him?' Firebrand asked her.

Brightleaves considered. Coin was the easiest to carry but the hardest to use, as it was only accepted by people who travelled. As for livestock, what was an experienced cowman worth? Six cows perhaps. She didn't really want to travel with another six cows. So jewellery would be easiest. Then again, Firebrand would know that and would try to beat her down in the bargaining. And would jewellery be the best for her in practice? If she were to buy the son of a small farmer, wouldn't he rather be paid in cattle?

The bargaining began.

Willow and Cherry watched it with a sense of shame. Thus they had been bargained for, at Rayfort market. They wondered how it made Fadge feel.

Fadge grinned and chuckled as he watched the bargaining. He wanted Lady Brightleaves to win, but he wanted his new owner, Chief Firebrand, to think he had won. Surely Lady Brightleaves could manage that? He had great faith in her.

Fadge's faith was justified. Chief Firebrand was a skilful bargainer but he bargained on the assumption that Lady Brightleaves would want jewellery. She let him think so, and with apparent reluctance accepted another dozen cattle into her already large herd, and the temporary loan of a herdsman. When they shook hands in farewell, she bowed her head slightly as if to acknowledge his superior bargaining powers. She looked back, as they rode away, and saw him smiling, pleased with himself. She gave him a finger-ripple wave and drove on.

As usual when they reached a ford in winter, the riders took off their shoes and pulled up their skirts or trousers to keep them dry. The borrowed herdsman drove the cattle across the ford without incident. The women in the chariot sat watching the horses in front of them; if the water rose too far up the horses' rumps, it would cover the floor of the chariot, whose passengers would have to stand up.

Once they were across the river, Dainty relaxed. She looked back at the opposite bank. Then she looked down at the baby in her arms.

'We've done it!' she told him. 'We've escaped!'

'Are you not going back, then?' said Brightleaves.

'Sometimes the unknown is less frightening than the known,' said Dainty.

Brightleaves made no comment. Whether or not Dainty should return to her husband must be decided by someone wiser than she was.

* * *

The first place on the other side of the ford was Greenslope Fort. Brightleaves did not want to ride in there with her entire procession, because that would involve offers of hospitality which it would be rude to refuse. Stopping for a cup of mead and a chat would delay her more than she wanted. She sent Hooky into the fort on his own, with a message explaining that she was passing through on her journey north, wanted to get as far as she could that day, but was in need of a cowherd.

He came back with a polite message of thanks for the information, regret that she could not stop for a chat – and sorry, no cowherd to spare.

It was the same at every place where they stopped to ask. The journey was taking far longer than Brightleaves wanted, with all these stops; and the further they went from Rushglen, the longer it would take for the borrowed cowherd to get home.

The stops were helpful to Dainty, though. It was easier for her to feed her baby when the chariot wasn't bumping along the track. She had to be shown how to change his wet loin-cloth, clean him and pad him with clean moss. The stops were a chance to throw the dirty moss away and wash the cloth in the river.

'I'm so grateful you advised me to pack that bag of moss, and all this linen!' she told Brightleaves.

'Normally you would have a slavegirl change the baby for you,' said Brightleaves, 'but it's nice to know you can do it yourself.'

The washed loin-cloths were tied to the arches of the chariot-frame to dry. They fluttered in the breeze as the procession moved along, giving a tatty yet grotesquely festive look to the smart little vehicle. Brightleaves suppressed her irritation at this. She confided to Dainty her worry about the Rushglen cowherd being able to get home if they went too far before they found a replacement for him.

'Oh, don't worry about him!' said Dainty. 'He'll be

enjoying seeing the world. And we haven't come so very far, have we? He'll be able to walk back in half a day.'

It had been raining in the night. Brightleaves prayed to the Rain-god to keep the rain off until she had reached her destination. If it rained too much, the wheels of the chariot would stick in the mud.

They reached Crowhill, where their road turned eastwards. The cattle had been driven far enough that day, and Brightleaves sent Hooky into Crowhill Fort to ask if they could stay the night. Lady Crowhill came out to greet them, a small vivacious russet-haired lady.

'Of course you must stay the night!' she said. 'I love entertaining and knowing everybody's business, that's why I married a border guard!'

Anyone crossing a border into another country had to stop and tell the border-guard his or her business as a matter of courtesy. If a warband rode across the border without stopping, the border guard would send messages to nearby chiefs who would come to his aid with their warriors while another messenger went galloping to tell the king.

There was no reason to expect hostile warbands at the moment. But there was always crime to watch out for. Someone crossing the border with a herd of cows might be stealing them.

Travellers who needed to stay the night were the best. They provided the border guard and his family with novelty – a new face, new stories – and after being plied with drink they would speak freely, so the border guard could find out more about them and their intentions.

The High Priestess and her school for healers, in a northern glen of the Hunters' country, had such a high reputation that most of the travellers crossing the borders these days were on their way to see her. People travelling with herds of cattle and other valuables were usually parents of a trainee priestess bringing the school fees for their daughter's education. Chief and Lady Crowhill had seen cartloads of timber, wool, linen, goblets, hides, rushes, oats, wheat and barley being pulled along the track towards the school in Wildcat Glen. The track was therefore a good deal wider and smoother than it would otherwise have been.

The normal time of year for such offerings, however, was the summer, when the tracks were relatively dry and the rivers relatively low for fording. It was unusual to see a lot of goods being taken there in the winter when the tracks were muddy and rivers ran high. There was definitely a story here!

The Crowhills welcomed their guests and saw to it that the cattle, horses and baggage were safely disposed and the slaves housed and fed. Dainty asked if a quiet place could be found for her baby to sleep. Lady Crowhill looked at her in astonishment.

'You don't want him to think that he can only sleep when it's quiet! How often is it quiet, in a normal household? Keep him with you, then he'll be contented. I'll get you a cradle to pop him in when he drops off. And my slaves will bring you water for washing him, and a pile of clean moss.'

The Crowhills served their guests a feast of roast pork. There were goblets of mead, horns of beer, the Crowhill bard to sing songs and tell stories. By now they were on first-name terms; Chief Crowhill's name was Dignity, which suited him, and his wife was called Gentian.

Then the point in the evening came when Gentian

turned to Brightleaves and asked, 'Are you going to visit your daughter at the Healing School?'

Brightleaves hesitated. It would have been so easy to answer Yes. But one of the diners was the local priestess-healer, Whitepath. It was said that the priestesses knew when people were lying.

'No,' said Brightleaves, 'I don't have a daughter. I'm taking Lady Dainty to see the High Priestess. Her local healer can't seem to help her.'

Dainty was in a bedspace changing her baby's loin-cloth.

Whitepath looked at Brightleaves as if she knew this wasn't the main motive for the journey. But the mention of the healer interested her.

'That's unusual,' she said. 'Mother Swan trains us all very well. It's a ten-year training! Even a newly graduated healer ought to be able to deal with most things, unless she's been called in too late. What's the healer's name?'

'I don't know,' said Brightleaves. 'They're down at Rushglen.'

'Rushglen?' said Whitepath. 'I knew the healer there. Mullein, she was called. A highly respected healer. I was so sorry when she died. She hasn't been replaced yet, has she? I suppose they're sharing a healer with another settlement for now.'

Dainty came back to the fireside holding her baby, who had fallen asleep in her arms. She laid him gently in the cot beside the bench and sat down. A maid brought her a goblet of mead.

'Which healer are you using in Rushglen now?' Whitepath asked her.

'The new one, Wintergreen.' said Dainty. 'She's only young, perhaps that's why she can't get it right.'

'Wintergreen.' Whitepath sat musing. 'Wintergreen… never heard of her.'

'You can't be expected to know who all the new healers are!' said Gentian.

'But I can be expected to know where they are,' said Whitepath. 'Excuse me for a moment.'

She took her cloak from its peg, left the house and shut the door behind her.

'Probably gone to sit in the porch and think,' said Dignity. 'She does that sometimes. And if people disturb her there, she goes home.'

'So, what are you going to call your baby?' Gentian asked Dainty. 'Have you decided yet?'

'I think I shall call him Traveller,' said Dainty, 'as he's started his life with a journey!'

'Oh, that's a good name! Will your husband like it, do you think?'

'He'll probably like it. Whether his mother will like it is another matter.'

'But surely it's none of her business?'

Dainty sighed. 'She lives with us.'

'Ah,' said Gentian. 'So she runs the house?'

Dignity turned to the bard. 'I think we could do with a jolly tune.'

'But not too loud, please!' said Dainty.

The bard played a quiet jolly tune, and then another. It was some time before Whitepath came back into the house. She hung up her cloak, looked at Dainty and said,

'You must not go back to Rushglen until Mother Swan tells you it's safe.'

There was a babble of enquiry and surmise from the three women. Chief Dignity sat waiting for Whitepath to explain. Whitepath sat down.

'I have been looking at Rushglen,' she said.

'She can send her mind out, you know, to other places!' Gentian told Brightleaves. 'They're all taught how to do it but Whitepath is exceptionally good at it.'

'I was hoping to make contact with a healer,' Whitepath continued. 'I made contact with several, in the areas around Rushglen. None of them has ever met Wintergreen. And that's very strange.'

'Why?' Dainty asked.

'A healer usually meets other nearby healers.'

'Perhaps she's just been too busy with patients?' said Gentian.

'Unlikely,' said Whitepath. 'Dainty is her only patient.'

'Oh, that's not true!' said Dainty. 'Wintergreen is for ever going off to see people. My mother-in-law is always saying, Oh Wintergreen's gone here, she's gone there...'

'Your mother-in-law is a liar,' said Whitepath. 'Her aura is muddy with lies. As for other patients, Mullein's former patients have been going to other healers, even if it means a much longer journey for them. Wintergreen is no use. She doesn't know how to treat animals, she doesn't know how to treat children, she's like a child playing Healer with her dolls. That's what the patients tell the other healers.'

'Well, she is young,' said Dainty.

'Girls at Mother Swan's school learn how to treat both animals and children before their first bleeding,' said Whitepath. 'Wintergreen is not a child, I assume.'

'No,' said Dainty.

'Worst of all, she doesn't hear distress signals. When someone sends out a distress signal, the nearest healer hears it and she has to answer. Healers who live near Rushglen are having to ride there to answer distress signals because there's nobody there to do it.'

'Distress signals?' said Dainty. 'Nobody ever told me about those! What are they? How do you make one?'

'You make it without knowing,' said Whitepath. 'It's like a scream but it's silent. You can't hear it. Your energy-body makes it when you have an accident, or when you're hurt or ill or in distress. Your energy-body has been sending distress signals for some time now. The healers find it very upsetting. When you first started sending them, the nearest healer got on her horse and rode to your house, but your mother-in-law said, 'We've got our own healer, thank you,' and wouldn't let her in. The same thing happened with all the healers within half a day's riding distance. They couldn't believe your distress signal wasn't being answered, and each in turn went to find out why, and each was turned away and had to ride home still hearing the distress signal.'

'Am I still making it?'

'No. You don't make it all the time. But the healers also told me that when they were turned away from your house, they could not sense the presence of a healer inside, whatever your mother-in-law said. And when I flew over the house, there was a girl who looked like Wintergreen there, but there was no healer.'

'When you flew?'

'They can turn themselves into swans and fly, you know!' said Gentian. 'That's why they like to live near water.'

It was only in meditation that the healers flew; but everyone wanted to believe that they really flew, so they had given up denying it.

'Are you saying Wintergreen's not really a healer?' said Dainty. 'But she's been giving me remedies!'

48

'She's probably been giving you poison,' said Whitepath. 'Mother Swan will be able to tell you more about that. All I can tell you is that your mother-in-law is plotting something, and she's using Wintergreen, and your husband doesn't know what's going on.'

'Let's assume,' said Dignity, 'that Wintergreen has been poisoning you, Lady Dainty. She's a young girl, you say – has she got her eye on your husband, perhaps?'

Dainty considered this. 'I don't think so. She doesn't look at him in that way. And I don't think my mother-in-law would want Wintergreen as a daughter-in-law. She treats her – now I come to think of it, she treats her more like a slave. I can't imagine her treating you like that!' She looked timidly at Whitepath.

'So your mother-in-law is using this girl, who is acting on her instructions,' said Dignity.

'Yes, I suppose so.'

Whitepath nodded. 'That's what it felt like.'

'Why would your mother-in-law want you dead, Lady Dainty?' Dignity asked.

Tears came to Dainty's eyes. 'She's never liked me. But I didn't think she wanted me dead!'

'Did you bring him a good dowry?' Gentian asked. 'Mothers-in-law are very keen on dowries.'

'It wasn't particularly good. My father was a chief but his land wasn't very productive; and he loved feasting and making displays of wealth he didn't have. And I was the youngest of several daughters, so the wealth was pretty much used up by the time it was my turn for a dowry. Everyone sighed with relief when I married Firebrand.'

Tears were trickling down Dainty's cheeks and she began to sob. 'I can't go back there, can I?'

49

Traveller whimpered and stirred in his cradle.

'Perhaps your mother-in-law has come across a girl who could bring in a large dowry, so she's trying to get you out of the way,' said Dignity. 'It seems the most likely explanation.'

'There must be a way to sort this out!' said Gentian. 'We can't do much, it's not Hunter business. Brightleaves, couldn't you could send a message to your husband? Then he could alert the king of the Livelies.'

'The fact is,' said Brightleaves, 'I am leaving my husband.'

Whitepath smiled at her, sensing the relief Brightleaves felt at no longer concealing this. 'That's why I have so many cattle with me and so much baggage,' Brightleaves continued. 'I stopped for the night at Dainty's house, and that's when I suggested she should come with me, because I'm going to Wildcat Glen.'

She felt her cheeks blushing.

'So you're not going to see the High Priestess?' said Gentian.

'No. I'm going to—'

'You're going to marry Chief Hardy! His wife died, I remember. I went to the funeral – Dignity couldn't go, of course. So you're bringing your dowry with you! Oh, this is so exciting!' Gentian clapped her hands like a pleased child. 'Imagine,' she said, turning to her husband, 'if I wasn't married to you, I'd be sitting weaving in some hilltop fort, getting the bard to sing me the Lay of Lady Lily yet again, bored stiff!'

Dainty waited for all this joy to be over so that the company could focus on her problems once again. She sighed loudly. 'What am I going to do?' she asked them.

'What you need,' said Dignity, 'is a Druid.'

'There is a Druid in the north, beyond Wildcat Glen,' said Whitepath.

'Then that's where you must go, Dainty, after you've seen the High Priestess,' said Brightleaves. 'Now, about my cattle–'

'They'll be all right in that outhouse,' Dignity assured her.

'I'm sure they will, and it's very kind of you – but what I want to ask is, do you by any chance have a spare cowherd you could sell me?'

She explained her problem with Fadge and how the present cowman was on loan from Chief Firebrand.

Dignity nodded. 'Things are quite complicated enough without you being in debt to Chief Firebrand,' he said. 'Can you think of anyone, Gentian?'

'We can lend Brightleaves a cowman!' said Gentian. 'He can go with them as far as Wildcat Glen, then come back here. So Chief Firebrand's cowman can set off home tomorrow morning. There, that's settled.'

The next morning, the cowherd from Rushglen set off to walk home. Then it was time for Brightleaves and Dainty to say their goodbyes and thankyous. Dignity and Gentian Crowhill stood at their gate waving until the travellers, their baggage train and their cattle were out of sight.

Whitepath accompanied the travellers. 'I'll just come with you for part of the way,' she told them. They did not ask her why. One did not ask a priestesses why she was going here or there, doing this or that.

They had only ridden for a few miles when they met another priestess coming the other way. The two priestesses conversed secretly for a few minutes, then Whitepath introduced her colleague, Harmony, an earnest young woman with straight brown hair held back from her face with large horn combs.

'Would you consider taking on a boy to herd your cattle the rest of the way?' she asked Brightleaves.

'I might.'

'It's not so much for your sake as for his. He's called Robin, he lives at Bogend farm, not far from near here. He's been working with cows since he could walk. But he needs to get away.'

'Tell me more.'

'His parents died when he was younger, and his aunt Pansy, who was living there anyway, took over their farm and looked after him. Pansy's not the brightest bead in the basket but she has a good heart. She was struggling, running the farm on her own, with Robin and her own children to care for.'

'What about her husband?'

'I don't think she's ever had one. No-one knows who or where her children's father is. But the other farmers lent a helping hand, and she was managing all right. Then last year she came home from the Midsummer Fair, smiling like the sun, with a big strong man in tow. He would never say where he came from.'

'An outlaw?'

'That's what we all suspected. But most people were pleased for Pansy, and the other farmers didn't need to lend a hand any more.' Harmony sighed. 'The man turned out to be a disaster. All he wants to do is drink. Pansy still has to do all the farmwork, the house is falling down, and she can't ask the other farmers for help now that she's got Bluff. If the farm produces anything worth trading, Bluff takes it away and trades it for drink. And he beats Robin.'

'Why don't the local chief and his wife do something about it?'

'Chief Hookhill has a policy of what he calls non-interference,' said Harmony. 'And his wife is a shy person, she doesn't like to exert authority.'

'So who organizes things in Hookhill Glen?'

'The local bard and I do our best.'

'Someone should have informed the King,' said Brightleaves.

'The boy is covered in bruises,' said Harmony. 'You'll be saving his life if you buy him. And I'm sure he could herd your cattle to Wildcat Glen.'

'What should I offer for him?'

'Preferably something that Bluff can't trade for drink.'

'Is there anything that can't be traded for drink?' Brightleaves wondered.

Bogend Farm was a depressing sight. The roof sagged. The thatch looked rotten. There was no haze of smoke rising from the roof, suggesting no fire within even on this chilly day. The smell of the latrine wafted from behind the house. There were four sheep grazing near the house; three of them were lame.

There was a woman standing in the doorway, a skinny woman with a bruised face and a dress full of holes, shivering in the cold. Beside her were two skinny children, naked except for scraps of fabric knotted around their necks as makeshift cloaks. One clutched at the woman's knees and buried its snotty face in her dirty skirt while the other gazed open-mouthed at the visitors.

Pansy too stared in amazement at the scene before her: the two ladies in the red-and-yellow chariot, one with a fur cloak; the warriors in their splendour; the pretty girls on horseback; the two priestesses in their white cloaks; the lines of pack-horses; the large herd of cattle who had passed the farm first and whose sounds had brought her to the door.

She had never seen so much wealth.

Brightleaves had never seen such poverty, and was shocked. How could any chief allow one of his people to get into this state?

'Pansy?' said Harmony.

The woman nodded.

'I'm Harmony the healer. You know me, don't you? And this is Whitepath, who is also a healer.'

Pansy put an arm round each of the children. 'Don't take them away! Please! Please don't take them away!'

'We're not here to take them away, Pansy.'

'You're not?'

'No! Why would you think that?'

'Bluff said that if I ever complained to anyone about his – his little upsets – then warriors would come and take away the children. And I haven't complained, really I haven't, but Goodwill Riverside saw the bruises and asked about them, so I told her about Bluff's little upsets and she said I should complain to the chief and if I didn't, she would. But I don't want Bluff to think it was me who complained! He'll just get upset again!'

'No-one is going to take your children away,' said Brightleaves. 'But we would like to know if you'd be willing to sell us your nephew Robin, as a cowherd. If you don't want to part with him, perhaps we could just hire him, and then he can come back when he'd taken these cattle to Wildcat Glen.'

Pansy stood and thought about it.

'I will miss him, milady,' she said, 'but it would be good for him to go. Better for him.'

'What would you like us to give you in exchange for him?'

'Oh, take him!' said Pansy. 'I'll call him and you can take him!'

'But Pansy,' said Harmony, 'won't Bluff be a little bit upset if you don't let us give you anything in exchange for Robin.'

Pansy looked frightened. 'Oh yes! Yes he will be! Oh, I can't let Robin go.'

'But perhaps if we give you two cows for him?' Brightleaves suggested.

'Two cows!' Pansy opened her eyes wide. 'Two cows!' she repeated, wonderingly, as if such wealth was beyond her wildest dreams. She detached the child clinging to her ragged skirt, went around the side of the house and called, 'Robin! Robin!'

Brightleaves turned to look over her shoulder at Willow and Cherry.

'Girls!' she called, 'where did you put the fresh bread Lady Gentian gave us?'

Cherry dismounted, identified the relevant pack-horse and stood beside it. 'On this one!' she called.

'Unpack it, please, and bring it to me.'

Cherry pulled the loaf out of one of the panniers slung over the horse's back. The wonderful fragrance of newly baked bread spread though the clear air. All the travellers had eaten a hearty breakfast but nonetheless they felt their mouths watering. Pansy, returning to the porch, looked at the loaf with big, longing eyes. Cherry carried it to Brightleaves, who waved her on – 'Take it to Pansy, please!'

Pansy grasped the loaf reverently, clutched it to her breast and stuttered her thanks while her eyes filled with tears.

'I'll keep it for Bluff, he'll be so pleased!'

'No you will not keep it for Bluff!' said Harmony 'You will eat it here and now, in front of me, and give some to your children. If there is any left I'll take it back.'

'But what will Bluff say?'

'Say about what? How will he know? It will all be gone and you will sweep up every crumb, won't you? So he'll never know there was a loaf here. And when you've eaten it, you might think it was a dream.'

Pansy and the children crammed chunks of bread into their mouths and chewed. But so ingrained were Pansy's habits of putting a bit by for hard times to come, she automatically pulled off part of the loaf and hid it away in the filthy folded rag that served as her belt-pouch, tucked into the piece of twine around her waist.

The boy Robin came running around the side of the house. He was a thin, weather-tanned child with dark hair, blue eyes, and bruises on his face. His cloak was a rag tied around his shoulders. His shirt and trousers were not so much garments as scraps of fabric connected by fraying threads; when he got up in the morning, it must have been a puzzle where to insert his arms and legs. But he probably slept in these rags. Some of the bruises on his arms and legs showed through the holes. The skin of his bare feet, or what could be seen of it through the dirt, was blue with cold on this frosty day.

'Robin,' said Harmony, 'your aunt and cousins have their mouths full at the moment, so I will explain what's happening.'

Robin looked at the bread.

'We need to talk, and then you can have some bread,' said Harmony.

'Yes ma'am,' said Robin, with a sigh.

'Now, Lady Brightleaves, that lady there with the red hair—' Harmony indicated Brightleaves, who smiled at Robin. 'She wants to buy you.' Robin had bowed his head to the red-haired lady and now looked up in surprise.

'Buy me?'

'To drive her cattle to Wildcat Glen. Then, because she's bought you, you'll stay on there as her cowherd.'

'Wildcat Glen? Where the High Priestess has her school?'

'That's right. Or Lady Brightleaves will just borrow you, and you can walk back from Wildcat Glen, if you don't want to leave your Aunt Pansy and your Uncle Bluff.'

Robin bit his lip and stared at the ground. He did not want to leave his Aunt Pansy but he couldn't wait to get away from his Uncle Bluff. He looked up at Lady Brightleaves in her chariot.

'If you buy me, milady, what will you give Aunt Pansy?'

It had taken Pansy time to finish her mouthful, because so many of her teeth had fallen out or broken during her years of starving and being beaten. Now she said, 'Two cows!'

'Two cows?' echoed Robin.

'Well, Robin, is it yes or no?' Whitepath asked him.

'Yes!' said Robin. He would see the mysterious magical Wildcat Glen. Aunt Pansy would get two cows. And best of all, he would be away from Bluff.

'You pick out two cows now,' said Brightleaves. 'Show me what you can do.'

Robin went among the herd, inspecting each animal. He

57

did not choose the very best ones, because that would look greedy, but he chose good solid beasts. He couldn't help feeling sorry for them and wondered what their fate would be with Bluff around. He separated them from the rest of the herd.

Brightleaves nodded. She held out her hand to Pansy.

Pansy approached the chariot, wiping her hand on her skirt, which did little to improve it. The two women shook hands.

Brightleaves promised herself that she would stop and wash her hands in the next stream they came to.

'Now, give Robin some bread, please, Pansy,' said Harmony.

Pansy broke off a large chunk of the loaf and passed it to him. The boy ate it with the eagerness of the perpetually hungry, while Pansy gazed in wonder at the fine beasts that were now her own.

'Two cows!' she said.

'They are good milkers,' said Brightleaves, 'and their milk makes fine butter.'

'Butter!'

Robin demonstrated his skills by herding the two cows off the track and on to the farm, where they began to graze, resignedly he thought, on the meagre turf. Then he turned his attention to the remaining cattle, keeping them on the track.

'Here you are, lad,' said the Crowhill cowherd, dismounting from his horse and holding out the reins to Robin.

Robin had never ridden a horse. He had ridden cows. People had been surprised at how easily the cows accepted him on their backs.

'I thought I was just going to walk them,' he said.

'They'll go a bit faster if you're trotting,' said the cowherd.

Robin gritted his teeth and climbed on to the horse's back. It didn't feel the same as a cow. He sat there, quietly getting to know it, while the people around him talked, saying goodbye and thankyou and generally carrying on. It felt like quite a nice horse. It it had been a person, it would have been the kind of person he liked. It seemed a bit bored with all this waiting about. It started grazing, but soon lifted its head, wrinkled its nose and sighed.

Yes, horse, thought Robin. You're right. The grass here isn't much good.

Harmony, Whitepath and the Crowhill cowherd rode away westwards.

'All ready?' Lady Brightleaves called to the rest. 'Off we go!'

The procession set off. The horse began to trot. Robin was so busy adapting his body to this motion, and wondering about Wildcat Glen, and watching the herd in front of him, that he almost forgot to turn and wave goodbye to Aunt Pansy and his cousins and the house where he had lived since he was born.

Chapter 3. Wildcat Glen

Mother Swan, the High Priestess, had woken just before first light knowing that she must speak to Chief Hardy. She got up, put on her grey workaday cloak, and sat in her porch watching the other houses in the compound to see which of the trainee priestesses would wake up first. She suspected it would be one of the youngest ones, the Cygnets, as they were called. Small children tend to wake up early, whereas older ones often need to be encouraged to return from the land of dreams.

Sure enough, a small figure tiptoed out of the Cygnet house in the predawn dimness and ran round to the latrine at the back. Mother Swan went over to door of the Cygnet house and stood waiting for her, enjoying the deep quietness of this early hour, as if the day were taking a breath of being before it began to do.

Poor little Pickle nearly jumped out her skin when she came back from the latrine and found the actual High Priestess herself standing outside the Cygnet house waiting for her.

Mother Swan put her finger to her lips so that the child would not burst into high-pitched speech and wake everyone up.

'It's all right, you're not in trouble,' she whispered. 'Now, have you been issued with a new dress recently?'

The little girl nodded. 'Yes Ma'am – but I'm not to wear it yet, Curly said.'

'You may wear it now. I'll explain to Curly. Go and put

it on, then put your cloak on and come over to my house. Don't bother about washing,' she added, 'you can do that when you get back. I don't want you waking up any of the other girls.'

A cauldron of water was kept hot all night on the glowing embers of the fire, ready for the girls to wash with in the morning; but the small girls were not allowed to help themselves to hot water in case they tipped over the cauldron, scalded themselves and put out the fire. Ladling hot water into bowls and supervising the washing process was one of the jobs of whichever senior girl was looking after the little ones that week.

The Goddess whom the priestesses served was the goddess of (among other things) water, fire, and metalwork: clearly, then, hot water was one of Her gifts. Or so Mother Swan said.

Inside the Cygnet house, moving as quietly as possible so as not to waken any of the sleepers around her, Pickle pulled out the wicker storage basket from under her bed. She took out the new dress and unfolded it reverently. It was a plain grey dress, such as all the Cygnets wore, but it was new! No-one else had ever worn it! She had never had anything new before.

She pulled it over her head, groped for her belt, found it, fastened it, put her cloak back on and hurried out of the house. Nobody had woken. She'd half hoped somebody would, so that she could share her excitement.

'Now then, Pickle,' said Mother Swan when the little girl stood before her, blue eyes round with curiosity, 'You're trying for your Messenger badge, aren't you?'

'Yes Ma'am.'

'Well, I have a message for you to deliver. It will give you a lot of points towards your badge. First you must learn it. Do you know how to learn messages?'

'Yes Ma'am.'

'Good. Here's the first line: "Mother Swan sent me to say". Now you.'

'Mother Swan sent me to say,' repeated Pickle obediently.

They went through the whole message, Pickle repeating each line after Mother Swan. They said all the lines together; Pickle said them on her own; they chanted the lines, like a song, clapping their hands to mark the beats. Mother Swan tested the child: 'What word comes after "say?" What word comes before "stay"?' and so on.

'I think you've got it,' said Mother Swan eventually. 'Now, you're to take this message to Chief Hardy.'

Chief Hardy! Pickle's eyes became rounder than ever.

'Don't dawdle,' continued Mother Swan, 'and don't get distracted. You might find it helps to recite the message in your mind while you're walking. And remember, although you're only a child, you are also a priestess, so people should respect you. If you behave like a priestess, they will respect you. If you behave like a child, they won't.'

Pickle stood biting her lip, looking up doubtfully at Mother Swan.

'Ask!' said Mother Swan.

'What if,' said Pickle carefully, 'I meet someone who needs help and because I'm a priestess I should help them but if I help them it will make me late taking the message?'

'If that happens, you must send a distress signal. You know how to do that, don't you?'

Pickle nodded. 'First, I see you inside my head,' she said, 'then I call you very loudly, inside my head, until you look at me, then I show you the injured person, and I show you where we are.'

'Good,' said Mother Swan. 'You're a quick learner. But I don't think you'll need to send a distress signal today. Off you go!'

She watched the small figure trotting out into the gold light of the rising sun. Pickle, indeed! Some women should not be allowed to name their children.

Pickle walked to Chief Hardy's house with the dignity attainable only by a six-year-old taking a message from one Very Important Person to another Very Important Person. When she reached the house, there were so many spears in the porch that she wasn't surprised to find a crowd of men inside the house, all talking in loud manly voices. She waited quietly until one of them noticed the small grey-cloaked figure; he smiled down at her, saying, 'It's a Cygnet!' and stepped back to let her pass. A way opened before her between the men until she could see Chief Hardy, who was sitting on a bench pulling on one of his boots. There were two large, long-legged, grey woolly dogs sitting on the ground, one each side of the Chief, watching him pull on his boots and looking up at him expectantly, tongues hanging out, tails wagging. Sitting on their hindquarters, they were as tall as Pickle standing; but she sensed their gentle nature and was not afraid of them.

The Chief looked up at Pickle questioningly.

Pickle recited:

'Mother Swan sent me to say

She wants to visit you today

So you must in your homestead stay.'

* * *

'And what did the Chief say to that?' Mother Swan asked Pickle when she was back at the school.

'Well, he said "Hmph!" and pulled the ends of his moustache, then he got up and stumped about, but he was only wearing one boot. So he sat down again and said "Hmph!" again and pulled it off. The boot, not his moustache. Then his housekeeper came and asked if I'd like something to eat, and I said Yes please, and she brought me some bread and butter. Then the men all said good-bye and went out, and one of them took the dogs with him, and the Chief just sat there. He asked me, 'Do you know why she wants to see me?' but my mouth was full of bread and butter so I just shook my head. Then I finished eating and bowed to the Chief and came home.'

'You've done very well,' said Mother Swan.

* * *

Meanwhile, Brook the Bard ('Never stops babbling,' his mother explained when she named him) was standing on a hill near his house at the top of the glen, gazing at the eastern sky. It was lighter now, an arc of luminous whiteness that merged into pale blue at the top and pale pink down on the horizon, where a flock of small fluffy grey clouds were drifting away on a dawn breeze.

'Soft fleece of fleeing sleep-herds,' murmured Brook and smiled, pleased by the conceit. He would use that somewhere.

He paced to and fro, muttering, and pulling his red and blue checked cloak tighter around his lean body.

Chief Hardy had once said to Brook, 'Why don't you come and live in my house? We would have a laugh!'

'We would,' Brook had said, 'but what about my work?'

'You don't work!' said Hardy. 'When you're not teaching, you just wander about the hills, muttering.'

'When I wander about the hills muttering, that's me working,' Brook explained. 'I compose new poems and stories or I recite all the old ones so I won't forget them.'

Hardy shook his head wonderingly. 'That's no way for a man to live,' he said.

'It is a great sacrifice,' sighed Brook. 'That's why I have privileged status.' Actually, he loved his work.

This morning he might set the boys a task and go fishing. It was one of the few sports he was allowed to indulge in. He could fish and he could hunt small game; but he was not allowed to hunt dangerous animals like boars, stags, bears or wolves. He was too valuable to the people. If the Chief was killed in a hunting accident, another chief could be found. But if anything happened to the Bard, the people's entire history would be lost. Brook was teaching history to his two apprentices. There was a thousand years of it, all the different chiefs and their battles, the reasons for their battles, and their political marriages; and it took a long time for all this to be inserted into a boy's brain, by repeated recitations, so that it would emerge all correctly described and in the right order.

Brook's sense of urgency about teaching was fuelled by the fact that his own teacher, Deep, had died nine years ago, in the massacre at Honey Isle, before he had finished teaching Brook everything he knew.

His musings were interrupted by the sight of a runner loping along the track that led to his house. It was one of Hardy's runners. Brook sighed. No fishing for him this morning!

He was right. When the man finally arrived beside him – barely panting; they were amazing, these runners – it was to say, 'Chief Hardy invites you to breakfast.'

The Bard and the Chief were equals, so Brook could have refused the invitation, although it might have offended his friend Hardy. But he was curious. Why hadn't Hardy gone hunting or fishing? He was not a man to sit indoors on a fine day, however chilly.

The runner set off homewards and was soon lost to view. Brook set his pupils a task, then walked to Hardy's house.

Hardy greeted Brook jovially. 'Come in, my dear chap, take off your cloak, sit down –' and so forth; but Brook was suspicious. He sat down by the fire and looked around. Something was missing...

'Where are your dogs?'

'Oh, one of the men has taken them out with him. It wasn't fair for them to be stuck in here having no fun just because I am.'

'And you are stuck here having no fun because...?'

'Well, I was about to go hunting when Mother Swan sent me a message saying she was coming to see me. So I've got to wait here until she turns up.'

'So you thought, who shall I get to entertain me? I know! I'll drag Brook away from his work!' Brook sat down on one of the carved benches beside the fire. 'What you need are inner resources.'

'What are those?'

In case Hardy wasn't joking, Brook began to explain. 'Well, you know how you have a store at the back of the house where you keep timber, spears, honey and so forth?'

'The tithes, yes.'

'Well, don't think of them as tithes,' Brook began, for this notion would spoil his simile – or would it? he paused to ponder, because perhaps all inner resources were tithes of a sort, portions of other people's poetry, music and wisdom...

'Tell me the story of the raid between the Hunters and the Founders,' said Hardy.

'Not that again!'

'It's a great story.'

'Can't you remember it for yourself?'

'Yes, but you tell it so well,' Hardy grinned. He knew that bards feed on flattery.

'At least let me have breakfast first.'

Hardy's housekeeper, a quiet grey-haired woman who had looked after his household since his wife died in childbirth, brought them an excellent breakfast: barley porridge sweetened with honey, bread freshly baked in the domed clay oven at the back of the house, slices of cold beef and rounds of soft white goats' cheese. They were happily full, sighing with satisfaction and sipping their beer, and Brook expected Hardy to say, 'How about that story, then?' when Mother Swan arrived.

'What's going on?' Hardy asked her, after her cloak had been hung up and she was sitting by the fire with them.

'I don't know yet,' said Mother Swan. 'We'll have to wait and see.'

'You don't know?' said Hardy, exasperated. 'You've got me to miss a morning's hunting and you don't know why?'

'I just knew I had to come and see you today,' replied Mother Swan calmly. 'I'm sure the reason will manifest in due time. Meanwhile we can sit and chat.'

* * *

The procession moved eastwards at a good pace. The track wound through woodland and along the edge of a steep drop into a glen far below. Then the land evened out again. They passed between hills and hills, they forded streams and streams, each hill and stream with its own magic and its own story.

'Not far now,' Lady Brightleaves told them.

They began to sing. It was Willow who started, catching the mood of the day; then she faltered in case this was not wanted – but Lady Brightleaves joined in, and the others followed her, men's and women's voices raised in song among the hills. Even the little cow-boy joined in, when he thought no-one else could hear him.

They reached the mouth of Wildcat Glen. The procession was quite noisy by now, what with the singing and the tambourine and the cattle making a fuss: Why-y-y-y-y-y-y are we being moved? Wha-a-a-a-a-a-a-a-a-at's it all about? Whe-e-e-e-e-e-en will it all end?

Following normal practice, craftsmen whose work fouled the water had their workshops at the mouth of the glen, so that the streams would flow fresh and clean by the farms and households further up. Noise pollution was included in this southward-siting. Visitors to the glen, therefore, passed the dirtiest, smelliest, noisiest places first.

The apprentices, hearing the music of the procession, came out to stare.

First there were the tanner's apprentices. They left the hides browning in the smoke house, the hides painted with sludge of wood ash and water, the hides rubbed with boiled brains, and the sickly-sweet smell of the tanning pit where hides were soaking in a creamy foam of water and oak-bark – left all these to stare at the beautiful woman in her otter-fur cloak, and the pretty girls; and then, hastily, in case they were asked later, at the horses' harnesses, the warriors' shield-covers, the chariot's plaited suspension straps.

One apprentice was so stirred by the sight of Lady Brightleaves' dainty little boots, tapping on the floor of her chariot in time to the singing, that he decided then and there to focus on shoemaking as his central career skill.

Heather Dyer and her apprentices watched as the procession went past her workshop. She admired the red and yellow cloaks of the warriors, the pink cloaks of the young musicians, the green and blue cloak of the older warrior. She could guess some of the plants that must have been used. But there were plants and lichens growing near the sea that also gave colours, if boiled in water or steeped in urine; sea shells too, and she hadn't used those. She had lived in Wildcat Glen all her life.

The sound of iron clanging on iron told the members of the procession that they were passing the smithy. Between the beats of their own metallic noise, the smith's apprentices heard the singing and came out to stare. They stared at the pretty girls and the beautiful woman; they observed the quality of bridle-bits, slip-buckles, tyres, lynchpins, terrets, spear-blades, shield bosses and swords. Their eyes were especially drawn to the young warriors' jewellery and the gold torc around Lady Brightleaves' neck.

The charcoal burner, grimy from his trade, stood beside his quietly smoking heaps staring at the colourful procession. The open mouth of his child-assistant was the only pink thing to be seen on his patch.

The trainee carpenters, wainwrights and wheelwrights, like the other lads, ogled the pretty girls and the beautiful woman: they inspected the cart as it passed, a good solid piece of work; and above all they gazed at the red and yellow chariot, the yoke, the chassis, the wheels, the halving joins tipped with carved leaves –

'It's a Shaper,' said the oldest boy.

'A Shaper!' echoed a second boy reverently.

'What's a Shaper?' asked the youngest.

'They live somewhere in the south, the Shapers,' said the oldest boy. 'They make the best chariots in the world. You have to wait ages to get one.'

Everyone, then, saw different aspects of the procession as it went clip-clopping, singing and jingling on its way.

It passed farmsteads where women were sitting at their doors to catch the light, spinning, grinding corn or churning butter. In most places there were several women gathered in one porch, because repetitive work is more fun if you have someone to chat with.

That's the lady who came in the summer. The one who fancied the Chief? Yes, that one. What a lot of luggage she's got! And there's another lady with her! And a wee baby, look! Aww! And all those cattle!

As it approached its destination, the procession doubled in size because so many children abandoned their play or their chores to join it.

At last the leading cattle reached a fork in the track. In front of them was a loch. To the left, the track led to the temple and school; to the right, to Chief Hardy's house.

The cattle stopped, because the little cowboy didn't know which way he was supposed to drive them.

Hooky and Badger turned in their saddles to look enquiringly at Lady Brightleaves, who paused, pulling the reins of her white horses. Her heart and body wanted to go right. Her sense of duty told her she should go left, to take

Dainty to the High Priestess.

Behind her, Willow and Cherry stopped, the packhorses stopped, Stern stopped. The gang of following children milled about, giving shrill directions to the school.

The faces of the young warriors, turned towards her, gave Brightleaves an idea. When she was at home at Roughrock (home no longer! she reminded herself) her chariot was stored in a special hut of its own and she was the only person allowed to drive it. But she wasn't at home all the time. She went out to visit friends or to keep an eye on problem families; and for such trips as these, she went on foot or on horseback, leaving her chariot in its shed.

Right next to the warriors' fighting-practice area.

What young man could resist having a go at driving it? But they always put it back exactly as she had left it – or so they thought, in their boyish folly, for with her housewife's eye of course she could tell that it wasn't the same.

'To the right!' she ordered everyone, and off they went.

'But the temple and the school are to the left, according to these children,' said Dainty, looking worried.

'If you don't mind,' said Brightleaves, 'I'd like to drop the cattle and all this luggage off first' (and see Hardy, she thought but did not say) 'and then Hooky and Badger can drive you to the school.'

'Can they drive this chariot?'

'Oh yes!' said Brightleaves. She saw the two young men exchange glances. 'They love driving it. I expect one will drive you there, and the other will accompany you on horseback, and then they'll change places on the way back.'

'But I thought you would come with me, to introduce me to the High Priestess!'

'You don't have to be introduced to the High Priestess.

You can introduce yourself, the way I did when I visited her.'

'Oh dear!' said Dainty.

Brightleaves began to feel some sympathy for Dainty's mother-in-law. But she was too excited at the thought of seeing Hardy to let Dainty manipulate her.

'Let's have another song, girls!' she said.

Willow picked up her mood and started singing. Cherry joined in, rattling her tambourine, then the warriors joined in, then the children, who clapped their hands or clacked sticks and stones percussively.

So the Bard and the High Priestess were sitting by the Chief's fire, in his large, comfortable home, chatting with him, when all three of them heard noises approaching. They went out into the forecourt, where Lady Brightleaves' procession came to a jingling clapping clacking singing mooing stop.

Hardy saw the cattle, packhorses, warriors, and in the centre of it all his ladylove, in her chariot, already standing up. Her cheeks were rosy from the cold and her eyes sparkled. Hardy ran over to her and held out his hand to help her down from the chariot. She stepped down easily in her dainty shoes and stood looking up into his eyes.

'Here I am,' she said.

Hardy began to pull her towards the house.

'Wait!' she said. 'I want to show you all the presents I've brought you! And I must introduce you to–'

'Introductions later! Let Brook take an inventory of your baggage train, and he can tell us all about it. Oversee the unpacking, will you, Brook?'

He was already striding back to the house, holding Brightleaves by the hand.

'Willow and Cherry must oversee it too,' she said, turning towards the two girls. 'Make sure that my personal belongings are kept separate from the rest, will you, girls? Dainty, Mother Swan is here! Mother Swan, this is Dainty – '

Hardy pulled her into the house with him, and shut the door.

Brook stood looking at the cows and pack-horses.

'How to begin?' he mused.

'The pack-horses must be taken round to the store to be unloaded,' said Mother Swan. 'And the animals must be put in a pasture.'

'Probably,' said Brook. 'I was wondering how to begin the song.'

'Song? Hardy asked you to take an inventory.'

'Making a song about something is the easiest way to remember it,' said Brook.

'Grace!' Mother Swan called, and when the grey-haired housekeeper hurried over, 'All this stuff needs to be unloaded and put away. And please will you allow Brook Bard to watch, so that he can make a song about it?' Then she turned to Dainty. 'How can I help you, my dear?'

Was this dumpy old woman in the old grey cloak really the High Priestess? She didn't have an aura of mystic power. She looked more like a slave. She didn't have that clear authority that the priestess Starlight had. And Dainty's mother-in-law, who wasn't even a priestess, could make you quail just by standing in front of you and looking at you in a certain way. Dainty was not very impressed by Mother Swan.

She looked around at the bustle of cattle being moved to a pasture, pack-horses being taken to the store at the back of the house, children milling around watching everything that was going on.

Traveller woke and wailed because the motion of the chariot had stopped.

Dainty wished she hadn't come. This great long journey in search of wisdom and serenity – and here she was surrounded by chaos and about to seek advice from a well-meaning old slave-woman.

'I wanted to talk to you in private,' she said, and was going to add something along the lines of, but perhaps I should go straight to the druid instead, when Mother Swan climbed into the little chariot and sat down next to her.

Traveller stopped crying. The children dispersed. The animals were led away. The warriors and maidservants faded into the background. There was complete peace in the forecourt of Chief Hardy's house. The only sound was that of the white horses munching the grass.

'We are in private now,' said Mother Swan.

Dainty had spent much of her two-day journey preparing her opening speech for Mother Swan. In her imagination she had told her story in great detail while the sympathetic High Priestess listened. After the evening with Jewel, her story was going to be even longer.

Instead she just burst into tears and gulped, 'I don't know what to do!'

Mother Swan nodded. 'You have already done something,' she said. 'You have made the first move. Now it's time for other people to do things. You can stay in the Temple guesthouse for as long as you need to. When you're able to ride again, you can visit Druid Northway and get his advice about what your choices are. Meanwhile, other people will have done things and the situation will have changed. So you can just rest and concentrate on your baby.'

She climbed out of the chariot. 'Now,' she continued, 'I expect you would like to go to the guest house, wouldn't you?' While she spoke, Mother Swan was looking around as if expecting something or someone. Hooky appeared, followed by Badger leading his horse.

'We just came back to—' Hooky began.

'To drive Lady Dainty to the Temple guesthouse,' said Mother Swan. 'Back down to the foot of the loch and then turn right. Drive slowly! And tell the Cygnet on the gate that I sent you.'

Mother Swan watched the brightly-coloured chariot drive away. Dainty waved, smiling through her tears. Then Mother Swan went back to where Grace was supervising the unpacking and storing Lady Brightleaves' wealth: horses, cattle, shields, swords, spear-heads, hides, linen, salt, goblets...

Brook was making a song about all this.

'What about the little cowboy, sir?' Grace asked.

'Oh yes!' said Brook. 'Where is he?'

'I'll find him,' said Mother Swan.

The boy was standing just beyond the store-house, watching the cattle in their winter pasture.

'What is your name?' she asked him.

'Robin Bogend Hookhill, Ma'am.'

'What were you beaten for, Robin?'

He hung his head.

'It's all right, you can tell me,' Mother Swan reassured him. 'I won't be cross with you.'

'Singing,' whispered the boy.

'You were beaten for singing?'

'For singing!' cried Willow and Cherry, fluttering towards him in their pink cloaks. 'Beaten for singing? Oh, the poor little thing!'

'That's why he didn't join in the singing, on the way here!' said Cherry. 'I thought he was just shy!'

'He did sing, actually,' said Willow. 'He sang very quietly – I only heard him once or twice, for a moment at the end of a line.'

'Were you beaten for anything else?' Mother Swan asked.

'Muttering. Making up stories.' The boy was blushing with shame.

'Muttering and making up stories!' echoed Mother Swan, unfolding herself and standing up. 'Brook!' she called over her shoulder, 'I think this one's for you!'

Brook came loping towards them, long-legged and lean. He reminded Robin of a heron. Mother Swan met him on his way towards Robin and murmured a few words of explanation.

'So you like making up stories, do you?' Brook asked when he reached Robin.

Robin nodded warily. The man was being quite nice to him; but in his experience men could turn nasty in a moment.

'I like making up stories,' said Brook. 'In fact, I make up stories every morning. And every day, someone invites me to dinner. Do you know why they do that?'

Robin shook his head.

'Because they want to hear one of my stories. People love stories. Do you like stories?'

'Yes,' said Robin.

'All right, let's go and sit down and I'll tell you one.' They walked back towards the buildings. 'Is there a fire we can sit by?' Brook asked Grace.

'You could sit in the men's house, sir, if you don't mind it. They're all out and about at the moment.'

As Brook led Robin to the men's house, Mother Swan said quietly to Grace, 'Perhaps you could find that child something to eat? He looks as if he doesn't see food very often, let alone taste it.'

In the men's house, Brook sat down on one of the benches around the fire and poked the fire so that it flamed up brightly.

'Sit down,' he told Robin, nodding towards a bench. Robin sat. He glanced around at the house. This was where the menservants lived. It was much more comfortable than his own home. The fire was huge! He felt his body relax in the warmth.

'Once upon a time,' said Brook, 'there was a little boy who loved to sing songs and make up stories. But his uncle beat him when he heard him singing or making up stories. So the little boy only sang and told stories to the cattle, who wouldn't criticize. Then one day a lady hired him to herd some cattle for miles and miles to a glen where he hadn't been before.'

Mother Swan came into the house and, seeing that the story was in progress, motioned to Brook not to get up, walked quietly to a bench and sat down to listen.

'When they got to the top of the glen,' continued Brook, 'he met a bard, who said to him, "Would you like to be my apprentice?" "Yes please," said the little boy. So he stayed in that glen, working for the bard and learning lots of useful things. He was allowed to sing and make up stories as much as he liked. When he was grown up he became a bard himself and people gave him dinner every day. And even the Chief couldn't boss him about! So he lived happily ever after.'

'Did you like that story?' Mother Swan asked Robin.

'Yes,' said Robin, 'but it couldn't come true.'

'Why not?' Brook asked.

'Because my uncle would never sponsor me. And my aunt could never.'

During his years of training, an apprentice had to be fed, clothed, and (in winter at least) shod. Normally a boy was apprenticed to his father, whose trade he learned while his family supported him. For fatherless children or the talented sons of slaves, sponsorship had been devised. Sponsoring a bard's apprentice could be an expression of gratitude, a gift, or a way of showing off one's status. It meant one had wealth to spare.

'But your uncle and aunt have nothing to do with this,' said Mother Swan. 'Because Brook made a mistake in his story, didn't he? When he said the lady had hired you.'

Robin didn't want to say that Brook Bard had made a mistake, so he sat with his head hanging and said nothing.

'Ah, so Lady Brightleaves bought you!' said Brook.

Robin nodded.

'Perhaps she'll be willing to sponsor you.'

'She's already spent two cows on me!' said Robin.

Grace came in with a plate. She looked disapproving when she saw Mother Swan sitting in the men's house, but as it was the High Priestess, she said nothing. She brought Robin the plate, a wooden plate bearing a chunk of fresh bread and a grilled pork chop. His eyes widened.

'Is this all for me?' he asked.

'Yes,' said Mother Swan.

Robin had never seen so much bread and meat for one

person. He ate a couple of mouthfuls, then tried to hide the rest inside his belt-pouch when neither of the grown-ups was looking.

Brook had a belt-pouch of red leather tooled with spiral designs.

Mother Swan had a belt-pouch of tightly-woven wool in many colours.

Robin's belt-pouch was just a piece of sacking, scrunched up and tucked under the length of twisted honeysuckle vine that served him as a belt.

He wasn't sure where this sudden awareness of belt-pouches had come from; but because of it, he wasn't surprised when Mother Swan asked him,

'Why have you put that food in your belt-pouch?'

'To save it for later.'

'It will get dirty in there,' she said. 'I expect you put all kinds of things in there, don't you? Dead mice, bits of fleece, dead birds...'

He stared at her wide-eyed. This woman knew everything!

'So it won't taste very nice,' she continued.

'It will be better than nothing,' said Robin.

'You expect to get nothing later, then,' said Mother Swan. It was a statement rather than a question. 'Brook, I think you'd better take this boy home with you. But first – give me that bread and meat, Robin. And the plate.'

Robin pulled the food out of his pouch, certain he was going to be punished. Both bread and meat were covered in tiny bits of stuff – hairs, a small feather, brown leaf-fragments, grass-stalks, a dead beetle. Mother Swan flicked off the dirt as best she could, then took a sharp stick from the woodpile, impaled the bread on the end and began to toast it over the fire. The smell made Robin's mouth water. She laid the toasted bread on the plate, then stuck the chop on the end of the poker and re-grilled it until all the rubbish burned off.

'There,' she said, passing the plate back to Robin. 'Eat it all, when it's cool enough. You will certainly get more food later. If you don't, you can come and complain to me.'

The two grown-ups talked while Robin ate the food. Then Mother Swan stood up, saying,

'Time to go. They won't be coming out again today.'

Chapter 4. The bards

As Brook and Robin approached Brook's house, they could hear the sounds of two voices reciting poetry and the soft twanging of a lyre.

Brook grinned. 'They've seen us coming and they're putting on an act for me, to show me how hard they've been working in my absence.'

Inside the house, two boys were sitting on a bench by the fire. The older one put aside his lyre when Brook and Robin came in. The younger one went on reciting, with his eyes closed, as if so absorbed in his task that he didn't realize anyone else was there.

'Over-acting, Marten!' said Brook. 'Wake up, I want you both to meet Robin.'

Robin, who'd been hiding behind Brook's cloaked figure, emerged quietly at the bard's side.

'Hi, Robin,' said the older boy. 'I'm Raven.' The name suited him; he was tall and lean with black hair and a hooked nose.

'And I'm Marten, as you heard,' said the younger boy, who had light brown hair and a round freckled face. 'But I want to change my name. Don't get me wrong, I like martens! I like their quickness, and the way they put their heads on one side to listen for things, and the way they stand like little bears, and the way they can climb trees going down as well as up – that's brilliant. But I'd like my name to be more – more shiny.'

'Shiny?' echoed Robin.

'Yes, you know, like Flame or Glitter or – '

'Twinkle?' suggested Raven quietly. Marten glowered at him.

'Well, I can see you're going to get on all right,' said Brook. 'I need to go off and compose a poem, to celebrate Chief Hardy's forthcoming wedding. I want you two to teach Robin a bit of history while I'm out. And help yourselves to some food – but don't forget to put the cheese back in the crock, unless you want the mice to eat it.'

When he'd gone, Robin and the two boys stood looking at each other for a moment. Then Marten said, 'Well, you'd better take your, er, cloak off.'

Robin untied the knot at his neck and hung up the greyish rag on one of the pegs to the left of the doorway, beside the two cloaks that were hanging there already. One was grown-up size, with red and yellow checks. That must be tall Raven's. The smaller one was blue with red lines woven through.

A farmer's wife in Hookhill Glen had given Robin a cloak once. His Uncle Bluff took it to Chief Hookhill's steward and swapped it for a flagon of beer.

Raven's and Marten's shirts and trousers, also woven of wool in bright criss-crossing colours, did not have a single hole in them that Robin could see. And both boys wore shoes. His feet just wore a layer of dirt.

'So we've got to do some history,' Raven was saying, 'and have a snack, and then – '

'Snack first,' said Marten. 'We can't do history on an empty stomach.'

In a partition at the back of the house was a broad shelf bearing several large lidded pots and a few knives. Raven took the lids off three of the pots and lifted out some oatcakes, half a wheel of cheese and a pile of barley biscuits.

'Tuck in,' Marten advised Robin, cutting himself a generous slice of cheese. 'Eat as much as you like.'

'Are we really allowed to eat as much as we like?' Robin asked.

'Of course we are,' said Raven.

This had never happened to Robin before. It was a day of new experiences for him. He'd already been given bread and meat by Grace and here he was being offered something more to eat. It was amazing.

'Where does all this food come from?' he asked, between mouthfuls of oatcake and cheese.

'Grace sends some from Chief Hardy's house because Brook is his bard,' said Raven. 'And my sponsor sends some – he's Chief Quickwater, in the next glen.'

'And my sponsors are the Thornridges, they're farmers,' said Marten. 'Mrs Thornridge made these biscuits – try one.'

Robin's eyes widened when he bit into a biscuit.

'They're good, aren't they?' said Marten. 'It's the honey.'

Robin had never tasted honey before. He had sucked the nectar from flowers in the woods and fields, but this was a much more intense sweetness.

He decided to eat as much as he could, while he was here. It would all come to an end soon. He would be sent home to be cold and hungry and not allowed to sing.

'Now we'd better teach you some history,' said Raven, when they had eaten as much as they wanted. He sat down on the bench beside his lyre. Marten, with his drum, sat next to him and Robin sat on the bench opposite. The fire warmed the whole house. Marten got up and threw on an extra log. Robin watched in wonder and fear, expecting

Raven to get angry and say that the log should be saved for the evening.

Instead he said, 'We're going to start at the beginning.'

'Not the beginning of time!' said Marten, sitting down again. 'Just the beginning of history.'

Raven strummed a sombre chord on his lyre and intoned, 'It was one thousand, two hundred years ago –'

'One thousand two hundred years!' echoed Marten, and beat a roll on his drum.

'When a Great Darkness rolled in from over the sea and covered the land!' continued Raven.

'A Great Darkness!' shouted Marten. 'It covered the land!'

'And the air was full of poisonous smoke, so that when people breathed – '

'They choked and died!'

'And when the rain fell, it did not refresh!'

'It burned like fire!'

'Mothers died,' chanted Raven, 'fathers died, children died.'

'Sheep died in the field,' sang Marten, 'wolves died in the woods. Great eagles fell from the sky!'

'And the land was laid waste,' Raven intoned gloomily.

'Laid waste!' echoed Marten.

'But one man did not die!'

'Father Hunter!'

'And one woman did not die!'

'Mother Hunter!'

Then they sang in unison: 'The ancestors! The ancestors! All hail to the ancestors!'

'We'd better not go on too long to begin with,' said Raven in an ordinary voice. 'Let's see how much of that you can remember, Robin.'

'Do I have to do the chanting?'

'No, you can just say it. Once you've learned it you can start adding the sound-effects.'

'One thousand two hundred years ago,' began Robin.

'That's right,' said Marten, 'but every year you have to add one. So after next Winterbrink, you'll be saying "One thousand, two hundred and one years ago." You have to remember that. And you have to think of a way of reminding yourself.'

'Never mind all that for now,' said Raven. 'Let him carry on.'

'A great darkness covered the land,' said Robin.

'That's right. Where did it come from?'

'Oh, from over the sea.'

'And by the way,' said Marten, 'when you get to the animals and birds, you can put in any you like. Choose ones you think your audience will care about.'

'Stop interrupting him, Marten, he's got to do the poisonous smoke and the burning rain first.'

'How did the ancestors survive when everyone else was dying?' asked Robin, after he had talked his way through the story.

'Nobody knows,' said Raven. 'We can make up reasons. Any ideas?'

'Maybe they put cloths over their faces to breathe through?' suggested Robin.

'And hid in a cave to keep out of the burning rain,' said Marten. 'But what would they eat if everything was poisoned?'

'Maybe they had stuff in storage pits.'

'But then they had to live through three years of

darkness when the sun never shone!' said Raven. 'And it got so cold that nothing would grow. We'll teach you that bit next. How did they live? It's a mystery.'

'I like mysteries,' said Marten, 'but I don't like trying to think about how they could happen; it makes my mind ache.' He got up, ran to the door and peeked out. 'No sign of Brook yet,' he said. 'Let's sing Robin our song!'

'My song,' Raven corrected. He picked up his lyre and stood back, away from the bench. Marten sat down on an upturned bucket next to him, hands poised over the drum.

They sang:

'You can milk cows, girl,
but you can't milk me!
You can milk co-ows,
sweetie, but you can't milk me!
You can milk all the cows in the field but girlie,
you can't milk me!

'You can shear sheep, girl,
but you can't fleece me!
You can sheer shee-eep
sweetie, but you can't fleece me!
You can sheer all the sheep on the hill, girlie
but you can't fleece me!

'You can pluck chickens, girl,
but you can't pluck me!
You can pluck chick-chick-chickens
but you can't pluck me!
You can pluck all the chickens in the hencoop
but girlie, you can't pluck me!'

The singing stopped. Raven plucked a final riff on his lyre; Marten beat a last drum-roll, and they both looked at Robin.

'What do you think?' Raven asked.

'I've never heard anything like it,' said Robin.

'Raven wrote it for his girlfriend,' said Marten.

'You must really hate her!' said Robin.

'Nah, he's nuts about her,' said Marten the worldly wise.

'Brook hates that kind of music,' said Raven. 'He calls it "mindless noise". That's why we only play it when he's away in the hills.'

'But what did you think of it, really?' asked Marten. 'Did you like it?'

'I found it quite–' Robin tried to think of a word. 'I can't really explain. It sort of made my mind fly away.'

This seemed to please them. Raven nodded and Marten said, 'I think that's what it's supposed to do.'

'It should be played in a bigger space, though,' said Robin, 'maybe outside, and with more people listening.'

'At the wedding feast!' said Marten, his eyes sparkling.

'Chief Hardy's wedding feast?' said Raven. 'I don't think so!'

'Not at the beginning. We can wait till after all the usual stuff; then the grown-ups will go into Hardy's house to talk about politics, or they'll go home, and we can play our song.'

Raven thought about this and began to smile.

'Why not?' he said.

'Whee!' said Marten, and beat an excited drum-roll.

'Maybe we should do some more history before Brook gets back,' suggested Raven. 'There are forty-two kings to get through after Father Hunter. Including the bit where everyone got so hungry that lots of women died in childbirth so the men had to share wives!'

'I'm still wondering how Mother and Father Hunter survived,' said Robin.

'Yes, it gets to you, doesn't it?' said Marten. 'Maybe they ate birds that had flown in from somewhere that wasn't poisoned?'

'Maybe they were helped by the Goddess or one of the gods?' Robin suggested.

Raven shook his head. 'Brook says that divine intervention is a questionable narrative device.'

Robin frowned. 'What does that mean?'

'Well, divine intervention means a god or a goddess helping.'

'Or hindering, as the case may be,' said Marten.

'Narrative means a story,' continued Raven, 'and a device is like a tool. A god helping is a questionable tool to shape a story with, because people can question it. Like, why did the god help those people rather than some other people? Why didn't he help sooner rather than later? Then they start giving the gods offerings, to bribe them to do stuff. When that doesn't work, they think they have to give bigger offerings. And so it goes on, until the whole system destroys itself. That's what Brook says, anyway.'

'That's what happened to the Druids, he says,' Marten put in.

'What, they made bigger and bigger offerings?'

'No, when they started trying to look into the future with human entrails,' said Marten, with ghoulish delight.

'Brook says a really good Druid doesn't need entrails to look into the future, he can do it with anything,' said Raven. 'Anything to hand – a few leaves blown into a corner, the grain in a piece of wood, a wind-ripple on a pool. And he says the future isn't set anyway, but it has tendencies and you can see these if you know how. Some Druids used animal or bird entrails to look into the future – and they didn't like what they saw.'

'Because what they saw was the Romans coming!' said Marten, lover of drama. 'So they decided those entrails couldn't be good enough, they'd have to use human ones. And of course people didn't like that.'

'Well, to begin with they just used criminals' entrails,' said Raven, 'and people didn't mind about that so much, except the criminals of course. But the Druids were getting in a panic and wanting to look into the future more and more. Every time they did it, they didn't like what they saw. They had to check again, and that meant having more entrails. Then they started making more people into criminals and condemning them to death for really silly reasons.'

'So people started hating the Druids,' said Marten. 'Which was bad luck on the nice ones who didn't use human entrails to read the future.'

'The result was,' said Raven, 'that when the Romans came to attack the Druids on High Island, nobody came to help them. Everyone thought, good riddance! Let the Romans get on with it and we can't be blamed. But of course the good Druids got killed as well. Brook's teacher was killed.'

'Some of them escaped,' said Marten. 'There are still a few, wandering around. But they have to sneak about disguised as pedlars.'

'The problem is,' said Raven, 'the Druids knew all the laws. The people who were taught by Druids try to remember what the laws were; but of course they can't remember them all, not unless they're fully trained Druids themselves. So chiefs and kings are making up their own laws now.'

'Is that bad?' Robin asked.

'Well it is in a way,' said Raven, 'because it depends what the king or the chief is like. If he's a good bloke, he'll make up decent laws – but if not...'

Brook came into the house, emanating that fresh-air glow that people have when they come in from outside on a crisp day.

'I've got it!' he said as he took off his cloak and hung it up. 'The poem is complete! What have you boys been up to?'

'We've done ancient history and some modern history!' said Marten proudly.

'We were just explaining about chiefs and kings having to make up their own laws now,' said Raven.

'The lucky ones,' said Brook. 'In the countries that have been taken over by the Romans, the people have to live by Roman laws – even the chiefs and kings.'

'The Romans won't take us over, will they, Sir?' asked Marten.

'Let's hope not,' said Brook. He strode over to the food shelf and helped himself to cheese and biscuits. 'Time for some bodily exercise, boys. You can all go out wood-collecting. Raven, please bring some water from the stream. You're all going to have a bath.'

'Oh no!' groaned Marten. 'Do we have to?'

Robin looked nervous. He had never had a bath.

'I want you to be clean for the chief's wedding,' said Brook. 'Hair washed too. Consider it part of your bardic training, boys.'

He knew that Raven and Marten were relatively clean. But he wanted Robin to wash all over in hot water before he went to bed. Fleas in the house were just a nuisance.

Marten and Robin collected firewood. Raven fetched the water and poured it into three cauldrons. Three cauldrons! Brook must be rich, Robin thought, even though he wore simple clothes and no jewellery. One cauldron hung from a tripod, the others were wedged at the edges of the fire, supported by stones. Raven and Marten dragged a big wooden tub from the back of the house to stand it near the fire. It was big enough for a person to sit in. When the water in the cauldrons began to bubble, Brook and Raven emptied them into the tub. Brook scattered herbs into the water – tansy, groundmint, wormwood, all known to deter fleas, then Raven added some cold water to the tub.

Robin recognized the smells of the herbs although he did not know their uses. Raven and Brook refilled the cauldrons and put them back on the fire. Then Raven took all his clothes off, stepped into the tub and sat down in the hot water. Robin watched in amazement. He had never seen anyone do this.

Marten handed Raven a lump of pale stuff. Raven rubbed himself all over with it, handed the lump back to Marten, then rinsed the traces of it off his face, neck, shoulders and chest.

Perhaps this is a special bardic ritual, Robin thought.

Raven wetted his hair and reached out his hand. Marten put the lump of pale stuff into the outstretched hand. Raven rubbed some of the pale stuff into his hair while Brook filled a jug with warm water. Marten took the jug and emptied it slowly over Raven's head, so that the pale stuff trickled out of his hair.

It must be a ritual, Robin decided.

Raven stood up and stepped out of the tub, dripping. Brook handed him a large square of coarse-woven linen, with which he rubbed himself dry.

'Next!' said Brook, while Raven put on his clothes.

Marten had taken off his clothes. Naked, he swung first one leg then the other over the side of the tub, and sat down. He sloshed water over himself in a business-like fashion, humming merrily.

'Where did you put the soap, Marten?' said Brook, looking about.

'Er… oh, never mind,' said Marten. 'I can do without. I'll find it when I get out.'

'Marten!' said Brook.

'I don't need soap,' said Marten. 'I'm quite clean really.'

'Surely by now you've learned not to get it in your eyes?' said Raven. 'You're acting like a two-year-old.'

'It's under the bench,' Marten sighed. Raven found it and handed the pale lump to Marten.

So that's soap! thought Robin. He had often heard Aunt Pansy say, 'Oh, if only I had some soap!' But she never did, so he had never seen it. He knew it was made from beef fat. They could have made some when their cow gave birth to a bullock, but Uncle Bluff took the bullock to Chief Hookhill's steward and that was the last they saw of it. Whatever he exchanged it for, he didn't come home for days.

Marten soaped and rinsed himself as Raven had done, then washed his hair.

'Your turn, Robin,' said Brook when Marten climbed out of the tub.

Robin took off his ragged clothes and dropped them on the floor. Raven and Marten stared at him.

'How did you get all those bruises?' Marten asked.

'From Uncle Bluff,' said Robin.

'I'm glad I don't have any uncles!' said Marten. 'I used to feel sorry for myself, not having a family, but now I think I'm better off without one.'

Brook was pouring more hot water into the tub. He threw in some more herbs.

'Marten,' he said, 'while Robin's in the tub, I want you to have a look through your clothes basket and see if you have anything spare that might fit him. Shirt, trousers, cloak.'

Marten went to one of the bed-spaces and pulled out a basket from under the bed.

'Come on, Robin,' said Brook. 'In you get.'

Robin's legs were slightly shorter than Marten's. He put one leg over the edge of the tub and felt the water with his toe. It wasn't too hot. But his foot couldn't reach the bottom unless he lifted the other foot off the floor.

Firm hands gripped him under the arms from behind, lifted him up and plonked him down in the tub.

'Thank you, Raven,' said Brook. He handed Robin the soap. 'Give yourself a good wash, now. You've seen how it's done.'

'Don't get soap in your mouth!' Marten warned.

Robin sat in the hot water, rubbing soap over himself and then rinsing it off. On one side of him was the fire, reflected in the sides of the cauldrons. On his other side the glow lit up the friendly faces of his new companions. He felt as if he was in a dream. When he woke up it would be cold and dark, and Uncle Bluff would be shouting, and Aunt Pansy saying, Oh please don't Bluff, please...

The soap smelled of heather. How did they get beef-fat

to smell of heather? he wondered. Then he realized that, in this dream, it was safe to ask such questions aloud.

'How do they get soap to smell of heather?' he asked.

'I don't know,' said Brook. 'It's women who make soap. We can ask Lady Brightleaves, she'll know.'

They were going to ask Lady Brightleaves something he had asked! This was definitely a dream.

'Wash your hair too,' said Brook. 'I should think it'll need two washes.'

'Shut your eyes when he pours the water on your head!' Marten shouted in warning.

When the hair-washing was over, and Robin was out of the tub and drying himself, he looked for his clothes. They were nowhere to be seen. There was a smell of burning cloth coming from one corner of the fire.

Marten offered him a linen shirt and wool trousers. The shirt had been red but was now a soft pink. The trousers were grey-green. 'They're faded,' said Marten, 'but there aren't any holes in them.'

They were the smartest clothes Robin had ever worn.

'He'll need a belt to keep his trousers up,' said Raven. 'I've got an old one he can use.'

'And then there's this,' said Marten. He held up a cloak, the colours of foxes and buttercups. Robin gasped.

'Yes,' said Marten, 'Mrs Thornridge used to say I looked like a little ray of sunshine in this. She won't need it back until she has grandchildren. Here, catch.' He tossed it to Robin. 'It'll be a bit small,' he added. 'But better than the one you had before.'

The cloak had a proper bronze clasp to fasten it. No more struggling with damp swollen knots on a finger-chilling day.

'Now he just needs some shoes,' said Brook. 'We'll take him to Crag Tanner in the morning.'

Then they had to empty the tub, which meant carrying out buckets of water to throw away down the hillside. 'Don't splash your clothes!' Brook warned; but of course they ended up splashed, standing around the fire laughing as they steamed.

Chapter 5. Dream-Blossom

When Pickle told her little friends about her early morning adventure, they were amazed. 'While we were asleep!' 'To the Chief's house!' 'In your new dress!' 'And you sat by the Chief's fire!' 'What was the message?'

'I can't tell you that!' said Pickle. 'We're only supposed to tell the message to the person it's for.'

A slightly older girl, whose mother had seen fit to name her Dream-Blossom, looked across the Cygnet house at the group around Pickle – the little rosy faces, the sparkling eyes, the general air of excitement. Stupid children! Getting so worked up about a little thing like that. 'Oh Pickle aren't you wonderful!' she mocked inwardly, 'Took a message! That's certainly going to change the world, isn't it?'

Dream-Blossom, with her perfect oval face and smooth dark hair, would have been pretty, except that her expression was usually unpleasant. Her eyes, fringed with long dark lashes, tended to flick rapidly about like blue fish, seeking things for their owner to criticise and sneer at.

It was house-tidying time. Dream-Blossom hated housework, which she thought was beneath her as well as boring, and she resented having to do her share. Today she was in a worse mood than usual as she swept, dusted, shook, folded and tucked. It wasn't fair. Why had Pickle been chosen to take the message? It would have been much more suitable if I had taken it, she thought. At least I know how to behave in chiefs' houses, unlike Pickle! I don't suppose she's even been in a chief's house before.

'And did the Chief speak to you?' a child asked.

Pickle hesitated. Yes, the Chief had spoken to her – but if she said that, the next question would be 'What did he say?' and if she answered that one, it would give away what the message had been.

'Of course he didn't speak to her!' said Dream-Blossom coldly. 'Why would he want to speak to a brat like that?'

All the fun and fizz went out of the group of little girls. They got on quietly with their individual chores and then went out, one by one, to their next lesson. Pickle was the last to leave. She had changed out of her new dress and was folding it up to put it away. Dream-Blossom suddenly leaped across the room, grabbed Pickle's hair, twisted it round her hand and tugged it viciously.

'That's for showing off!' she hissed.

'I wasn't showing off,' whimpered Pickle, with tears of pain in her eyes. 'I was just telling them – '

'You were boasting!'

'No I wasn't –'

'Don't contradict me! I heard you! "I was allowed to wear my new dress!" As if that made you special!'

'I wasn't *allowed* to wear my new dress,' Pickle explained. 'I was *told* to.'

This pedantry seemed to enrage Dream-Blossom still further. She let go of Pickle's hair and snatched the dress out of the child's hands.

'Well you're not special, d'you hear me? You're nothing! And as for your new dress, I'll take it to the latrine–'

'No!' wept the child.

'Yes! And it's just a question of where I'll drop it – into the piss bucket? Or down the shit pit?'

'Neither, I think,' said a voice from the doorway. There

stood Curly, the priestess in charge of the juniors.

How does she do that? wondered Dream-Blossom in the midst of her shame. Some of the teachers seemed to be drawn to wherever they were needed, as if they could see through walls and hear what people were thinking.

Curly reached out her hand in silence. Dream-Blossom gave her Pickle's dress.

'Get your cloak and wait for me outside,' said Curly quietly. Then she turned her back on Dream-Blossom and started comforting Pickle, helping her to refold the dress and put it back in its basket, whispering to her so that Dream-Blossom couldn't hear what they were saying. The two of them ignored Dream-Blossom while she put on her cloak and left the Cygnet house.

If Dream-Blossom had to be caught by any of the teachers, she was especially sorry it was Curly. She heroine-worshipped Curly and wanted the young woman to like her. Curly was a princess; her sister was a queen somewhere in the far north where the hills were impossibly high. Her people were called the Doughties. Her long dark hair was very curly and on her round white arms she wore gold bracelets and armbands, which somehow looked more like armour than jewellery, as if they were designed to ward off sword-slashes and spear thrusts.

Dream-Blossom wanted Curly's respect more than anyone's and now it seemed she had lost all hope of it.

It wasn't fair.

While she stood outside in the cold, waiting for Curly, Dream-Blossom soon managed to convince herself that she was the one hard done by in this situation. Curly would never like her now – and it was all Pickle's fault! She had worked herself up into a state of tearful self-righteousness by the time Curly appeared.

Curly took no notice of Dream-Blossom's tear-filled eyes and martyred expression.

'Come with me,' she said in matter-of-fact tones, and led the girl across the compound to Mother Swan's house.

Dream-Blossom began to feel nervous.

The house was quiet when they entered. Mother Swan was out and it was as if she had created this stillness in her house and left it there for them to experience. Curly did not speak, and Dream-Blossom did not dare to. They took their cloaks off and hung them on pegs beside the door. They left the door open to let in light. Curly sat down on a bench at one side of the fire; Dream-Blossom sat opposite her.

At first, she was looking around with her friends in mind, in case there was anything interesting in Mother Swan's house, so that she could tell them about it. She was already looking forward to seeing them afterwards, when she'd had her scolding and been sent back to her class. They'd get together in break as usual; Joy-of-Spring would giggle and Rainbow would make a clever remark. So Dream-Blossom had to find something juicy to tell them.

But she couldn't see anything interesting in Mother Swan's house. It was disappointingly ordinary. She remembered thinking how ordinary it was when she first saw it, on the day her father brought her to be enrolled in the school. That first visit had been quite a shock.

She'd heard so many amazing stories about the Swan Priestesses: they could turn themselves into swans and fly; they could heal people by singing magic songs; they could hear what people were thinking; plants talked to them. Then she had actually seen one of these marvellous beings. It was in the time of the old king, who was dead now. Her father was in charge of all the King's ships. He took her to Highplace for the day because he had to see the King on some official business. While he and the King settled down for their talk, the Queen was most gracious to Dream-Blossom, speaking kindly to her and giving her a piece of hazelnut cake flavoured with clover flowers. She was halfway through eating it when a Swan Priestess appeared in the doorway, wearing a white cloak covered in swan feathers. A hush fell on the house. Everybody bowed. Even the King and Queen bowed before the Swan Priestess.

For a long time afterwards, Dream-Blossom associated the taste of hazelnuts and clover with that hush, everybody bowing, that atmosphere of awe and respect.

Then she heard that there was a school where girls could train to become swan priestesses. After that, her father had no peace. She tried every ploy known to a spoilt only daughter. She pleaded, cajoled, pouted, wept, sulked, bargained with promises of good behaviour, refused to speak, and so on.

In spite of all this hard work – and she was very persistent – she might not have succeeded, had it not been for the appearance in her life of a potential stepmother. This lady soon realized that if she was going to get any attention at all from the First Sea Lord, his daughter would have to be elsewhere. So she took Dream-Blossom's side in the debate about the school. Why not let the child go there? It might be a great advantage to have a swan priestess in the family. And so on.

That was how Dream-Blossom had ended up here in Mother Swan's house, that first day. She wasn't sure what she had been expecting, but it certainly wasn't such an ordinary-looking house. Nobody was wearing feather cloaks.

The bigger girls wore brown cloaks. And the High Priestess, who wore a grey cloak, looked like a dumpy old farmer's wife (except that her eyes went right through you, as if she could see what you were thinking). Dream-Blossom was in that state of slowly increasing shock created by the incoming tide of reality nibbling at the sandcastle of illusion. Only pride prevented her from asking her father to take her home again.

More shocks were to follow.

Some of the girls in Cygnet House were the daughters of rich important men, as she was. Others were the daughters of craftsmen, farmers, even slaves. Yet they were all treated the same! She, Dream-Blossom, had to make her own bed, help to tidy the house, and bring in logs for the fire!

Then there was the milking...

The Cygnets were divided into twos and threes for their 'milking groups'. Dream-Blossom thought this must be something esoteric, until the morning when one of the Pens, as the senior girls were called, woke her and said, 'Come on! Milking time!' Off they went to a nearby farm to milk cows. This happened every few days. Sometimes they went to a different farm and milked goats. Mother Swan thought it was a good idea for them all to learn this skill but Dream-Blossom couldn't imagine why she would ever need it.

One of the older girls explained: 'It's so that, when you're a healer, if you get called out to a little farm where the woman's lying ill and the man's away and the children are too small to do milking, you can milk the cows or goats – which will stop the animals getting ill and provide food for the children and for your patient.'

Dream-Blossom and her friends Rainbow and Joy-of-

Spring made a secret pact that they would never go out to a small farm where they had to do the milking.

You could even get a Milking Badge, if you cared enough. Images of the badges people could get were painted on the wall of the Cygnet House. Dream-Blossom thought the badges were silly. But the other girls looked at the pictures and chattered about which badges they'd got and which ones they were working for and which one they longed to have. The badges were made by the senior girls, embroidered in coloured wools on small scraps of coarse-woven linen. When you earned a badge, you sewed it onto your cloak. Dream-Blossom had actually earned a badge (which she was secretly rather proud of, although she would never have admitted it). When she was much younger, her granny had taught her to spin. 'If you're going to sit around day-dreaming, you may as well do it with a spindle in your hand,' the old lady had remarked. Dream-Blossom had found it rather soothing, once she'd got the knack of it, and could now spin a beautifully even thread from wool or flax. So she had a badge, with a picture of a spindle on it, sewn on to her grey Cygnet cloak.

But Dream-Blossom hadn't come to here to get a Spinning Badge. She had come here to get a white feather cloak, to learn how to fly, and to have magic words that would give her special powers whispered in her ear.

Well, she was given a white cloak. But it was grown-up size.

'You will grow into it,' the Pen in charge of cloaks told her. Meanwhile, she would wear the grey cloak of a Cygnet.

Dream-Blossom's white cloak had no feathers on it!

'You have to collect the feathers yourself, in your free time, and sew them on. That's all part of the training.'

That would be all very well if you lived in a place where there were hundreds of swans. But the small loch in Wildcat Glen could not support many swans, so the girls were in competition for the feathers. Sometimes, on a free afternoon, a group of girls travelled to a more distant loch or river and wandered along the banks, looking for signs of a swan's landing place or nesting spot, where feathers might be found.

'At this rate it's going to take me years to finish my swan cloak!' Dream-Blossom complained to a Pen.

'That's the point,' was the unsatisfactory reply. 'That's why we give you the cloak while you're still little, so you've got years to work on it. It's symbolic: when you work on the cloak, you're working on yourself.'

Dream-Blossom had done very little work on her cloak. She was just too indignant about the whole thing. If it had been any other kind of bird, she would have sent a messenger to her father asking him to have one killed for her, so that she could have all its feathers. But swans were sacred, so nobody was allowed to kill them. It wasn't fair.

'It's all part of a plot to make us feel inferior,' said Rainbow. 'We're forever being reminded that we're not as good as the special girls.'

'What d'you mean, the special girls?' asked Joy-of-Spring who, unlike Dream-Blossom, didn't mind showing her ignorance.

'Every summer,' said Rainbow, 'Mother Swan travels all over the country talent-spotting. Sometimes she even goes to other countries. It depends where she's "called", you see!' and Rainbow whispered the word 'called' in fake awe, rolling her eyes.

Joy-of-Spring gasped in admiration of Rainbow for daring

to make fun of the High Priestess.

'So,' continued Rainbow, 'she finds girls who have natural talent as priestesses. And they come to the school. But most of them are poor. And the school' – here Rainbow did an imitation of the solemn, semi-chanting voice used by one of the Pens when she led the Meditation class – 'the school exists in the ma-ter-ial world and so it needs ma-ter-ial things.' (This made Joy-of-Spring giggle so much that when she remembered it during the next meditation class she couldn't stop giggling and was sent out.) 'That's where we come in,' Rainbow concluded. 'Our parents donate the material stuff the school needs and in exchange, we are allowed to come here. So there are basically two kinds of pupils – poor and clever, or rich and stupid.'

'So we're the rich stupid ones?' said Dream-Blossom indignantly.

'That's us!' said Rainbow.

In fact, even rich girls were only accepted if Mother Swan felt they had a glimmer of talent.

The trio decided that if they were seen as stupid, they were going to act stupid. They pretended not to understand the simplest instruction from their seniors. In class, they tried not to take in anything at all; but the teachers were subtle and cunning, and the girls, almost against their will, began to find themselves fascinated by the shapes, colours, flavours and smells of herbs, and of course by the dramatic diseases that they alleviated. Meditation, too, became more than merely permission to daydream, because at the end of each class, the teacher would go round the circle, asking each girl in turn to describe what she had seen during her meditation. Then she would comment, perhaps explaining the symbolism of what a girl had seen. If you made up stuff, she didn't comment, she just said, 'Next!' and moved on to the next girl. Dream-Blossom and Rainbow were both too competitive to be satisfied with this for long; in the end they had to do it properly, just to earn a comment. Joy-of-Spring had never been able to make things up in any case, so she always reported exactly what she saw in her meditations, even if that was nothing.

Acting stupid for the prefects was one form of amusement. Another was taunting the 'special' pupils, the poor and clever ones. Remarks like 'Why are you carrying those logs in? Can't you make them fly here from the woodpile?' or 'Going feather-hunting? Why not just collect some hen-feathers and say a magic word over them?' seemed terribly clever and provoked storms of rather nervous giggling in Joy-of-Spring.

Today, Dream-Blossom had gone too far.

Curly reached for one of Mother Swan's fire irons and poked the fire.

'So, Dream-Blossom,' she said, 'do you want to leave the school?'

'No!' said Dream-Blossom in alarm.

'Then we have to decide if we want to keep you.' said Curly.

'You have to,' said Dream-Blossom. She was confident about this. 'My father donated all that timber for rebuilding the temple.'

Curly shook her head. 'Lots of parents give generous donations. We always make it clear that their donation doesn't guarantee their daughter can stay here, if she turns out to have unsuitable qualities. As you have.'

'Unsuitable?' echoed Dream-Blossom indignantly.

'We are training to be healers here,' said Curly. 'Cruelty

is an unsuitable quality in a healer.'

Dream-Blossom hung her head so that she wouldn't have to look Curly in the face.

'So, you need to develop compassion,' continued Curly, as if this was just a practical problem with a practical solution.

'How do I do that?' Dream-Blossom asked humbly.

'Well, there's a huge obstacle in your way at the moment,' said Curly.

Dream-Blossom relaxed. If there was a huge obstacle, then it wasn't her fault. Someone else would sort it out. 'What is it?' she asked.

'Your sense of superiority,' said Curly. 'We are training to be healers, remember. Superiority is an unsuitable quality in a trainee.'

'I don't understand,' said Dream-Blossom.

'Well, would you have treated Pickle the way you did if she was a chief's daughter? Of course not. If she'd been a princess, you would have been flattering her. But you knew she was a slave's child, so you felt superior to her, you felt it was all right for you to take out your vicious jealousy on her.'

The part of that speech which hurt Dream-Blossom the most was the sentence: If she'd been a princess, you would have been flattering her. She wanted to tell Curly, I don't flatter you because you're a princess! I think you're wonderful!

Vicious jealousy was a bit hurtful too. As if she would be jealous of someone like Pickle!

'Healers are in service to all of humanity,' said Curly. 'If you're training to be a healer, you're training to be a servant.' She stood up. 'There are two things I want you to do for me before I come back. One is a simple practical task. Tend the fire. You may think it's beneath your dignity but I need you to prove to me that you can do it efficiently. The second thing is a mental exercise. Imagine that you're a grown-up priestess and you're in charge of the Cygnets at a school like this. One of the girls has behaved as you have today. What could this girl do to show that she's sorry? And what tasks would you set her to allow her to prove that she deserves to stay at the school?'

Curly put on her cloak and went out, without looking back.

* * *

Hardy and Brightleaves had been left undisturbed. A servant occasionally crept into the house, to put wood on the fire, and crept away again unnoticed. Only the upper half of the door was left open, to let in light. Once when Brightleaves got up to use the piss-pot, she found a table placed just outside the bed-curtains, with a plate of bread and cheese and two cups of mead on it. She and Hardy ate the food in bed, giggling like children as the crumbs fell, then licking them off each other's bodies.

While they lay resting, Brightleaves became aware that there was a lot of activity outside the house; people shouting instructions, heavy objects being dragged about, feet running to and fro.

'What's going on?' she asked.

'I think they're getting the wedding-feast ready,' said Hardy.

'What?' Brightleaves wanted to sit up, to spring into action, but there was such a strong pull between her body and his, she could only prop herself up on her elbow for a

moment then fall back again with a sigh on the soft heather
mattress.

'What's the matter?' he asked.

'I don't want to have my wedding-feast today.'

'Oh, it won't be today,' Hardy assured her. 'The whole
glen will want to come, so Grace will cook a whole bullock.
The wedding feast will be tomorrow.'

'Tomorrow!'

Now she sat up. 'But I want to go and talk to the druid
tomorrow!'

'Why do you want to talk to the druid? You've were
married seven years, you're allowed to leave.'

'I know that, but I want a druid to confirm it. Then if
Sparky decides to follow me and argue with me, I can say, I
have talked to a druid and he says it's legal. And if Sparky
doesn't believe me, he can go and talk to the druid.'

'Oh well, if you must,' said Hardy, relaxing into the
mattress and trying gently to pull her down towards him.
'He's only half a day's ride away. You'll be back before dark.'

'But Hardy, it's winter. The days are short. And it's not
just the feast, there's the wedding itself, I don't want that
to be in the dark or even in the nearly-dark.'

'If it was a fine night, with firelight and stars?'

'But it might be raining, and people will have to find
their way home in the dark and wet.'

She pulled away from him, climbed out of the bed and
ran her fingers through her tousled hair. Then she wrapped
herself in a cloak, slipped on her shoes, and went outside.

Grace had the fire blazing in the fire-pit, and aspen
branches and reed mats soaking in the river. Now servants
were bringing the dripping wet aspen branches up from the
river, some still bearing their golden leaves. They laid them

on the red hot stones in the firepit. With a hiss, a surge of white steam arose, curling out like wings from under the long roof over the firepit.

'That's enough!' said Grace. 'A mat or two now.'

Women unrolled the sodden reed mats.

Brightleaves stepped forward, feeling guilty for disrupting all Grace's well-made plans.

'Grace,' she said.

'Milady,' said Grace, bending her knees under her brown dress so that she bobbed down for a moment. 'What can I do for you?'

'I'm sorry, but we'll have to postpone tomorrow's feast until the day after.'

'Leave the mats!' Grace called to the women.

Two men appeared through the steam, carrying a carcase of beef.

'Take that back and hang it up again,' Grace told them.

'I am sorry to upset all your excellent arrangements,' said Brightleaves.

'Don't worry about it, milady. So will it just be the household tomorrow night?'

The two women had a short discussion about the various foods available, what could be served next evening, and food for the feast. Brightleaves went back to the house feeling that she had taken a first step towards becoming the mistress of the household.

After she had shut the lower part of the door behind her, she looked up at the platform that ran all around the interior. It was partitioned into sections that served as small rooms with various purposes. Some were bedrooms, curtained off with woven hangings, carpeted with rush matting. Others were store-rooms full of baskets and pots of all shapes and sizes. Ladders here and there around the house gave access to these upper spaces. This was the same as in her house. She tilted her head back to see the hams and cheeses hanging from the rafters in the smoke that lingered under the thatch before it filtered out. Just as in her house. But she had not organized the way the little up-ladder spaces here were used, furnished and decorated; she had not supervised the filling and stacking of these baskets; she had not overseen the hanging of these cheeses and hams. Grace had done it. There was nothing wrong with the way Grace had done it. Brightleaves couldn't fault it. But she would have done it differently. One way in which it would have been different was that Brightleaves would know exactly what was in each space, each basket and pot, and she would know the logic of why it had been placed here rather than there. As she had done in her own house.

Brightleaves felt homesick. She had not just left a man. She had left a house; and that was a very different matter. All the habitual daily actions of her body-mind, engaged in this task or that, were suddenly stopped short; all the invisible threads of usage and familiarity, which connected her with hundreds of humble everyday objects and small places, were broken; not put aside to be resumed later, as when she went away on a visit, but broken for ever. She was a walking bundle of broken tendrils.

When spring came she would have to look for the best places in the landscape to find what she needed; the best hazel-trees for making egg-whisks, the best part of the river-bank for scooping up cooking-clay, the best place to pick nettles for cloth, the best butter-bog, the best places to gather moss.

And tomorrow, before she went to see the Druid, she

would set up a loom. That would make this house feel more like her own.

She shut the upper door, found her way over to Hardy's bed by the soft white glow of a rushlight fixed to the wall, took off her cloak and shoes and climbed in beside him.

* * *

Grace was having the reed mats hung up to drip when Curly the priestess arrived and took her aside for a quick chat.

'We'll be bringing you an extra servant today. A child called Blossom.'

'Oh, another "spy", is it?' Grace asked, with a smile.

'That's right.'

'She'll come in useful,' said Grace. 'The wedding feast will be the day after tomorrow, now. It would have helped if I'd known earlier. These mats will freeze folded if there's a frost tonight!'

* * *

Dream-Blossom decided to do the mental exercise first, because that meant sitting by the fire with her eyes closed. Trying to imagine she was a grown-up priestess would be easy; she used to do that before she came to the school.

She closed her eyes and pretended she was walking into the King's house, wearing a white feathered cloak, with everyone bowing before her.

But she was supposed to be a teacher at a temple school. The teachers only wore feathered cloaks at festivals. The rest of the time they wore plain white cloaks. So, she must see herself as a teacher in a plain white cloak. Where was she?

Was she on a herb-walk? Who were her pupils?

This was difficult. She got up and went out to get some wood. The woodpile was next to the latrine, which reminded Dream-Blossom of her threat to Pickle, and she was sorry. Sorry about being caught, being in disgrace, being thought badly of by Curly. She would have been sorry about hurting the feelings of another child, like Joy-of-Spring for instance, but she couldn't quite believe that slaves had the same feelings as real people.

As Dream-Blossom came around the house with her armful of logs, she saw girls coming out of the temple and walking towards the Cygnet House. They were going for their midday meal. She shrank back out of sight. She didn't want anyone to see her. When they had all gone past, she darted into Mother Swan's house and put some of the logs on the fire.

Perhaps now that she'd done the first thing Curly had asked her to do, the second would come more easily.

She sat down on the bench by the newly fed fire, straightened her back, and closed her eyes. She tried doing the exercise that was always given at the start of a meditation class. After a while her attention began to wander. When she finally noticed it was wandering, she drew it back to focussing on the idea of herself as a priestess.

She expected to find herself looking out of a priestess's eyes at admiring crowds, as in her daydreams. Instead, she became aware of a tall priestess image standing behind her, like a woman with white swan-wings outstretched. Sitting in the aura of this being, she felt totally safe, loved and protected. Is this my dead mother? she wondered. Or is it my Higher Self? We're being trained to get in touch with our Higher Selves so that we act from them and not from our personalities. Not that there's anything wrong with my personality, of course.

In her mind's eye, she watched herself being nasty to Pickle earlier that day. She must go to Pickle and apologize. And what task could she do to prove that she should be allowed to stay at the school?

She was still wondering about that when she heard Mother Swan's voice, saying calmly,

'Come back into the house and open your eyes.'

Dream-Blossom opened her eyes. Mother Swan smiled at her.

'The fire is going well, I'm glad to see. And what did you learn in your meditation?'

'I have to apologize to Pickle, Ma'am.' said Dream-Blossom.

'Good,' said Mother Swan

'But I can't think what I can do to prove that I deserve to stay here.'

'Don't worry,' said Mother Swan. 'I can help you there. You go and say you're sorry to Pickle now – she'll be in the Cygnet house. Then come back here.'

Dream-Blossom was feeling quite cheerful as she put on her cloak and walked over to the Cygnet house. There was Pickle – and – oh no! – Rainbow and Joy-of-Spring were there too! She would have to apologize to Pickle in front of them!

Her two friends were sitting by the fire, already eating.

'Hi, Dream-Blossom,' called Joy-of Spring, 'we've kept you a place!'

She waved to them and walked over to the serving area, where Pickle was collecting a bowl of broth and a spoon.

The child shrank back as Dream-Blossom approached her.

'Pickle,' began Dream-Blossom in a voice so quiet it was almost a whisper, 'I've come to say – '

The whole house had gone quiet, because everyone wanted to hear what Dream-Blossom was saying to Pickle. Rainbow and Joy-of-Spring were smiling, ready to have a good laugh.

'I'm really sorry about the way I spoke to you this morning,' muttered Dream-Blossom. 'I do hope you can forgive me. And I'll never do it again.'

Pickle looked amazed. She didn't say, 'Oh, don't give it another thought!' or 'Of course I forgive you!' or anything like that. She was waiting for Dream-Blossom to turn into her usual nasty self.

Dream-Blossom didn't look to see how her two friends reacted. She turned and ran out of the house, back to Mother Swan's.

'Sit down, child,' said Mother Swan.

Dream-Blossom sat down obediently on the bench opposite Mother Swan.

'Now then,' said Mother Swan, 'You asked your Higher Self to show you what you could do to prove that you deserve to stay here?'

'Yes, Ma'am.'

'And she didn't tell you.'

'No, Ma'am, she didn't.'

'Fortunately,' said Mother Swan, smiling, 'she told me. I'm going to send you on a mission. It's very important and very secret.'

Dream-Blossom, who had been sitting in a humble, apologetic posture, sat up straight, her eyes glistening with excitement. An important secret mission!

'So I'm not being punished?'

'What would be the point of that?' said Mother Swan. 'Your lack of compassion is caused by ignorance. It's no use punishing the ignorant; we have to teach them to know better. Meanwhile, you want to prove that you deserve to stay here and I have found a way you can be useful to us. It's quite simple. Do you understand?'

'Yes Ma'am.'

'When I say this mission is secret, I mean you can't tell your friends about it. You can't tell anyone. Is that clear?'

'Yes Ma'am.'

'I must have your solemn promise that you will not tell anyone about your mission, no matter how much you want to. Not friends, not strangers, no-one.'

'I promise I won't tell anyone!' said Dream-Blossom earnestly.

'Good,' said Mother Swan. 'If you break that promise, you will be sent home.'

Dream-Blossom began to feel that the situation was serious.

'Now,' Mother Swan continued, 'I'll tell you what we want you to do. Listen carefully.'

Dream-Blossom put on her best listening face.

'We need to send a spy into Chief Hardy's house,' said Mother Swan.

Dream-Blossom gasped in astonishment. 'To spy on Chief Hardy?' she said.

'Oh no. No need for that! We want someone to spy on the slaves. Your task will be to live in the women's house, work with the slaves and keep your eyes and ears open, until you find out something important. Then one of us will come to collect you. Nobody there must know who you

115

really are. You'll be in disguise. Your name will be shortened to Blossom. And we'll teach you a story to tell, in case anyone asks about your background.'

Curly came in, carrying a pile of clothes.

'I think these should fit,' she said, laying them on the bench beside Dream-Blossom.

The clothes were not dirty. But they were worn, shabby, and in horrible dull colours.

'Are these the clothes I have to wear?' said Dream-Blossom in dismay.

'You have to look like a slave,' said Mother Swan.

'And here are the shoes,' said Curly, pulling a pair of shoes from her basket.

Dream-Blossom would not be seen dead in shoes like that.

'Really you ought to have bare feet,' Curly continued, 'but there isn't time to get your soles toughened up. We'll have to think of a reason why you wear shoes.'

This is a nightmare, thought Dream-Blossom.

'You'd better get changed,' said Mother Swan. 'You're going to start work at Chief Hardy's house today. Grace will be delighted to have some extra help for the wedding feast.'

'You should leave your bronze hairclip here,' said Curly. 'No slave could afford such an ornament. If you want to tie your hair back, you can use a length of wool.'

Dream-Blossom's mind was racing as she tried to think of a way of getting out of this. She could feign illness – but with so many experienced healers around, would anyone be convinced?

'It is a great honour, you know, being given this mission,' said Curly.

'I don't deserve it!' said Dream-Blossom.

'But surely,' said Mother Swan, 'the whole point of this is to prove that you deserve to stay here at the school. Are you now refusing a job we're giving you?'

'No, Ma'am,' said Dream-Blossom.

'She must have a meal before she goes,' said Curly. 'I'll bring some food.'

Dream-Blossom changed into the awful clothes, put on the awful shoes, and ate her bread and stew in silence.

Chapter 6. A visit to the druid

Dream-Blossom arrived at Chief Hardy's house to find a strange scene: poles set between forked sticks with reed mats hung over them, dripping; the firepit open but with only sullen wisps of smoke coming out and no delicious smells of food. There was a tall, grey-haired woman ordering people about. Dream-Blossom approached her.

'Excuse me, are you Grace? I was told to report to you.'

'Ah!' said Grace, 'you must be Blossom.'

Dream-Blossom nodded. She wasn't sure whether she should call Grace 'Madam'.

'Come with me,' said Grace, 'and bring that bucket with you.' She pointed to a bucket of pine-needles sitting near the firepit. Dream-Blossom paused for a moment, shocked, then took a deep breath and ran to fetch the bucket, congratulating herself on how well she was acting her part.

'Shall I empty it into the fire-pit?'

'No, bring it just as it is.'

As she picked up the bucket, it occurred to Dream-Blossom that she should put it on her head. That was how slaves carried buckets. They practised from childhood. But the bucket would dirty her hair. She could not bring herself to do it.

Grace led her to one of the houses in the compound, where two young women were sitting over a bowl in the porch.

'This is Blossom, girls,' said Grace. 'She will shell the hazelnuts for you, and then roast them and chop them up, if you can show her where everything is. Introduce yourselves, please!'

She took the bucket of pine needles from Dream-Blossom and went into the house. They could hear the splashing sound of water being emptied into a cauldron.

'Hello, Blossom,' said the taller girl, who had light brown hair. 'My name's Willow.'

'And I'm Cherry,' said the shorter, dark haired girl.

'The hazelnuts are just here,' said Willow, showing Dream-Blossom a basket. 'There's a flat stone here, to bang them on, and a rag to wrap them in. You just need to find a round stone to bang them with. And there's a plate here for the bits of shell and a bowl for the shelled nuts.'

Grace came out of the house and said, 'There's a cauldron of pine-water heating on the fire. I want you to keep it in mind, Willow, and when it boils take it off the fire and leave it to steep.'

Grace hurried away. Dream-Blossom searched the ground for likely-looking round stones. Once she had found her stone, she knelt down, spread the cloth on the clean side of the flat stone, wrapped some nuts in it and began to hit them with a round stone. It was harder work than she expected. She was exhausted after shelling four – and there was a whole basketful of them. She sat back on her heels and sighed.

'Shall we take turns?' Willow suggested. 'It seems a bit mean, Blossom doing the hardest bit when she's the youngest.'

Cherry shrugged.

'Swap with me, Blossom,' said Willow. 'We're just rubbing beef-fat into flour, it's not difficult.'

Dream-Blossom sat opposite Cherry and rubbed fat into

flour. Each girl was trying not to let her fingers touch the other's fingers while they rubbed the fat and flour.

'You have to keep rubbing it in until it all looks like breadcrumbs,' said Cherry. 'No! Not like that! Do it gently! It needs a light touch!'

A slave had never spoken to Dream-Blossom like this. She was about to say, I will have you whipped! when she remembered that she was supposed to be a slave too.

Willow started humming a tune while she banged the nutshells.

'What's that song?' Cherry asked.

'It's a nutshell-cracking song,' said Willow. 'I'm making it up as I go along.'

They spoke with strange accents. Dream-Blossom wondered where they came from.

The song came to a stop. 'The really fiddly bit is getting the nut out of the shell when I've cracked it,' said Willow.

'Would you like me to do that?' said Dream-Blossom.

They rearranged themselves. Dream-Blossom knelt opposite Willow and picked nuts out of their broken shells. The girls chatted to Dream-Blossom. They told her that their mother used to own Lady Brightleaves' chariot. She didn't believe that for one moment! Everyone knew that slaves always made themselves out to have been grander than they really were.

They told her their father had been killed in the war.

'What war?'

'You must know about the war!' said Cherry. 'It was only a few months ago – and the whole country was involved!'

'Yes, but not this country,' Willow reminded her sister.

'Some warriors from this country came to fight in it,' said Cherry.

'Did you see the Romans?' Dream-Blossom asked.

'No,' said Cherry, 'we just heard about them.'

'I talked to a woman in the market who'd seen Romans,' said Willow. 'Do you know what she told me? The Romans don't use soap!'

'They don't even know how to make soap,' said Cherry.

This was astonishing. Soap-making was one of the winter occupations of every household.

'They must be very dirty!' said Dream-Blossom.

'This woman said,' continued Willow, 'that when the Romans want to get clean, they sit in a very hot room and rub themselves all over with oil!'

'Ugh!' said Dream-Blossom, 'how disgusting!'

'You'd think they would fry,' said Cherry.

'Fried Romans!' said Willow, and they began to giggle. Then Willow ran into the house to check the pine-water.

When the hazelnuts were all shelled, the girls took them inside the women's house to roast them. Dream-Blossom breathed in the scent of pine wafting from the cauldron.

'That will be for cleaning the latrines,' said Willow.

'We won't have to do that, will we?' said Cherry.

'Why shouldn't you?' said Dream-Blossom.

They explained that they were Lady Brightleaves's personal slaves. They looked after her clothes and helped her with her hair. 'We might tidy her bedspace or fetch her washing water,' said Cherry, 'but we don't do heavy housework.'

Grace came to check the pastry mixture and the hazelnuts.

'Now, Cherry,' she said, 'empty the pine-water into this bucket, then you and Blossom take it with you and clean the latrines. They were done first thing this morning, they just need freshening up. Wipe round the seats. Here's a cloth each.'

Grace delved into her apron pocket and produced two cloths. Cherry and Dream-Blossom glanced at each other, united by mutual disgust. Dream-Blossom waited for Willow or Cherry to say, Oh no, we don't do heavy housework! But they didn't say it.

'Start with the Chief's latrine,' Grace continued, 'then do the one behind this house, then the men's one. Check the moss baskets and the earth-buckets, and let me know if any need refilling.'

Dream-Blossom carried the cloths, Cherry carried the bucket, and they set off to the back of the Chief's house. Cherry didn't carry the bucket on her head either, Dream-Blossom noticed. And she knew, with a sinking heart, that Cherry would give her all the worse jobs because she was younger and smaller. If there were any stray bits of poo or pools of pee on the wooden seats, she would have to mop them up.

I can't do this, thought Dream-Blossom. I'll have to tell them I'm not really a slave.

But I haven't found out anything important yet!

Her pride saw her through the task. And the latrines turned out not to be as bad as she expected.

'I expect the piss-buckets are emptied every day, in a household this size,' Cherry remarked.

'They are at the Temple School.' Dream-Blossom's story was that she was a slave at the school, on loan to Chief Hardy's house for a while.

'I'm glad I don't work for a tanner or a dyer,' said Cherry. 'Their slaves spend all day carrying buckets of piss about.'

The girls threw extra earth into each shit-pit to take

away some of the smell before they started cleaning the seat. They were glad to get outside into the fresh air when they had finished.

On their way back to the women's house with the bucket and cloths, they met a well-dressed girl of about Cherry's age, with dark hair and blue eyes, pretty but for her rather pointy chin.

'I've come to see Lady Brightleaves,' she said, smiling. 'Would you be kind enough to tell her I'm here? The name is Vetch Oxhill.'

'I don't think her ladyship is available at the moment,' said Cherry. 'You'd better ask Grace—'

At that moment Grace appeared. She had, as Dream-Blossom was beginning to notice, an almost priestess-like ability to appear where she was needed.

'Mrs Oxhill!' she said. 'What can I do for you today?'

'I was hoping for a quick word with Lady Brightleaves.'

Grace shook her head. 'I'm sorry, Ma'am, she's not receiving visitors just now. You'll see her at the wedding the day after tomorrow.'

'I was just wondering if there was anything I could do to help, or anything you need.'

'That's very kind of you, but it's all under control. Only a loaf for the feast, that's all we're asking guests to bring.'

'Only a loaf for the feast!' the young woman echoed, dismally, as if it were the chorus of a tragic song.

They watched her until she was too far away to hear them. Then Grace murmured to Dream-Blossom,

'Follow her and make sure she goes right out of the gate. If she starts wandering about instead, nip back and tell me.'

Proper spying at last! Dream-Blossom dropped her cloth and ran off. Mrs Oxhill passed the firepit, paused, glanced at the stables. Dream-Blossom crouched down, pretending to pick up something from the grass. Mrs Oxhill looked straight at her, shrugged, went out of the gate and shut it behind her.

Back at the women's house, Dream-Blossom washed her hands in a bowl of lovely hot water. There was even a cake of soap to use, and a clean length of linen for drying her hands.

Willow had roasted and skinned the hazelnuts. The next task was to chop them into tiny pieces and stir them into the pastry mixture.

'Why can't we grind them on the quern stone?' Dream-Blossom asked.

'Because their oil will squeeze out of them!' said Cherry. 'Didn't your mother teach you things like that?'

'My mother died when I was a baby,' said Dream-Blossom.

Over the years she had grown grateful to her mother for doing this. People were always so sympathetic when she told them.

After an interval of respectful silence, Willow and Cherry talked about Mrs Oxhill, telling Dream-Blossom all the gossip they'd heard from Grace.

'She's only sixteen.'

'She's got a crush on Chief Hardy.'

'She married a rich old farmer so that she could have nice dresses and things and could be – how did Grace put it? "part of the Chief's social group".'

'She was planning to marry Chief Hardy when the old farmer dies.'

'And now Chief Hardy is going to marry Lady Brightleaves!'

'So Mrs Oxhill probably came here to try and poison her!'

Grace came in with a pot of honey and a jug of beer to stir into the hazelnut-and-pastry mixture.

'Leave that to rise for a bit,' she said, and sent them to fetch water. Cherry and Willow went to the river for washing water. Dream-Blossom went up the hill to the spring, for drinking water, with a girl called Dawn to show her the way. Dawn was about her own age, a thin, mousy girl. She led the way to the spring without saying anything. Dream-Blossom was glad of that. She was tired of pretending to be a slave when people spoke to her. It was easier when they didn't speak.

The work never seemed to stop. Trays of food were carried to the chief's house, to the warriors' house, to the men's house. Finally it was the women's turn to eat. They sat around the fire eating delicious clay-baked fish with their fingers, while the hazelnut muffins bobbed in one cauldron and the crab-apple halves simmered in another. But they still had to serve the muffins, which were scooped out of the cauldron with slotted spoons and piled on to trays.

Cherry was chosen to take a few muffins to the Chief's house. Willow took a tray of muffins to the warriors' house. As she approached it, she heard the deep male voices, talking and laughing. She went in, tray first. It was rather daunting, going into a house full of men. Even when they were clean, men smelled different from women, especially when they were all together like this.

'Hello, you're new!' said one of them.

She stood holding the tray of muffins, looking around in the firelight for somewhere to put it down.

'Come on, lads, help her!' said another voice.

A tall man with red hair stood up and took the tray from her. She smiled at him.

'Grace says these are best eaten warm,' she said.

For a moment she and the tall man looked at each other. The others started whistling. Willow turned and fled.

'I saw this man,' she told Cherry.

'Really? In the warriors' house? How extraordinary!'

'No, listen. I think he liked me.'

'Well, a warrior can't marry a slave,' said Cherry. 'So that's the end of that.'

Dream-Blossom only caught snatches of this whispered conversation because she was almost asleep. A manservant brought the bowls back from the men's house and they had to be washed, dried and put away. The cauldron of crab-apples was taken off the fire and carried outside for the contents to cool overnight.

When at last Grace told them they could go to sleep, Dream-Blossom was glad to lie down on the floor and roll herself up in a blanket, as the other slaves did. It was a shock, though, to wake next morning and have to roll up her blanket and put it away, leaving the floor clear for the comings and goings of the day's work. She had no private nest here. She stood looking at the cleared floor with a sense of lack.

'I know how you feel,' said Willow quietly. 'We used to have such a lovely bedspace at home.'

'Did you?' said Blossom, doubting it. How could slaves have a lovely bedspace?

'Oh yes!' said Cherry. 'We had a bed, for a start!'

'A bed each!' said Willow. 'And there was plenty of room for clothes-baskets, and we had little tables with our mirrors and combs on them – bone combs, they were.'

'And the mirrors were bronze, really pretty,' said Cherry. 'My hand can remember the feel of my mirror even now. The back was engraved with lovely curving patterns. They were birthday presents from our father.'

'And there were beautiful murals on the plaster wall,' said Willow, 'and lovely woven hangings on the wicker walls —'

'And gorgeous furs on the bed!' said Cherry.

'It sounds a bit grand,' said Blossom, thinking they were making it up, like the story about Lady Brightleaves' chariot.

'Well, we were chief's daughters,' said Willow.

Slaves were always saying things like that. Was it suspicious?

'Get on with your work, girls!' Grace called to them.

* * *

When Brightleaves went out to the latrine first thing in the morning, she had to hurry through the rain. The sky was covered in grey, not just a few clouds drifting by but an all-over greyness with some slightly paler patches here and there like glimmers of hope. The hills were veiled in rain-mist.

'What shall I take as an offering for the druid?' she asked Hardy while they were having breakfast by the fire.

'Take anything you like from the store,' he said.

People paid their tithes to Hardy in goods, which he put into his store-house. If he needed more of their products or skills after they'd paid their tithes, he would pay them in goods (which their wives chose) from his store.

When goods were brought into the store, Heron the steward organized them as follows:

Timber, raw and dressed, all qualities from furniture to firewood.

Timber products: benches, buckets, bows, Woodwit boards, cups, shuttles

Hazel & willow wands, for wickerwork.

Woven wicker products.

Heather for thatching, basket-making, brooms, mattresses etc.

Heather products.

Rush-lights, rush mats.

Iron products: spearheads, arrowheads, knives, axes, hammers, nails, cleavers, sickles, cauldrons, fire-irons, snaffles, bridle-bits, slip-buckles, lynchpins, terrets,.

Bronze products: cauldrons, goblets, mirrors, cloak-brooches, arm-bands.

Pottery products: beakers, flagons, loomweights etc.

Horn & bone products: combs, needles, fishing hooks.

Furs: bear, lynx, wolf, fox, beaver, otter, marten

Hides & skins: cow, horse, deer, pig, goat, sheep

Leather products: shoes, boots, bridles, belts, buckets, laces, and of course kickskull balls.

Wool unspun, spun, dyed,

Wool products: woven cloth, blankets, clothes.

Smoked meats

Cheeses

Honey

Corn & barley

Beer

Herbs, culinary & medicinal

Exotic imports:

Salt (brought from the coast in pots wrapped in protective leather inside bags slung across a pony's back)

Quernstones (very expensive, these: the sort of thing you'd give your daughter as a wedding present; and sisters would fall out over Who Got Mother's Quernstone)

Grace then reorganized the goods in the store into sections or 'departments', as it were:

Women's wear & jewellery
Children's clothes
Toys and games, including kickskull balls
Menswear & jewellery
Furs
Home furnishings
Kitchen equipment
Food & drink
Herbs
Craft materials & accessories:
    wool, linen, looms, spindles, loomweights, needles;
    hazel, willow, heather & basketry tools;
    leather & leatherworking tools;
    Building materials
    Building tools
    Farming tools
    Horse harnesses
    Weapons
    Firewood

What would be a suitable gift for a druid? Any farmer's

wife could give him a length of woven wool or a good cheese. Would he value jewellery?

Brightleaves went back to the house and asked Hardy.

'How would I know?' said Hardy.

She sent a messenger running through the rain to Brook Bard. Her message was: What should I take as an offering to Druid Northway?

The messenger returned with the reply: He likes a drink.

Brightleaves went back into the store. There were flagons of mead in there, Grace's mead, very good no doubt – but it wouldn't feel like a gift from her.

Then, in the feasting utensils section, she saw the bronze goblets that she had brought with her from Roughrock. They were so elegant! She couldn't bear to part with any of them.

She looked around for other things but her eyes kept going back to those goblets.

Any man of taste would appreciate them.

But how many to give him?

One would be enough, surely? She wasn't going to take up much of his time. It was a straightforward case. I've been married seven years, I have left my husband, I want to get married again, am I acting within the law?

But one goblet would seem mean. Legal advice is never cheap.

Four, then. A nice set.

No, four would be overdoing it.

She chose two of the goblets, then went to find Grace.

'Would you get someone to wrap these for me please, Grace?'

'Do you want them gift-wrapped, milady?'

Gift-wrapped meant that the wrapping material itself

was a gift, a nice piece of linen, perhaps, or a length of woven wool.

'They're for Druid Northway. I'll leave it to you to decide on the wrapping.'

The goblets were wrapped in useful leather and strapped to Stern's saddle. He would accompany her, together with one of Hardy's warriors, a tall young man known as Shorty.

Brightleaves' horse was saddled. The warriors mounted and waited in the rain. Young Shorty was bare-armed to show off his muscles. Stern, older and wiser, wore a waxed cloak. Brightleaves put on a wool cloak, undyed and tightly woven so naturally waterproof.

'Here yesterday, gone today!' said Hardy.

'I'll be back this evening, gods willing.'

She kissed him goodbye. He followed her out of the house and watched her mount her horse. She waved to him, then they set off.

The sound of the raindrops pattering on the earth mingled with the sound of the horse's hooves. They rode down the glen, forded Wildcat Water, rode north-east and across Fox Water. The hills were blurred, like cloud-hills. They rode east past Meet Hill, then north-east again until they came to Steep Water, where they turned north-west and rode up Steep Glen. Hills appeared out of the mist then vanished again. The riders kept their hoods up while the horses trotted along, splashing through puddles, mud spreading up their legs and spattering the riders. Occasionally they passed a house, but there were no cheerful spinners sitting in the porch. On a day like this people would be inside around the fire.

The travellers reached a track leading down to a ford. They rode across Steep Water, then the track forked.

'It's the right-hand fork,' said Shorty.

They forded a stream and there was the druid's precinct: the usual arrangement, a gated enclosure containing a main house with other buildings around it – slaves' houses, a store, a granary and so on.

The main house was not as imposing as the druid houses that Brightleaves remembered from her childhood in the Land of Plenty. It didn't look as if it would have room for the druid's pupils. Perhaps they lived in a separate house. Or perhaps here, in the land of the Hunters, chiefs had given up sending their sons to be educated by druids.

The trio dismounted. Stern untied the gift-parcel from his saddle and handed it to Brightleaves.

A woman came to the door.

'I am Lady Brightleaves–' Brightleaves began, and paused. She could not yet introduce herself as Brightleaves Wildcat Hunter but nor could she use her old name, Brightleaves Roughrock Lively. She left the name unfinished and continued, 'I've come to consult Druid Northway, if he's available and willing to see me.'

'Please wait.'

The woman hurried away. Shorty and Stern ducked into the porch beside Brightleaves, out of the rain. They could hear the woman speaking to someone inside the house. She came back and nodded to Brightleaves. 'Please come in.'

'What about my bodyguards?'

'I'll look after them,' said the woman. 'I'll show you in first.'

The house was full of the delicious smell of newly baked bread. The woman took Brightleaves' cloak, hung it on one of the pegs near the door, went into the centre of the house and announced:

'Lady Brightleaves!'

Then she indicated the bench where Brightleaves should sit.

Does she think I don't know how to behave and might sit on an inappropriate bench? Brightleaves wondered. But such thoughts were too trivial to have in the presence of a druid.

On the far side of the fire sat an old man with a wrinkled face and a long white moustache. Brightleaves curtseyed to him, walked sunwise around the fire and presented him with the parcel.

'A small gift, Druid Northway,' she said.

'Thank you.'

She sat down where she'd been told, and waited for him to open his present. But he set it down on the bench beside him, unopened, and said,

'What can I do for you?'

Brightleaves was childishly disappointed.

'Before I ask my question, sir,' she said, feeling in her belt-pouch, 'I've brought you something else that I thought you might like.' Her fingers found the parcel she was looking for. She pulled it out. 'I'll have to check that it's survived the journey,' she continued, unwrapping the layers around it: leather, linen, more leather, more linen, and finally a horn cup. She peered into it, tilting it towards the fire so that she could see the contents. 'Yes! I think it's alright.'

She passed the horn cup to Druid Northway. He looked into it.

'Salt!' he said. 'Thank you. This is indeed a thoughtful gift for an inland-dweller.'

He picked a single grain out of the cup, dropped it onto his tongue, and sat savouring it.

'An extraordinary substance, is it not? How one grain can fill the mouth with that startling flavour. Like a spark of the sea.'

He put the cup down on the bench beside his unopened gift.

'Now, Lady Brightleaves who is of no community or people, you have what you wanted – a pleased reaction from me. Perhaps now you will give me what I want? Your reason for this visit?'

Brightleaves felt herself blushing. 'I'm sorry, sir. I was Brightleaves Roughrock Lively. I was married to Chief Roughrock Lively for seven years. Three days ago I left him. I cut our wedding blanket in two and took my half away. I also took half our joint wealth. I want to marry Chief Hardy Wildcat Hunter. But first I want to make sure that I'm acting within the law. I can't call myself Lady Roughrock Lively any more but I can't call myself Lady Wildcat Hunter yet either. That's why I didn't give a full name. I haven't got one at the moment.'

Druid Northway nodded. 'Well, that all seems to be in order,' he said.

She stared at him.

'So that's it? It's legal? It's all right? I can marry Chief Hardy? I mean, Sparky didn't ill-treat me or anything. I've got no cause for complaint against him.'

'Were you hoping for a longer interview?' said Druid Northway. He glanced at the parcel on the bench beside him, picked it up and called, 'Mallow!'

The slave woman appeared. Druid Northway handed the parcel to her.

'Take these elegant goblets, unwrap them, wash them if need be, and bring them back filled with mead.'

'How did you know they're goblets?' Brightleaves asked as Mallow went away with the parcel.

'Perhaps it was my druidic wisdom,' said Druid Northway, 'or perhaps it was because I could feel them through the wrappings.'

'But how did you know they're elegant?'

'A woman like you, Lady Brightleaves no-name, would not give anyone goblets that lacked elegance.'

'Thank you, sir.'

'It's not a compliment. It's just an observation.'

Brightleaves did not know how to reply to this, so she said nothing. She sat in silence. Druid Northway also sat in silence. Brightleaves felt awkward, sitting there saying nothing, but she could not think of anything to say. She rehearsed various possible remarks in her head, but they all sounded banal and pointless. Druid Northway looked perfectly contented, gazing at the fire. She wondered about asking him, Can you see things in the fire? But he would probably say, Yes, flames.

He smiled at her as if he could hear what she was thinking. Mallow came back with the goblets on a tray, carried one to the guest and the other to Druid Northway.

Brightleaves sipped. It was quite good mead. She smiled at her host but stayed quiet. She could do this not-talking thing too!

'Bring us something to eat, please, Mallow,' said Druid Northway. 'Some cheese, I think, and some of that bread whose scent is making our mouths water.' As Mallow went away, he turned to Brightleaves. 'So, Lady Brightleaves from nowhere,' he said, 'when you cut your wedding blanket in two, did you do so in anger?'

'No, sir,' said Brightleaves. 'I did it as a message, to show

Chief Roughrock that I was divorcing him.'

'As a message,' said Druid Northway. He sighed deeply. 'If you could have left him some thoughts, other than "I divorce you", what thoughts would you have left? If you were sending a message, say, with a very able messenger.'

'Oh!' said Brightleaves. 'Let me think. Well, I would have said, No hard feelings, it's not your fault, I'm really quite fond of you, and I would probably have been happy with you if only we'd had children. But the High Priestess says that if I want children I must find another husband. And perhaps you'll be able to have children with another wife? We've had some fun, over these seven years, and I will always be grateful for that. I hope you will not think too unkindly of me but instead remember the happy times we shared.'

'I think he would have liked that,' said Druid Northway. Then he shook his head. 'We have done a terrible thing.'

'Who?'

'We, the druids.'

'What do you mean?'

'Oh, I'm not talking about the sacrifices. The Romans have made a big fuss about those, of course, pretending to be so shocked – and all the while they practise something called crucifixion!'

'What's that?'

'You don't want to know. No, our great crime was one of with-holding. We kept a secret from you all that we should not have kept. But we had so much justification for it!' He sighed.

Brightleaves waited. She wanted to know the secret. But she felt that she mustn't rush him by saying, Oh, tell me! Tell me!

'Life is not just about surviving, is it?' he said. 'It's not just about things that are useful. The urge to make music is strong. Equally strong is the urge to make marks. When you, Lady Brightleaves, weave a length of wool, you weave it in patterns of colour. Men carve patterns in wood, leather, stone. They paint patterns on their skin. They forge patterns in metal. But the marks that carry thoughts, the marks that make words – we druids have kept these secret. This was our power and our downfall. The Romans are coming, pitiless conquerors. They will take your lands, kill you, enslave you, impoverish you. But they will let you make marks. This was our sin of pride, that we did not let you make marks. We feared that if everyone could make marks, they would mark only rubbish – shallow, trivial stuff lacking depth and elegance. All of you have excellent memories, and our pupils have the best memories of all. But marks last longer than memories.'

There was silence then, except for the occasional crackle of the fire, and a log shifting as the log below it burned away, and the pattering of the rain on the thatch. Mallow came back with the food; fine firm yellow cheese, with wheat bread, soft and still warm from the oven.

Brightleaves ate with enjoyment. She was sorry that Druid Northway was so distressed about this business of markings. But she did not share his distress. She liked weaving colours but she had no interest in making marks.

While they ate, she made desultory conversation about this and that: cheeses, and how the flavour of the grass the cows ate must affect the taste of the milk and hence the cheese; how everything tasted more salty by the seaside.

Once she had eaten her bread and cheese, she wanted to get back to Wildcat Glen and make sure everything was

137

ready for her wedding feast the next day.

She finished her mead and put the goblet on the bench beside her, trying not to look wistfully at it as she did so. Such an elegant goblet!

'Thank you,' she said, standing up. 'That was delicious. And now I really must be getting back.'

'Of course,' said Druid Northway, and clapped his hands. Mallow appeared. 'Our guests are leaving now,' he told her.

Mallow went to fetch Brightleaves' warriors.

'Would you like to come to the wedding, sir?' Brightleaves asked Druid Northway. She thought perhaps a wedding and a feast might cheer him up.

'It's very kind of you, but no thankyou,' he said. 'My presence might put a damper on the festivity. You will have Mother Swan, won't you, to perform the ritual?'

'Oh yes.'

'Well then, I would be superfluous.'

She had never met such a humble druid.

As they rode away through the rain, Brightleaves felt cheerful. It had been worth the effort of this extra journey, worth giving up two of her beautiful goblets. Her divorce was legal, her new marriage would be legal. As for Druid Northway's rant about making marks – it didn't affect her in any way, so she wasn't going to worry about it.

Chapter 7. The wedding

The day of the wedding was a fine day, Goddess be praised. The trees lifted bone-bare boughs to the pale blue sky, the rain-filled river roared – and Dream-Blossom was at the grindstone again.

The slaves had spent part of the previous day making crab-apple butter, for the crab-apple butter tarts that were to be served at the wedding feast. Now they were making flour for the pastry. Buckets of grain had been scooped up from the underground grainstore, all to be ground into flour. There were three querns in the household. Dream-Blossom sat at one of them, Willow and Cherry at the other two, turning the stones in a rasping rhythm that soon prompted them to sing.

Someone went to the nearest bog and dug up one of the casks of butter stored there. The three girls, having created a hill of flour, now began to turn it into a mountain of pastry. Dream-Blossom was taken off pastry-making for her lack of a light touch. She and Dawn were sent up to the spring for water. Today, with the river rushing so fast, a grown woman had to be sent to fetch river water, for the bucket would have been snatched from a child's hands and whirled away.

Men were building a fire outside and setting up benches in a semi-circle. Inside the women's house, the women were patting the pastry into little cakes and singing cake-patting songs. Guests began to arrive. Farmers' wives brought loaves of bread, which they laid on the long table outside.

Dream-Blossom wondered at this. Surely Chief Hardy, of all people, didn't need to be given bread? Then it occurred to her that she had been making flour all morning, for the pastry. If they'd had to make flour for bread as well, she would still be at the grindstone.

Mother Swan came in through the gate. Dream-Blossom's heart leaped! Perhaps the High Priestess had come to take her away? Following Mother Swan were the other teachers, then the Pens... Oh, Goddess, Dream-Blossom prayed, please don't let the Cygnets come! I don't want my friends to see me like this!

Her prayer was not answered. The Cygnets followed the Pens through the gate. They all looked happy and excited, having the day off school to come to the wedding.

Dream-Blossom fled into the women's house. During the wedding ceremony, she lurked at the back of a crowd of servants and missed much of what was going on.

Mother Swan had organized a small fire some distance away from the great feasting fire. Around this small fire the guests stood in a large circle. Chief Hardy walked around the inside of the circle, followed by his ribbon man, Brook Bard, carrying the ribbon that he would hand to Chief Hardy at the crucial moment. Then came Chief Hardy's warriors. The Chief looked very smart in a green cloak, a red shirt with red-and-green trousers, and a gold torc around his neck. He wore a crown of holly leaves over a protective leather headband. Some men, when wearing holly-crowns, wore no protective headband underneath, to show how tough they were. Chief Hardy knew he was tough and felt no need to prove it.

The warriors looked splendid, of course, with their cloaks flung back to display their muscles in spite of the goosepimpling cold. Even Brook Bard had made an effort to be crowd-pleasing, in his beaverskin cloak and all his jewellery.

After this procession around the circle, Hardy stood waiting at one side of it with his men around him, while Brightleaves took her turn to walk around the inside of the circle. She wore a blue dress and had a crown of ivy on her bright hair. She also had a gold torc around her neck. She carried a bouquet of gorse, the only flower in bloom at this time of year; one of Willow and Cherry's tasks that morning had been to cut all the thorns off the gorse-stalks without damaging the flowers. It had taken them a long time. They were Lady Brightleaves' attendants and were happy, despite their gorse-pricked fingers, in the new pink-and-blue dresses she had given them for the occasion. The Smiths' eldest daughter, Hazel, was the ribbon girl, carrying the blue ribbon that would fasten the lady's hand to Chief Hardy's.

The purpose of these processions was so that everyone in the glen could see exactly who was getting married. Yes, that was Chief Hardy, they recognized him. And this was Lady Brightleaves. They would know her now.

When both groom and bride had completed a circuit, they stood at opposite sides of the circle. Hazel held the bride's bouquet while Willow and Cherry helped her to pull her skirt up through her belt so that it hung only halfway down her thighs. Everyone could see her legs, but they were shapely legs, the skin smooth and milk-white, so she didn't mind showing them. She just hoped the ceremony would be over quickly so that her skin didn't start getting goose-pimples in the cold. She took the bouquet from Hazel again and stepped forward to receive Mother Swan's blessing. When she reached Mother Swan, she threw the bouquet backwards over her shoulder, high into the air. As it arced down, Willow caught it.

In spite of the girls' work of de-thorning the gorse, and then binding all the stalks together with a strip of leather, one thorn must have escaped their notice. It had worked its way through the leather and now it pricked Willow's finger. She repressed a squeak of pain and sucked at her finger. Cherry noticed and sighed. This was somehow typical of Willow.

Hardy took Brightleaves' right hand in his left. Mother Swan invoked the Goddess. Everything went quiet. Dream-Blossom could hear the wood crackling in the two fires. Mother Swan invoked the Goddess, not in her aspect of the goddess of fire, water or metalwork, but in her aspect of the goddess of hearth and home (and motherhood, added Mother Swan secretly, just between the Goddess and herself). After the invocation she waited until she could feel the presence of the Goddess.

Of course the invocation did not bring the Goddess. She was there all the time. The purpose of invocation was to make the people in the ceremony aware of Her presence. Once they were all aware of Her – the moment was easy to detect by the way the atmosphere changed – Mother Swan asked Her to bless the union of Brightleaves and Hardy. Then she tied their hands together, pronounced them man and wife, and thanked the Goddess for her blessing.

The married pair ran to the little fire and jumped over it. This was to show the people of Wildcat Glen that their chief and his new wife were healthy and strong and therefore fit to rule.

As they jumped over the flames, through the faint upcurling smoke, memory-beings jumped with them. Hardy couldn't help thinking of his first wife, a shy little creature with wispy blonde hair, so different from the tall confident red-head whose hand was now tied to his; and Brightleaves remembered a very different wedding, all her family and the people of Two-Lakes standing around watching as she leapt over the fire with Sparky, the sense of relief (we have found her a suitable husband in spite of everything!) so palpable that she thought Sparky must feel it; and she had been sorry for him, this innocent and likeable young man, marrying a girl of sixteen without knowing how much passion and heartbreak she had already experienced.

This new leap over the flames was like a cleansing for her.

They landed on the grass at the other side. The people cheered.

The Goddess left their awareness quietly, without making a fuss, like a mother leaving the children to play their games.

Cherry ran to help Lady Brightleaves pull down her skirt. Willow didn't, in case her finger put blood on the blue cloth. Then Chief Hardy looked around at the waiting crowd.

'What is your name?' he asked his new wife.

'I am Lady Brightleaves Wildcat Hunter,' she said, in a clear voice so that everyone could hear.

They cheered again; some of them exchanged smiles, because her statement sounded funny in the Land-of-Plenty accent that she had not managed to lose even after seven years in the land of the Livelies.

There was a rhythmic whooshing sound from the sky. Everyone looked up. A flock of geese was flying overhead, from the north, heading for their winter quarters on the shore of the Saprush Firth. A good omen, people said, nodding to each other in agreement with their own opinion.

Dream-Blossom felt a sense of kinship with these winged skyriders. Did the other priestesses feel it too? She wished she could ask them. Instead, she went back inside the women's house and stayed there, spreading crab-apple butter on to a seemingly endless number of little pastries.

'Well done, Blossom!' said Grace, when she came in and saw that all the crab-apple tarts were ready. 'And now I need you to come and help outside.'

'I don't feel very well,' said Dream-Blossom

'That's a shame,' said Grace, 'but you'll be pleased to know that we have a crowd of healers outside – all the priestesses are here. I'll get one of them to come and see you.'

'No!' said Dream-Blossom.

Grace looked at her enquiringly.

'It's just a passing thing,' Dream-Blossom invented desperately. 'I'll feel better in a minute.'

'That's all right, then,' said Grace. 'Come on!'

As Dream-Blossom followed Grace out of the house, she reached up to the hair-tie at the back of her neck, untied it, and bent her head so that her dark hair fell down on either side of her face like curtains.

Outside, the cooking pit was being opened up and some people were taking their seats around the large fire. Others were queuing up to congratulate the happy couple. Women were carrying jugs of beer to people who had brought their own cups. As Dream-Blossom hurried along, trying to keep Grace between herself and the crowd, she thought of feasts she had been to with her father. Had she even once looked at any of the slave girls? No, of course not.

* * *

Brightleaves was introduced to the most important people first, beginning with Brook the Bard.

'Gracious lady,' he said, 'in this your hour of happiness, will you grant a boon to a poor bard?'

Brightleaves favoured him with her dazzling smile. 'What do you want, Brook Bard?'

'It's about the boy Robin,' he said. 'He's spent two nights at my house.' Brook smiled, remembering how amazed the boy had been at having a special tunic for sleeping in and a bed to sleep on. 'I've been observing him, and so has my student-teacher, Raven. We both think he has bardic talent. But he needs a sponsor. Will you free him and sponsor him?'

'I'll be glad to,' she said.

Everyone cheered.

'That's a relief,' said Brook, under cover of the cheering. 'I've already got him a new pair of shoes from Crag Tanner.'

After Brook Bard came the chiefs and bards from the neighbouring glens, and their wives; then her fellow-traveller Dainty Rushglen stood in line to congratulate her.

'I'm glad your story has ended happily,' she told Brightleaves.

'Ended?' said Brightleaves. 'This is just the beginning!'

Brightleaves introduced her to Hardy and asked after baby Traveller.

'He's flourishing, thank you. What was the Druid like?'

'I think you'll find him easy to get on with.'

'That's a relief. But I do wish you'd waited so that we could go together!'

'What, and postpone my wedding?' What a spoilt child

145

this young woman was! It was a relief to turn away from her to be introduced to the craftsmen – the smith, carpenter, tanner, waller – and their wives; and of course the craftswoman, Heather Dyer.

'It's lovely to have you here,' said Goldie, the smith's wife. 'Someone else to organize the festivals!' It was the job of the Chief's wife to organize the festivals but while Hardy was a widower, Goldie, as the wife of the second most important man in the glen, had undertaken the task.

'Thank you so much for letting Hazel be my ribbon girl,' said Brightleaves.

'She was delighted to be asked,' said Goldie.

Brightleaves could have used Willow or Cherry as her ribbon girl, or even Dainty. But she wanted to use a local girl, to link her with her new community. Hazel was already popular in Wildcat Glen.

Next in the queue to congratulate the couple and be introduced to Brightleaves came the teachers at the Temple School, and some of the wealthier farmers and their wives. Old Farmer Oxhill apologized for his wife not being with him. She wasn't feeling well.

'I quite understand,' said Brightleaves. 'Especially at this time of year! Aching bones, is it?'

'Oh no!' said Farmer Oxhill. 'My wife is only a young lass.'

'Well, I'm sure I shall meet her soon. Do give her my good wishes.'

After meeting some more farmers and their wives, she was introduced to Hardy's warband. There was Smudge, who spent so much time polishing his weapons that his colleagues' favourite remark to him was, 'You've missed a bit.' There was a tall warrior called Tallspear but known as

Shorty, who had accompanied her to the Druid's house, and a short, stocky warrior called Lofty. Dawdle's real name was Swift. Rocky seemed to have escaped without a nickname but turned out to have a very smooth manner. Whistler couldn't whistle. Brightleaves was familiar with this military humour. Stern, for example, was a mild, easy-going man.

Over at the serving-table, Dream-Blossom heard the cheer when Brook Bard was granted his boon. She wondered what it was about.

Men squatted by the open oven-pit, hooked out pieces of meat and laid them on wooden plates, which women brought to the table. An old man cut loaves into slices. Dream-Blossom put a slice on each plate before it was carried away.

'I always get this job,' the old man told her with a toothless smile, 'cos I'm the best bread-slicer in the house. Best in the glen, Grace says!'

Oh, Goddess! thought Dream-Blossom, how long will I be doomed to talk to people like this?

She, Rainbow and Joy-of-Spring would have had fits of laughter about him – 'the best bread-slicer in the glen!'

The servants carried plates over to the people who were sitting down. More people hastily took their seats. When every guest had a plate of food, the slaves were allowed to eat.

Dream-Blossom was hungry and glad of the meal, but it made her sleepy. The day was growing dusky now and stars were appearing in the sky. There were all those crab-apple tarts in the women's house... She yawned. She remembered feasts at her father's house, where she would be sitting beside him, by the fire. She felt a pang of homesickness.

Perhaps she would tell someone she was a spy on a mission. Then she would be sent home.

'Are you tired, chuck?' said the bread-slicer. 'We're allowed to sit down, you know, in the back row, when we're not serving.'

'I'm not really a slave,' Dream-Blossom whispered to him. 'I'm a spy on a mission.'

'I know, chuck. So am I! Isn't it fun?' He giggled.

She wondered if he was just joking. Mother Swan had told her to look out for anything suspicious. She would have to find out more about this old man.

Some of the slaves were bringing back plates and refilling them for second helpings. A few stood at the table, helping themselves to food. Others were cutting out parts of the animal to be taken to the underground, stone-lined cold-store and kept for tomorrow. When this had been done, the guests could cut slices or chunks to take home. Anything left would be given to Hardy's dogs.

Grace sent Dream-Blossom and others to the women's house to bring the tarts. There was a bustle of serving; Dream-Blossom carried a tray of tarts only to the outermost row of guests, well away from where the priestesses were sitting. She felt pleased when she heard people saying, 'Oh! These are delicious!' She wanted to say, 'I helped to make them!' so that the guests could say, 'Did you? What a clever girl!' But as a slave, she couldn't speak to the guests; and if she told them she had helped to make the tarts, they wouldn't think she was clever. That was the kind of thing slaves were supposed to do.

To Dream-Blossom's delight, Grace had kept a whole tray of tarts for the slaves. Dream-Blossom ate hers in silence, standing beside the bread-slicer. He stood with his head flung back, gazing up at the great wonder of the night sky. It was a clear night. The stars, white on black, were as thickly scattered as raindrops on wet grass. The 'Path of the Goddess' soared across all in a great milky track.

'Excuse me,' she whispered.

'Yes, chuck?' he said, looking down at her.

'Erm – I was just wondering – erm, where do you come from?'

'And where do you come from?'

'Furzefort,' said Dream-Blossom.

'Very nice too. I come from…' he paused. Then he said, as if changing the subject, 'Do you see that star up there?' He pointed.

Dream-Blossom looked where he was pointing. 'The big one?'

'Yes, and do you see the little one just next to it?'

'Yes.'

'That's where I come from.'

The slaves who had overheard this exchange laughed and muttered comments like, 'He's at it again.'

Dream-Blossom sighed. Then she thought, well, if he really is a spy, pretending to be mad is very clever.

Brook Bard recited a poem about the wedding. A tall boy chanted a bit of Wildcat history, accompanying himself on a lyre. Cherry and Willow sang. They had beautiful voices. A younger boy sang and drummed; the audience sang along with him, stamping their feet to the rhythm. Servants carried around flagons of yarrow-flavoured beer to refill people's cups. Someone started playing a bouncy tune on a pipe, the kind of tune that gets your feet tapping. The music became so lively that people had to get up and dance; their bodies would not let them sit still. One dance followed another.

Dream-Blossom almost went to sleep standing up, but the cold was keeping her awake. The Cygnets were led away. She wished she was going with them. Grace appeared at her side.

'You and Dawn must go to bed,' she said.

Dream-Blossom stumbled towards the women's house with Dawn. She was glad to feel the warmth in the house, glad to lie down on the floor and wrap a blanket around her. She would definitely not spend another night here, but now she just had to let her eyes close. Then she felt a quivering nearby. Dawn was shaking with sobs. Dream-Blossom wondered about this, for a moment, as she sank into sleep.

Brightleaves and Hardy went to bed when the important guests had gone home. After they had made love again, they lay side by side quietly.

'What are you thinking?' she asked Hardy.

'I'm thinking about the bear.'

'What bear?'

'The day I got the message from Mother Swan that I must stay here, I was about to go hunting. Someone had seen a bear at the salmon leap. Nobody got him that day. And yesterday, it was raining.'

'Don't you go hunting in the rain?'

'Yes, but you'd gone to see the druid...'

'And you thought I'd be really cross if I came back and found you being carried home on a stretcher?'

'Well, something like that, and then today was the wedding. But nobody's got that bear yet. He feels like mine. I might go after him tomorrow. Catch him before he hibernates.'

'Bears taste better when they haven't been eating fish,'

said Brightleaves. 'And we don't need the meat at this time of year, what with the bullocks being slaughtered and pig-killing starting. Mind you, bear fat makes the best pastry...'

'I wasn't thinking about eating it,' said Hardy. 'I wanted to present you with a bearskin.'

'Oh, Hardy!' Brightleaves felt herself melting, wanting him again.

Suddenly, outside by the fire, a young man's voice was raised in song: 'You can milk cows, girl...'

'What, in the name of the Black Hag, is that fearful racket?' said Hardy.

'It's probably just one of Brook's apprentices fooling about,' said Brightleaves.

They lay in silence listening to the song. Brightleaves giggled occasionally. Then there was a sound of screaming outside.

'He's upset the girls!' said Hardy, ready to rush gallantly to the rescue.

'I think, actually, they're making that noise because they like it,' said Brightleaves, laying a gentle restraining hand on her husband's tense body to prevent him from leaping out of bed.

'Really?' he said, relaxing. 'D'you think so?' He sighed, realizing that here he was at the ripe old age of twenty-seven, and there was now a Younger Generation and he didn't understand it.

Chapter 8. The bear-hunt

The next morning was mild and misty. Hardy went to get his bear.

First, he washed himself all over. People assumed this was a ritual purification to appease the god of hunting, but its intention was practical: to reduce his human odour as much as possible, because bears have a ferociously keen sense of smell. He put on his dull grey-brown hunting clothes and his special hunting boots. Then he set off. He took his spears, his hunting knife, two ghillies and two warriors, Dawdle and Lofty. He did not take his dogs, because a bear could kill a dog with a single blow of its paw.

Brightleaves sent a message to Brook inviting him to lunch. Instead of sending a runner, she sent Willow. Brook walked back with the girl. He arrived at Hardy's house to find Brightleaves weaving; she had set up a loom against the wall where it could best catch the light from the doorway.

His shadow falling across her work made Brightleaves turn to look at him.

'Thank you for coming!' She tucked the shuttle between two strands of wool to keep the weaving taut. Brook took off his cloak and hung it on a peg near the door.

'It's nice to see a loom in Hardy's house again' he said. 'It makes the place more like a home.'

'I'm weaving a blanket for our bed. It's going to tell a story. This top part is my arrival here. That red and yellow bit is my chariot, and those pink bits are the girls' cloaks, and those black bits are the cattle... That purple is Druid

Northway. That blue is the dress I wore at our wedding, these colours are the guests, those grey bits are the Cygnets.'

'That's really clever.'

'Thank you. And see this part here? This is you in your school. That purple is you, and the dark red is Raven, the yellow is Marten and the quiet blue is Robin.'

'With this to entertain you, why do you need me?'

'Because I'm frightened about what I might have to weave next. Hardy's gone after a bear!'

'You don't need to worry about Hardy. He's a superb hunter. He can be so light on his feet that a falling leaf makes more noise. He can empathize with the animal, so that he knows what it's going to do almost before it knows itself. And he's got far too much sense to put himself in danger. Hardy doesn't get reckless when he's hunting. It's not like when he's fighting. Out hunting, he's all cool caution.'

'But bears are very dangerous!'

'Yes, but Hardy knows that. He's experienced. He regards hunting as his job, you see. What he's for.'

'What he's for?'

'He feels that, as Chief, it's his job to protect his people's flocks and herds in the winter by killing wolves and lynx and bears, and then to feed the people in the summer by killing deer.'

'He's so noble!'

'You sound like a love-struck girl.'

'I am a love-struck girl,' said Brightleaves, 'even though I'm not exactly a young woman any more.' She was twenty-three.

'How about some mead?' Brook suggested. 'Nothing like

mead to brighten one's outlook.'

Brightleaves poured two goblets at the serving table beside her loom, and they sat on the benches by the fire, sipping.

'What did you think of Willow?' she asked him

'Who?'

'The girl I sent to ask you to come here.'

'Nice girl,' said Brook. 'Intelligent. Attractive. And she sang and played beautifully at your wedding feast. Why? Are you matchmaking, Brightleaves?'

'No, I'm apprentice-making.'

'Enlighten me.'

'Well, I'd like you to take on Willow and her sister Cherry as apprentices. They're wasted as maids, even though they do get to sing and play at feasts. They deserve a higher status and I think they'd make excellent bards.'

'Well, yes they would,' said Brook. 'But my skills are with words rather than music. I'm not the right teacher for them.'

'I wasn't thinking of the music so much,' said Brightleaves. 'They're already good at that. But they only sing folksongs. If you could teach them history and how to compose poetry – with that added to their music, they'd be amazing.'

'Yes,' said Brook, 'but they're girls.'

'You don't object to female bards, I hope?'

'No, no, but – my house, with girls in it – well, it just wouldn't work.'

'You seem remarkably inarticulate on this subject. Can't you be a bit more bardic about it?'

'My house is a bit rough-and-ready. The boys don't mind; in fact I think they quite like it. I think they like not having women around, fussing over them. It gives them a feeling of independence. We're just casual; we don't have to mind our manners. And that suits us fine. We have fun! We have a good time! And that's the best atmosphere for learning. Also, if I started taking in women students, the boys would be hopelessly distracted. It would be very bad for their intellectual development. So I really couldn't allow it for that reason alone. And finally, on a practical level, the latrine is quite unsuitable for girls.' Brook sat back with a satisfied air.

Brightleaves burst out laughing. 'I knew you were going to bring the latrine into it. I thought, first he'll plead that girls would spoil the fun, then he'll say they'd be a distraction, and then he'll bring in the latrine.'

'Perhaps I should ask you to compose my poems for me in future.'

'There's no need for you to get huffy with me. I'll tell you what,' she got up and went to the door, 'We'll walk back to your house now, and then I can inspect it, to see just how unsuitable it is.' She took her cloak from its peg.

'No!' said Brook, getting up quickly. 'Not today!'

'I'm not going to give you a chance to tidy it first,' she said. 'That would give me a false impression, wouldn't it?'

'If I'd known you were such a bully,' he said, as they walked back to his house together, 'I'd have warned Hardy not to have anything to do with you!'

'D'you think he'd have taken any notice?'

'No, probably not.'

They walked on in silence. Brightleaves was wondering about Hardy, perched in a tree downwind of the salmon leap. Brook was sending frantic telepathic messages to his apprentices – 'Tidy the place up! Tidy it!' – but bards, unlike the Swan Priestesses, were not trained in telepathic communication, so his signals were not received. This became apparent the moment he and Brightleaves walked into his house.

Robin, who as the youngest had taken over the job of look-out from Marten, had seem them coming, so the boys had time to prepare themselves for this visit. But it would never have occurred to them to make the beds, for instance, or sweep the crumbs off the shelf where they helped themselves to biscuits. They prepared themselves by sitting on the benches and looking knowledgeable while they chanted a section of history.

No-one knew how long the history was. It was said to take several hours to chant it all, from the Great Darkness to the present day, but neither hosts nor guests, at any feast Brook had attended, had ever asked to hear the whole thing.

The boys looked up in a laudable imitation of surprise when Brook and Brightleaves walked in. They stood up and bowed to Brightleaves.

'Lady Brightleaves has just come for – for a visit,' said Brook unconvincingly, immediately making the boys suspicious. Brook never had visitors. He visited other people's houses but his own was not designed to receive guests. There was no pot of broth on the fire, for instance.

'Do sit down, boys,' said Brightleaves. 'I'm just going to wander around for a bit. Carry on with what you were doing.'

The boys sat down and looked at Brook for guidance. He shrugged helplessly.

'Where had you got to?' he asked, while Brightleaves walked slowly around his house, inspecting things.

'We were doing King Hog the Great and how he played a game of Woodwit with the Cloudmaker,' said Raven.

'Oh yes. A very strange story, that. We'll have a discussion about what it means later. Just carry on with it for now –' for Brightleaves was beckoning to him. He walked round to where she stood, by the food-shelf.

Under the cover of the boys' chanting and the occasional 'pling!' of the lyre or roll of the drum, Brightleaves and Brook had a conversation about his domestic arrangements.

'You might at least teach them to make their beds!' she whispered.

Brook's house was a small one and had no sleeping-platform. Instead, a few wicker screens were attached to the right-hand wall of the house, dividing that area into sections, where the beds were. The sections were not curtained off from the central part of the house. This was because Brook liked to look at the embers of the fire when he was lying in bed; and he supposed that other people of a bardic temperament would like that too. The result was that anyone entering Brook's house could see the beds, whatever state they were in.

'It would be hypocritical of me to teach them to make beds,' said Brook. 'I never make my bed. What's the point? You get up, you live your day, you get back into bed again. I have never seen the point of making the bed. And I'm not going to start now.'

'You could put up curtains.'

'Whatever for? We don't mind seeing each other's beds.'

'You might not, but it looks so awful when people come in.'

'People don't come in,' said Brook.

'I shall send some nice cloth for you to hang up,' said

Brightleaves decidedly. 'In fact I'll bring it myself, to make sure you do hang it up. The place will look so much cosier.'

Brook groaned.

'And this food-shelf is disgusting!' Brightleaves continued. 'There's mouse-dirt all over it!'

'We always sweep that off before we have a snack,' said Brook.

'That's another thing,' said Brightleaves. 'Snacks can't be good for growing boys. Why don't you have a good pot of broth on the fire?'

'Usually we have our main meals out,' said Brook, 'because there's always someone in the glen wanting to be entertained; and in bad weather the nearby farmers' wives send over pots of food. If we had our own pot here, we'd have to stir it and worry about it and put stuff in it and generally faff about. This is a bardic school, not a cookery school!'

'It's a very dirty bardic school. When did anyone last sweep the floor?'

Brook just stared at her.

Brightleaves sighed. 'Do you even have a broom?'

'I remember seeing one,' said Brook, 'a few years ago. But I'm not sure what became of it.'

'I'll just go and inspect the latrine,' said Brightleaves, and out she went.

Brook sank down on the bench beside Raven. The boys stopped chanting and looked at him anxiously.

'Is anything the matter, Sir?' asked Marten.

Brook sighed. 'Yes,' he said. 'She wants us to hang up curtains and make our beds and sweep the floor and have a pot of broth on the fire! And in a moment she'll be coming in saying we need an extra latrine and she can easily get

Cliff Carpenter to make a seat for it. And d'you know why she wants all this done?'

They shook their heads quickly, to get the suspense over with.

'Because she wants me to have girls here,' said Brook.

'Girls!' they echoed. Then they sat in silence, mulling over this idea.

'I like it is the way it is now,' said Marten.

'So do I,' said Robin, loyally.

'Will they be pretty girls?' asked Raven.

Brightleaves came in, saying, 'You need an extra latrine. I can easily get Cliff Carpenter to make a seat for it.'

Brook and the boys all burst out laughing. Brightleaves looked at Brook enquiringly.

'I told them you would say that,' he explained.

'The exact words!' chortled Marten. 'Your Ladyship,' he added.

'And did you hear the boys' opinions, on your way in?' Brook asked her.

'I heard Raven's,' she said, flashing a winsome smile at Raven, who was blushing furiously.

'Would you like to repeat yours?' Brook asked Marten.

'I like it the way it is now,' said Marten, 'and Robin said he does too.'

'What did I tell you?' said Brook, looking at Brightleaves with a smugness he knew must be infuriating. But he had been right, so he might as well enjoy it.

'You don't have a piss-bucket,' said Brightleaves. 'That's not very public-spirited.'

'We've already discussed the logistical, economic and ecological aspects of the piss-bucket situation,' said Brook haughtily. 'This is not a stupid school. Tell her, boys.'

'With only four of us,' said Raven, 'it wouldn't be worth Heather or Crag sending someone all this way up the glen to collect it.'

'So we just pee anywhere, providing we're a certain distance away from the house,' said Marten.

'And?' said Brook.

'Oh yes!' said Raven.

'Let me say it!' said Marten, and hurried on before anyone could butt in. 'Male urine deters feline predators!'

Brightleaves chuckled. 'Well, it's not going to deter this one.'

'I thought not,' said Brook gloomily. He briefly considered asking Hardy, 'Can you reason with your wife?' but he knew what the answer was likely to be.

* * *

Hardy was up a sturdy oak tree beside the salmon leap, He was standing on a branch, wedged against the tree-trunk. For hours he had been doing the hunter's trick of remaining alert to every tiny movement in the woods around him while at the same time letting go of his self-awareness, as if he were not there, so that other creatures would not notice his presence.

He could not lose his awareness of parts of the tree pressing into his back, or the ribbed bark of the branch against his footsoles. But these were just things to be endured. He held his bear-spear ready. It was taller than he was, its iron head over a foot long, and sharp with hours of patient honing.

The bear was a big adult male. On its hind legs, it would stand about nine feet tall. At present it was standing four-legged on the rocks at the top of the salmon leap, its head down, watching the water.

Like the bear, Hardy was watching the water immediately in front of the animal. His view was partially obscured by the gold and rust-brown leaves that the oak still wore; but he could see enough through the gaps between them, and they veiled him from the bear. Standing against the tree-trunk in his bark-coloured clothes behind the random pattern of gold-brown leaves, he would look like a mere lump on the side of the tree.

A fish leaped, flicking its tail to propel it upwards. The bear opened its jaws wide and turned its head, following the salmon's soaring curve; but in doing so it was looking straight towards Hardy and would have seen his slightest movement. He kept still while the bear lunged at the fish and missed.

The salmon swam on, upstream to the loch to spawn. All around were the sounds of the forest. Below was the sound of the water, and from very far away came the cries of sheep. But it seemed to Hardy that these sounds were all around the edge of a circle of silence in which he and the bear waited for their prey.

This was the moment, Hardy knew from experience, in which one must not be lulled into simply experiencing the stillness and forget one's purpose. Instead, he used the stillness like a whetstone to sharpen his awareness.

Another salmon leaped, this time to the left of the bear, which turned its head quickly, away from Hardy, its jaws gaping wide, its neck stretching –

Hardy plunged the spear down into the stretched neck.

The bear staggered, turned its face towards him, then lumbered splashing towards the riverbank, with Hardy's spear still in its neck.

It scrambled out of the water and charged towards Hardy's tree. The spear bounced beside it as it ran. At the tree, it reared up on its hind legs, roaring, and scraped at the trunk with its huge curved claws. Hardy whistled for his men, who were hiding some distance away. The bear's claws alone were almost as long as his own hands.

He only had his knife now. He drew it from his belt and held it ready to throw into the bear's chest.

As he threw the knife, his men came running, knives and spears at the ready. The bear turned its head, pulling away from the tree a little. Hardy's knife bounced off its chest and fell to the forest floor.

The bear uttered a hoarse exasperated growl, like a final warning, dug its claws into the grey ridges of the bark and began to pull itself up the tree. This last effort was too much for it. It had fattened itself up for the winter, so it was big and heavy; and it had just been speared in the throat. The spear fell out of its neck, releasing a gush of blood. The bear's head drooped, its grip on the tree relaxed and it slumped to the ground.

Hardy climbed down from the tree. He and his men stood beside the bear in silence for a moment, acknowledging a brave adversary and thanking the god of hunting.

Then Hardy and Dawdle took off their clothes and hung them over a tree branch. This was not part of any religious ritual. It was because woven wool washed in winter takes a very long time to dry; and a man has to supervise the drying of his hunting-clothes, to make sure no woman hangs them where they would catch the scent of smoke.

He would have to remember to tell Brightleaves that,

Hardy thought as he removed his arrow from the bear's heart.

Then he cut open the bear's skin down its front and peeled back the thick fur, on both sides, to get a clear view of the flesh underneath. He and the naked ghillie began to gut the bear: they cut its throat to bleed it, slit its body open from breastbone to neck, broke its breastbone with an axe, sliced open its stomach, cut the skin of the stomach all the way to the pelvis, separated the anus and pulled it out along with the rectum, bladder and intestines, opened up the ribs and diaphragm, pulled out the food pipe, the wind pipe, the heart and the lungs.

Once it was gutted and the innards moved out of the way, the bear had to be skinned at once or, even on a cold day like this one, the hide would spoil and the beautiful fur would be wasted. It was too big to haul up and skin vertically, so they rolled it on to a clean patch of ground. Hardy on one side and Dawdle on the other skinned the bear, working down from the back legs to the head.

When they had got the bear's skin off, they spread it fur side down and scraped it to clear away the bits of fat and flesh that were still sticking to it. Meanwhile the ghillies cut the fat off the carcase in chunks. It would be useful for lamps; and in the deep dark of winter, who would care if the light smelled of fish?

Lofty cut a suitable branch off a tree. The two ghillies took one end each. Hardy and Dawdle draped the heavy bearskin over the branch. The ghillies, carrying the bearskin between them, each with an end of the branch on his shoulder, set off for Crag Tanner's workshop.

Lofty loaded all the fat into a bucket brought for the purpose. Hardy and Dawdle had a quick dip in the chilly river to rinse themselves, then put their clothes on again.

Without its fur, the long carcase looked like a person.

'Dawdle and I will stay here to watch it, with Rocky and Whistler,' said Hardy. 'We'll see who chooses to come and feast on it. Lofty, take this bucket of fat back to the house, give it to Grace, and come back here with Shorty, Smudge, more ghillies, and the dogs.'

Shorty and Smudge would halt the dogs well back. Only one of them would creep forward to let Hardy know they had arrived. Or, if a pack of wolves had already surrounded the carcase, they would know to loose the dogs and let them run at their enemies.

Perhaps a lynx would visit the carcase. Then the dogs would scare it up a tree. It would be another good fur. The meat was tasty too. But for a lynx they would have to wait until twilight.

Hardy and Dawdle sat behind a holly bush at some distance from the carcase. Rocky and Whistler were hidden not too far away. All four were downwind of the carcase. Hardy let his awareness sink into the leaf-strewn ground and spread out across the woods. They waited.

Crows found the bear first. They were driven away by a wildcat, who munched as much as she could before the shrill whistle of a red kite high above sent her scurrying into the undergrowth. The kite swooped down, followed by its mate. They landed a few yards away from the carcase, as if to check it out, then flapped towards it, clambered onto it, dug in their claws, pulled up fragments of meat with their hooked beaks and flew up again to eat in the safety of the sky. The crows, who were still hovering, took their chance and dived back to the carcase. The lazy kites let the crows do the work of pulling up meat and then fought the crows in the air to get it from them.

All this activity was bound to attract the attention of the wolf sentries. Hardy reckoned that by the time the wolf pack arrived, his own pack of warriors, ghillies and dogs would have arrived too.

Lofty, as the smallest of the warriors, was usually given any job that involved hiding behind leafless treetrunks or clumps of dry bracken. It was he who crept to Hardy's hiding place to let him know that the dogs had arrived. Creeping through the woods wasn't easy at this time of year when the forest floor was a carpet of crisp brown leaves that rustled under every step. Lofty moved slowly.

When he arrived behind the hollybush, Hardy pointed to the bear's carcase and murmured, 'We want the dogs down-wind of it.'

Lofty nodded and crept away.

What we need, thought Hardy, is a nice shower of rain to fall pitter-patter on the leaves, then the odd quiet footstep would go unnoticed.

But the rain-god did not consider the hunters' need important today.

* * *

The wolves came lolloping swiftly through the woods, sometimes bunching up close and bumping against each other while they ran, as if in play. When they reached the bear's carcase there was nose-wrinkling, snarling, and an upward-curling of black-edged gums to display long hook-shaped fangs; thus the leader reinforced his position while others scuffled among themselves for lesser seniorities.

The wolves tore at the bear's flesh with their teeth.

The white fur around their jaws became red. The pack's lowliest member, not permitted to eat yet, hung back watching hungrily – then turned tail and fled. Four grey dogs had come racing out from among the trees. The lesser members of the pack ran away. Only two wolves stood their ground. Brave wolves, thought Hardy approvingly.

The dogs leaped at the wolves, who stood up on their hind legs to meet them, snarling defiance. The dogs split their enemies between them, two dogs to each wolf. The men came running with their spears. Even if the two remaining wolves had wanted to flee now, they were locked in battle with the dogs. The animals had become two writhing bundles, growling, yelping, snarling and biting.

Although the dogs and wolves were grappling two to one, Hardy knew that a wolf could kill a dog with a single snap of its jaws. His dogs were quick, strong and well exercised; but the wolf lived wild, which was the best exercise of all. The leader wolf was a match for two dogs. Hardy drew his knife and ran towards the mass of snarling fur. Dawdle ran beside him. The wolf's jaw was gripped around the neck of his dog Shadow. His dog Misty was taking bites out of its shoulder but it would not be distracted, was focussed on killing Shadow. Hardy drove his knife into the wolf's throat. Its jaw relaxed then, it let go of Shadow and turned its head to snarl at Hardy. Their eyes met. The wolf's eyes were a golden colour, rimmed with black. The two leaders looked at each other for a moment. Then the wolf's eyes began to close.

The dogs got up and shook themselves, then turned to help their companions. But it was all over, the smaller wolf was dead too. Hardy checked his dogs. Shadow had toothmarks in his neck. Misty's leg was bitten. Scrap seemed to be unscathed. Gnasher's ear was torn. They would call at the Temple School on their way home to get some healing herbs from the priestesses.

* * *

At the feast in Hardy's house that evening, Willow and Cherry brought the warriors mugs of beer, and Lady Brightleaves wanted to hear all about the hunt. They were in a good mood by the time Brook Bard arrived with his three apprentices. Everyone shuffled up on the carved benches to make room for them and it turned into a jolly evening.

Up in the hills the wolves were howling, mourning the loss of their leader and his mate, but that made everyone appreciate the warm house, good food and companionship all the more.

Next day, Brightleaves wove into her blanket the colours of bears, wolves and winter trees.

* * *

Dream-Blossom had discovered what the worst thing was about housework. It wasn't the smells, dirt, heavy buckets, or tiredness at the end of the day. It was the boredom. Getting an object clean or a place tidy could be satisfying. But you had to do it again and again and again. Helping to prepare a meal was satisfying too, when you saw the result – but then it was eaten up, gone.

She missed being at school, learning things that were interesting and led somewhere.

The only thing that made housework bearable was if you had someone to chat with. Willow and Cherry were quite chatty. Dream-Blossom liked them. But Dawn never said a word. How could she bear this life of boring work if she never spoke to anyone? She never started a conversation and if you asked her a question, she answered as shortly as possible. Dream-Blossom thought it was just that Dawn didn't like her; but that didn't matter, she had Willow and Cherry to talk to.

Then Willow and Cherry were moved into the Chief's house to sleep. And rumour had it that they would soon be spending every day over at Brook Bard's house.

Dream-Blossom decided that if Dawn wouldn't speak to her, she wouldn't speak to Dawn. There was no point in trying to be friendly and being rebuffed. At bedtime they lay down and wrapped themselves in blankets without speaking. Dream-Blossom wondered how long it would be before she could have a clean under-tunic.

The work had not been so hard today and she didn't fall asleep straight away. After a while she felt a quivering beside her. Dawn was crying again, sobbing without making a noise. Dream-Blossom lay still so that Dawn couldn't tell she was awake. She didn't know what to do. Should she try to comfort Dawn? What could she say?

Dawn obviously didn't want to be heard. Dream-Blossom decided to ignore her and try to sleep. She rolled over; the quivering stopped abruptly.

They woke next morning to the sound of rain pattering on the thatch. Dream-Blossom groaned and pulled the blanket over her face – but it was daylight, so they had to get up. Dream-Blossom couldn't believe that she still had to go to the spring to fetch water, even in the rain.

But then she tried to imagine a slave at home saying to her, 'Surely I don't have fetch water in this weather?' What would she have replied? 'Of course you do. How dare you be so insolent? Be off with you!'

She suggested to Grace, 'Couldn't we just put the buckets outside and wait for them to fill up?'

'We do that in heavy downpours,' said Grace. 'But this isn't one of those.'

No, this was gusty, wind-driven rain that blew sideways at you while you climbed the hill. Dream-Blossom's poor-quality cloak was soaked through. Back at the women's house she hung it to dry, then ran to the warmth of the byre to do the milking. She found milking quite soothing, the regular hiss and plash of the milk squirting into the bucket, the warm flank of the cow against her head. She began to sing a milking-song.

The slaves often sang as they worked, songs that helped the rhythms of what they were doing. There were songs for milking, songs for grinding corn, songs for churning butter, songs for spinning. Once Dream-Blossom happened to be sitting next to Dawn when they were all singing. Dawn's lips moved but no sound came out.

When the slaves weren't singing, they talked. They talked about the Romans, strange mythical beings, not like real people at all. They talked about the Chief, Lady Brightleaves, and Brook Bard. They didn't gossip about Mother Swan in case this offended the Goddess.

They also talked about themselves. Each woman and girl came from somewhere and had a story to tell. Some of them told their stories. Dream-Blossom did not tell hers, because she felt embarrassed about telling a false story after hearing their true ones. Dawn did not tell her story either.

Thinking about this, Dream-Blossom wondered if perhaps Dawn didn't chat or sing not because she was unfriendly but because she was a spy like Dream-Blossom herself. If she was a spy, though, why did she cry in bed at night? Perhaps she was tired of waiting for whoever had sent her to summon her back. Perhaps she was crying because she hadn't found out anything yet and was beginning to despair. At this rate we'll be crying together, thought Dream-Blossom.

That night the silent sobbing started again. Dream Blossom was about to protest, or at least wriggle or cough to make it stop, when she remembered Curly saying, 'You are training to be a healer.'

She decided to try an exercise she had been taught at the school. She had no great hope of success. When she had tried it with Joy-of-Spring as her partner, they had both ended up in fits of giggles. But she had not really been trying then.

Now she lay still, breathed slowly, and did the meditation exercises used in the temple. When she was detached and surrounded by white light, she turned her head and looked at Dawn. She didn't turn her physical head or look with her physical eyes but she imagined herself turning and looking, so some part of her must have turned and looked. What she saw was not the girl Dawn but a sort of bundle, dark grey scarves wrapped around a ball of pain that glowed red-hot like metal on a forge.

She looked away again. She did not know how to deal with this. She breathed slowly and built up the white light again.

'Please help!' she asked the Higher Beings – not the gods and goddesses, who were busy organizing the movements of the sun, moon and stars, the changing seasons, the growing of crops, the weather; but the Higher Beings of a lesser order, who were close enough to people to understand and sympathize, and would help if they could.

Then she went to sleep.

The next morning was clear. Dream-Blossom's cloak was dry. She put it on and went to fetch drinking-water as usual.

The spring water came out from between two rocks in the hillside and fell as a small waterfall into a little pool no wider than the length of Dream-Blossom's arm. When she knelt beside the pool now, to put the pail under the waterfall, it suddenly came to her how strange and wonderful it was that pure clear water, for people to drink, should flow out of the hillsides like milk from a cow's teat.

When she had filled her pail she set it aside and simply watched the water flowing into the pool. She looked at the pool itself, with its rim of reeds and grasses. It was a quiet, peaceful little place.

The longer she knelt there, the quieter and more peaceful it became. The sound of the flowing water was like music and there was nothing else, just the little pool and the silence. As she grew more aware of the silence, it seemed to become a presence. Not the presence of a person; just the presence of the place.

The plants.
The pool.
The waterfall.
The stillness.

This is the Goddess, thought Dream-Blossom. When they talk about the Goddess, this is what they're talking about.

Suddenly she knew she must go and fetch Dawn. She left her pail by the spring and ran down the hillside, into the compound, dodging between the various outbuildings. Where was Dawn? What would she be doing this morning? I hope she's not churning butter, thought Dream-Blossom. Once you start churning butter you can't stop, you have to carry on until the butter comes. If you stop and start again, it doesn't work.

Dawn was cleaning out the cow-byre, with a shovel and bucket. All the dung had to be kept for plastering or fertilizer.

'Come with me,' said Dream-Blossom. 'Come quickly.'

Dawn didn't argue. Perhaps she thought that Grace or someone had sent Dream-Blossom to fetch her. Dream-Blossom didn't run on her way back to the spring; she felt that two girls running might attract attention. She walked briskly, looking like someone with a purpose. Dawn followed in silence. As they left the compound and began to climb the hill, Dawn looked questioningly at Dream-Blossom.

'Wait and see,' said Dream-Blossom.

They reached the spring. Dream-Blossom knelt down by the pool and patted the ground beside her. 'You kneel here.'

Dawn shrugged and knelt down.

Dream-Blossom waited. Nothing happened.

'This is a trick, isn't it?' said Dawn. 'You brought me up here to trick me.'

'No!' said Dream-Blossom, rendered almost tearful by the injustice of this accusation. 'I was up here just now and I felt the presence of the Goddess, here at the pool, and it was so peaceful – I wanted to share it with you – I thought it might help you.'

Dawn looked at her, curious. 'You wanted to help me?'
'Yes!'

Dawn burst into tears. Not the silent sobs that she did

every night into her blanket but proper crying. She cried and cried as if she would never stop.

Dream-Blossom didn't ask her to stop. She just put her arms round Dawn and hugged her.

After a while, Dawn's crying became quieter, slowed down and stopped. Dawn pulled back from Dream-Blossom, looked at her and said, 'Thank you.' Then she smiled. It was the first time Dream-Blossom had seen Dawn smile.

They walked back down the hill together, Dream-Blossom carrying the pail, Dawn looking around her as if she was seeing the beauty of the glen for the first time.

Dream-Blossom's next task was grinding corn. She had ground almost a crockful of flour when Grace came into the women's house and said, 'You've got a visitor.'

Dream-Blossom went outside. There in the porch stood Curly, smiling.

'It's time you came back,' she said

'May I say goodbye to Dawn before I go?' Dream-Blossom asked. Curly nodded. Dream-Blossom ran to the byre.

'I've come to say goodbye,' she said.

'Have you been sold?' Dawn asked anxiously.

'No,' said Dream-Blossom, 'I'm going to be a healer.' As she said it, she realized that she meant it.

Dawn nodded.

'I think you'll be a very good one,' she said.

The two girls hugged each other goodbye, then Dream-Blossom ran back to join Curly at the main gate.

As they walked back to the school together, Dream-Blossom waited nervously for Curly to ask whether she'd discovered anything suspicious – because she hadn't.

'So,' said Curly, 'what was the most important thing that happened to you while you were there?'

Dream-Blossom was surprised, because it wasn't the question she'd been expecting.

'Well, the most important thing that happened to me was when I felt the presence of the Goddess. At the spring.'

Curly nodded understandingly. 'She often makes herself felt at springs,' she said. 'She must like them.'

Chapter 9. New broom

Pig-killing began. The squeals of the pigs pierced the air up and down the glen. Each new squeal brought Crag Tanner or one of his apprentices riding or running to the relevant farm, to bargain with the housewife for the pig's bladder. He would get the pigskin to cure as a matter of course, but the bladder was a bonus. It could be blown up and turned into a kickskull ball. Crag Tanner's leather-covered kickskull balls were one of the most popular gifts in the glen.

The most proficient kickskull players were Hardy's warriors. Hardy believed in keeping them busy, because young men and boredom was a bad combination. So his warriors had regular exercises in sword-fighting, spear-throwing and slingstone hurling. He took them out on long treks into the distant hills hunting wolves, bear, boar or deer. When they weren't doing any of these things, he encouraged them to play kickskull.

The game was called 'Kickskull' because, according to Brook, the players used to kick the skulls of their enemies about; but then they decided that if their enemies had been brave men (and where was the honour in killing them if they were not?), it made more sense to stick their heads on posts outside the fortress, partly so that their brave spirits would guard the place and partly as a warning to other enemies – this could be you! After that, instead of a skull, the men used a pig's bladder, emptied, washed, inflated, and tied up tightly. This was great for playing games with until it burst. Then someone came up with the idea of covering the inflated pig's bladder with leather, to make it last longer. According to recited history it was one of the king's ancestors who had the idea about the leather covering, but Brook saw no reason to believe this. It could equally well have been a tanner's apprentice or a sports-loving bard.

One day while the pigs were squealing, Cliff Carpenter arrived at Brook's house with one of his apprentices. Between them they were carrying the materials for what Cliff described as 'the very latest in modern conveniences'. Raven, Marten and Robin stood watching Cliff and his boy erecting this phenomenon. Brook was out composing (or possibly visiting his lady-love in Quickwater Glen, an activity that the phrase 'out composing' sometimes covered).

'Haven't you lads got any work to do?' said Cliff after a while.

Raven was about to suggest that they should go back inside and do some more history, when Marten piped up,

'We are working! Brook says we should get to know the details of other people's trades so we can put them in our poetry.'

Cliff just grunted.

The boys watched as the building reached completion.

'It's like a little house!' said Robin. 'A person could live in there.'

'Not with the seats in the way,' said Raven.

'Why has it got two seats?' Marten asked. 'We've got one already.'

'Ah, this is just for the ladies,' said Cliff. 'You'll still be using your own.'

The boys looked ruefully at their own seat, tucked as far

as possible under the eaves of the house but still pretty much open to the weather. Nobody wanted to be constipated during a downpour, a gale or a snowstorm.

'So they'll have this all to themselves,' said Marten wistfully. The boys looked at the thatched roof, the weatherproof walls, and the smooth wood of the seat with its two holes, one with a pit under it.

'Take your last look,' said Cliff. 'I'm about to put the door on. After that, you won't see the inside again.'

At this point, one of Crag Tanner's apprentices arrived with a new leather bucket.

'Very good quality, this,' he said. 'It'll last you for ages. Stitching's been all sealed up, see, so the piss can't leak through.'

'Couldn't we test it?' said Marten.

'No,' said Cliff. 'You go on keeping the wildcats away!'

Then Brightleaves arrived, accompanied by Willow and Cherry.

'Brook's not here?' said Brightleaves. 'Oh well, while the mouse is away the cats can play, or whatever the saying is. Come on, girls.'

The girls were carrying all kinds of baskets and bundles. A basket of moss was installed in the 'modern convenience', then Brightleaves and the girls went into the house. The boys followed and sat on their benches in a daze while the girls made beds, shook out blankets, hung up bright woven curtains so that the beds were hidden, and dusted everything they could reach with rags they'd brought with them for the purpose. A new broom was produced and Cherry used it to sweep the floor. 'There!' said Brightleaves when all the activity had stopped, 'doesn't that look better?'

'It depends on your point of view,' said Brook from the

doorway. They all turned to look at him. 'It presents quite an attractive picture at the moment,' he conceded, 'but it won't stay like this. It'll get untidy again in no time.'

'You should have a slave to keep it tidy,' said Brightleaves, although during her wedding feast she had heard Brook's eccentric opinions on slavery.

'You know my views on that,' he said.

'You have to be realistic,' said Brightleaves. 'If we didn't have slaves, the community wouldn't function.'

'I agree that we need people to do what slaves do. What I don't agree with is the fact that we can buy and sell them, as if they were cattle or dogs. I don't think anybody should be able to own somebody else.'

'But it's a worldwide phenomenon,' said Brightleaves.

'That doesn't make it right,' said Brook. 'What do you think, boys and girls?' he asked, looking around at them all. 'Let's turn this into a proper school debate. Who agrees with me?'

The boys all raised their hands.

Brightleaves looked enquiringly at the girls.

'They daren't speak!' said Brook. 'You own their tongues, remember?'

'You can speak freely,' Brightleaves reassured them.

'No they can't,' said Brook. 'I know you're a kind mistress – but you could punish them or sell them if you got into a bad temper.'

Brightleaves reddened, remembering how on the journey she had punished Willow for causing a cow to be lost.

'All right!' she said. 'You've made your point. Now it's time to see if you'll put your principles into practice. I'll free these two, Willow and Cherry, on condition that you take them on as apprentices. I know I'm already sponsoring

Robin and I'll sponsor these two, at least partially; but they can also sponsor themselves, to some extent. They can do the sweeping and dusting for you and generally keep your house tidy. They can carry on sleeping at our place. What do you say?'

Brook looked at her in amazement. 'You've won!' he said. 'You've done it! I knew you were going to, I just couldn't work out how.'

'Thank you, Lady Brightleaves, thank you!' the sisters were saying.

'So it's all settled, then?' said Brightleaves. 'The girls can start here tomorrow?'

* * *

At her loom, Brightleaves repeated the colours she had chosen for Brook and his boys and now wove in the pinks of the girls among them. But her sense of achievement was accompanied by a sense of loss.

On a practical level, she had to find someone else to look after her clothes and dress her hair. This was not too difficult. Grace would choose someone suitable. There was that little girl Dawn, for instance, meek as a mouse but highly biddable. She might do. And if she turned out not to suit, when spring came Brightleaves would ride or drive to the nearest market and buy a new slavegirl.

But there was more to it than that. Willow and Cherry, before they became apprentice bards, used to sit with Brightleaves, spinning in the porch, or in the house on wet days. Grace sometimes joined them, and some of the other female slaves; every woman and girl in the household span wool, flax or nettle-yarn when she had an idle moment.

Brightleaves was not often alone when she sat spinning. But she missed two girls. They were young, but they were intelligent company. At Roughrock, her friends used to come and spin with her.

She had been so focussed on reaching Wildcat Glen and marrying Hardy, she had overlooked the fact that she was leaving behind all the friends she had made during her seven years at Roughrock.

Hardy led an active, energetic life. He took his men hunting, even in the rain, played kick-skull with them, or led them in fighting-practice. Only in the worst weather would he stay indoors and have a game of woodwit. His frequent hunts meant that there were frequent feasts, because once a boar or a deer was killed, it had to be eaten. The feasts were fun, under the stars on clear nights or crammed into the house in the rain. But being the hostess at a feast was not the same as chatting with one or two friends.

Now she had to make new friends.

On fine or mild days, Dainty visited, carrying baby Traveller. She was getting bored at the Temple guest-house and was hoping to be invited to stay at Brightleaves' house – as she made perfectly clear, by saying things like, 'Oh, if only I could come and stay with you!'

She was a chief's wife herself, so it would have been right and proper for her to stay with Hardy and Brightleaves. But Brightleaves found Dainty irritating. She could have put up with her for one night, a few even, if there was a definite prospect of her leaving. At the moment, however, Dainty could not visit Druid Northway because she was still not well enough to ride, or so she said. Brightleaves thought she was just putting it off and using her health as an excuse, so

Brightleaves did the same. 'I would love to have you staying here, of course, but I think until you're fit to ride, it would be much safer for you to stay near the Temple, with all those healers around you.'

The warriors Hooky and Badger, who had travelled to Wildcat Glen with Brightleaves, had been sent back to Roughrock. The original plan was that they should accompany Dainty on her way home, but it wasn't fair to deprive Sparky of two of his warriors while Dainty dithered.

'Mother Swan has advised me not to go home until the problem with my mother-in-law has been sorted out. She says if I go home now, I'll just let myself be bullied by her again and my husband won't believe she's trying to poison me. Mother Swan says I should wait until my husband comes to find me and then she'll tell him what's going on – he'll have to believe her!'

'Perhaps Druid Northway will agree with her.'

'I hope so!' Dainty was putting off her visit to Druid Northway from fear that he would order her to go home to her husband. He was a man and knew nothing of the terror – or rage – a mother-in-law could arouse in a young wife.

'Will your husband be allowed to come and find you? I thought Border Guards had to stay at their post.'

Dainty was horrified. 'I suppose they are! He would have to ask the King – then the King will know about it!'

'That might not be such a bad thing.'

'Firebrand might send his mother to find me!'

'I should think Mother Swan will be able to deal with your mother-in-law.'

Brightleaves wove Dainty as a fine line of soft nettle-green that sometimes flowed and sometimes went jaggedy with sharp points.

* * *

The women who had been introduced to Brightleaves at her wedding came to visit her, one by one; and she visited them. Each visit was a sort of test, for both visitor and hostess – could this woman become my friend?

The first visitor was a surprise. It was the one who had not been at the wedding, Vetch Oxhill. She was, as her husband had described, 'only a young lass'. Brightleaves was longing to ask why pretty young Vetch had married old Farmer Oxhill; but she didn't like to ask that straight out. From gentle, apparently random questioning she ascertained that there wasn't any cause in the family background for Vetch to have done such a thing.

Vetch was very friendly and at the same time touchingly hesitant in putting forward her opinions. She would begin to say something, then bite her lower lip and look anxiously at Brightleaves.

'I'm not sure if I should say this.'

'Oh, go on!'

So Vetch described the women of the glen to Brightleaves. Goldie Smith: 'She's very nice but she talks about nothing but her children, so it gets really boring after a bit.' Comfrey Carpenter: 'She boasts about how skilful her husband is all the time! It's as if she expects you to order something from him every time you visit her.' Woodrush Tanner: 'The house isn't far enough away from the tannery so it smells horrible.' Sunny Waller: 'She talks about cooking all the time!' Daisy Foxwood: 'She'll want to be your friend just because you're the Chief's wife.' Bracken Birchrock: 'If you aren't an expert on oxen, she won't be interested in talking to you.'

All this made Brightleaves laugh, of course; but she couldn't help remembering Vetch's remarks when she was visited by the various ladies.

Blonde-haired Goldie was a tiny, plump woman – 'my little bird,' Peak used to call her affectionately, forgetting how much little birds twitter, chirrup and tweet. She came from a country over a week's ride to the south and when Peak first met her, he found her accent sexy but barely understandable. In those days she was shy and didn't talk much. Now she was unstoppable.

She'd been married to Peak for nearly sixteen years and had borne him fourteen children, who had all inherited her fair hair and their father's large muscular build. The boys would make fine strapping smiths and the girls would make fine strapping wives for farmers. The oldest child was nearly fifteen, the youngest a babe in arms.

Brightleaves got on well with Goldie and hoped they would become friends. She also liked Daisy Foxwood, dark-haired, round-faced, rosy-cheeked, with a spirited way of talking which endeared her to Brightleaves. What did it matter if she boasted to her friends? To gratify Daisy, Brightleaves drove to her house in the little chariot.

But after she had visited all the women who had visited her, they did not come again, except as part of a crowd at feasts. They did not make individual friendship visits. Brightleaves could only conclude that they did not like her.

'Perhaps they're still missing Linnet,' Vetch tried to console her. 'After all, you are very different from her. She was little and shy.'

'Well, I'm not going to change who I am just to get them to like me!' said Brightleaves.

What she did not know was that, after her visits to the

women, Vetch had visited them, said, 'I'm not sure I should tell you this,' then told them: 'Lady Brightleaves thinks you're boring because you only talk about your children,' 'She thinks you're always trying to sell her your husband's work!' 'She thinks your house is smelly,' 'She thinks you've got cooking on the brain,' 'She thinks you're a snob,' 'She thinks you're obsessed with your oxen.'

After the conversation about Linnet, Vetch went round the houses again, saying, 'She doesn't care if you don't like her. She thinks Linnet sounds pathetic!'

The women of the glen could barely bring themselves to be polite to Brightleaves at feasts. The only one who defended her was Heather Dyer, because Brightleaves visited her so often to choose new colours. 'Say what you like, she's a good customer!' was Heather's verdict.

* * *

Brightleaves gave up trying to make friends and got on with her job of being a chief's wife. She put on her hooded cloak, set out in the rain, and visited every household in the glen.

The priestesses would be aware of any illness or injury, but there might be other needs. If a family member was ill, someone would have to look after them; and someone would have to tend the family's flocks and herds, plough, thresh, slaughter bullocks, bring sows to the boar and sheep to the ram. This sometimes meant that heavy or dangerous work was taken over by a child too small to do it safely. Then there would be another injury in the family, another person to look after, another set of jobs to fill. The chief could help by sending a man to work on the farm until the illness had run its course or the injury was healed.

Neighbouring families helped if they could, but sometimes they had problems of their own. Sometimes the help they could offer was not enough. Sometimes there was a neighbour-quarrel going on, which meant that no help would be asked for or given.

Because the communal team of oxen worked its way round the glen at ploughing times, not everyone's fields were ploughed on the same day, so the harvests were ready at different times. There might be only a few days' difference but the weather gods were so changeable in their moods, a smiling sunny day might cloud over and turn to rain, and while the field harvested yesterday was safely stowed in the granary, the unharvested field was soaked, a cause for concern unless the weather improved soon. If the rain did not stop for many days, the barley turned brown and was useless, except for the stalks which were uprooted for winter fodder.

A family's bad harvest meant hunger in the coming months, so the chief supplied them with grain from his store. A chief's wife looked out for cases of need. Some families were proud and would barter their last blanket or pot for food rather than ask for help. Other families hoped that with a little cunning, they could avoid doing anything but the minimum of work. A chief's wife had to discern. A newcomer like Brightleaves had to find out.

One way to find out about a family was to talk to their neighbours. Brightleaves visited Goodhill Farm; the farmer and his wife were out and about working on the farm but their daughter Iris was at home and entertained Brightleaves, bringing her a cup of ale and chatting to her.

'Can you tell me anything about your next-door neighbours?' Brightleaves asked.

Oh yes!' said Iris. 'They're called the Brindlehills. I'm going to marry Ray Brindlehill.'

'How lovely!'

'We've known each other all our lives. We're going to be handfasted this coming Brightfire Day.'

Next door at Brindlehill Farm, Brightleaves heard a different story.

'I understand congratulations are in order,' she said when she was introduced to the farmer's son, Ray.

The young man blushed and smiled.

'Thankyou, milady,' he said. 'Yes, Sorrel Carpenter and I are getting handfasted on Brightfire Day.'

'Sorrel?' said Brightleaves. 'I thought she was called Iris. I must have made a mistake.'

'Iris?' echoed Ray. 'Oh no! She's not still saying that, is she?'

Out poured a sorry tale of young love constantly disrupted by the jealous girl next door. 'I go for a walk with Sorrel and Iris walks along beside us, talking to me as if Sorrel wasn't there! I ask her to leave and she takes no notice!'

'I'm sorry to hear that,' said Brightleaves. If it was a case of physical want, she could help; but she couldn't think what she could do to ease this situation. 'Iris will have to accept it eventually, won't she?' she said.

'Perhaps you could say something to her, milady?' Ray suggested. 'She might take some notice of you!'

'I'll see what I can do,' said Brightleaves, although she was not looking forward to it. How would she have felt if some well-meaning older woman had tried to warn her off Longsword, all those years ago? But then Longsword had been in love with her, so it was completely different.

Her chat with Iris went remarkably well. Iris listened and seemed to accept what she said.

'I know that at the moment you don't think you could ever love anyone else,' Brightleaves told her, 'but you will! Take my word for it.'

'Thank you for being so understanding,' said Iris, and promised not to interfere between Ray and Sorrel any more.

Brightleaves went home feeling quite pleased with herself. She wove the love-triangle into her blanket.

Word went around the glen that Lady Brightleaves was a kind, helpful person – except that Iris Goodhill said she was a bossy interfering cow; but if anything, that served to enhance her reputation. It was a brave woman who gave advice to Iris Goodhill!

So while the rich women thought Brightleaves was snobbish and sneering, the middling ones and the poor ones thought she was tactful and understanding.

Chapter 10. Midwinter

The nights grew longer and the days grew shorter as Midwinter approached.

'So, what do we know about the Goddess of the Stars?' asked Brook, sitting on his nice clean bench in his nice clean school.

There were colourful hangings concealing the beds; the floor was swept; the food-shelf was crumb-free; and there was even a pot of broth simmering on the fire. When he'd argued that tending it would distract his apprentices, Brightleaves had replied, 'Nonsense, women can do more than one thing at a time.' And it was true that sometimes Cherry or Willow answered Brook's questions quite lucidly while stirring the pot.

Now they were just looking at it thoughtfully, sensing that it would probably need a stir quite soon, while they applied their minds to Brook's question: what did they know about the Goddess of the Stars?

'That white road across the night sky is hers?' suggested Cherry.

'Yes,' said Brook, in a tone that encouraged them to say more.

'I know, I know!' said Marten, bubbling with knowledge. 'She lives in a silver ship in the sky! It sails across the sky all through the year!'

'That's where you go when you're dead,' said Raven. 'Your soul goes there to think about the life you've just had, what you did right and what you did wrong. Then you decide what sort of life you need next time, to correct your mistakes. And when you're ready, you get born again as someone else.'

'Very good,' said Brook. 'So the Goddess of the Stars takes care of the souls between lives. Anything else? What does she do at Midwinter?'

'I know!' said Robin. 'She gives birth to the sun god.'

'Yes!' said Brook.

'You would think,' said Willow, now stirring the pot, 'that she would give birth to another star. The sun is so big! And so yellow and hot.'

'Perhaps the sun takes after his father,' said Cherry.

'But who is his father?' asked Willow.

'Can anyone answer that?' Brook asked the class.

'Perhaps he doesn't need a father,' said Robin.

'Everyone has a father,' said Cherry.

'I don't,' said Robin.

'But you did,' said Marten. 'He's dead now but you definitely had one. Everyone has a father. Lambs, puppies, everyone.'

'I think with gods and goddesses the rules are different,' said Raven.

Marten nodded. 'So that's why he has to get born every year,' he said.

'What d'you mean?' asked Willow.

'Well,' said Marten, 'when people get born, they stay born. They don't keep having to get born again every year.'

'They do when they die,' said Cherry. 'Raven just said; they go to the Star Goddess' silver ship and stay there until they're ready to be born again.'

'But then they come back as someone else!' said Marten. 'They come back as a different person! The Sun God doesn't do that. He doesn't come back as a Fish God or a Stag God. He comes back as the Sun God every time.'

'And he does it really quickly,' said Robin. 'He's only away for Midwinter night. I know it's a long night – but he's reborn the next morning.'

'Maybe people are reborn the next morning,' said Raven. 'They might be, for all we know.'

'But they've got a lot to sort out, before they come back,' said Marten.

'Time might feel quite different in the silver ship,' said Willow. 'Perhaps a single night there could feel like years and years.'

'Or maybe the Sun God hasn't made many mistakes in his life,' said Raven, 'so he doesn't have so much to think about before he comes back.'

'Poor Star Goddess!' said Cherry. 'She's been having babies for more than a thousand years and each one only lives for a year.'

'You're getting mystery confused with history,' said Brook. 'History is what really happened to ordinary people and it's recorded in memory. Mysteries are things we don't understand. We don't understand the gods and goddesses so we make up stories about them, to make them seem more like us, people in families. But we know they're not really people, so we honour them with ritual. The point of ritual is that it takes you outside ordinary time. We get older, we change, old people die, new people are born. But the ritual stays the same.'

The class was silent, pondering this.

Brook looked at his three oldest pupils. 'Willow, Cherry, Raven,' he said, 'how many Midwinters can you remember? Perhaps you can't remember the ones when you were very small; but you can probably remember some?'

They sat remembering, and nodded.

'Tell me something that happened in your household at Midwinter,' said Brook.

'We always had roast pork,' said Raven.

'We always used to sing special Midwinter songs,' said Cherry.

'There you are, you both said "always". If you look back over those midwinter festivals, can you distinguish one from another in your memory?'

They shook their heads. 'That's what made it nice,' said Willow, 'that it was always the same.'

'So when you look back,' said Brook, 'it's as if those Midwinter celebrations happened outside ordinary time.'

'Oh yes!' said Willow. 'I see what you mean now.'

Since Willow and Cherry had joined the classes (and since Brightleaves' makeover of his house), Brook had watched carefully to see if the presence of the girls or the new housekeeping arrangements had any negative effect on the boys.

Raven was certainly distracted. The girl who milked cows, sheared sheep and plucked chickens, whoever she was, seemed to have been forgotten. Raven was slightly in love with both girls, sometimes more with Cherry of the rosy cheeks and sparkling eyes, sometimes more with Willow and her slender grace, if his poems and songs were anything to go by. Also, his style had become more lyrical. But he only composed in the evenings, after the girls had gone back to Hardy's house. So, if anything, he was concentrating more on his bardic studies during the day than he had before the girls came.

The younger boys were slightly less wild than before,

when the girls were around, and slightly more wild than before when they'd gone, so that balanced out. All the boys, indeed all the male members of the group, whatever they might have said, enjoyed the increased comfort of the house and the hot food. Every day when Cherry and Willow walked over from Hardy's house, they brought with them something tasty to add to the pot; herbs, chunks of whatever animal had recently been slaughtered, wild garlic bulbs, the stored roots of wild turnips or wild carrots. The girls planned to plant garlic, turnips and carrots near Brook's house for a convenient source of vegetables.

Meanwhile, everyone was taken up with the preparations for Midwinter. Brook, Cherry and Willow were to spend the festival at Hardy's house, where all the servants would crowd into the main house with Hardy and Brightleaves for the midwinter feast. They would stay up all night around the fire, singing traditional midwinter songs to defy the darkness. Dainty and Traveller had been invited too; Brightleaves could not let them spend the feast alone in the Temple guest-house. The priestesses would be too busy to entertain them that night.

Raven, Marten and Robin had an energetic part to play, along with all the other apprentices and all the farmers' sons in the glen. They were getting their costumes ready.

The tanner's apprentices were the luckiest, because there were always a few tanning jobs that went wrong, so there were discarded, discoloured, half-tanned skins or hides in the tanner's store. The other boys wore rags dyed with soot. They rubbed animal fat into their hair, pulled it up into spikes, and stuck crows' feathers into it at odd angles. They painted their bodies and each other's faces with charcoal. Hardy had ordered that each boy must be issued with a thick woollen cloak dyed black or dark grey, to wear for the night. The cloaks were handed in afterwards and re-used the next year.

All the boys waited to see what the weather would be like. A clear sky was best, because then they could see their way up the glen by moonlight or starlight. If it was cloudy, the older boys were allowed to carry torches. Rain was the worst, as the veterans assured the first-timers, boasting of all-night downpours they had endured.

'D'you think we look fierce enough?' Marten asked, on Midwinter night, when they were ready to set out from Brook's house.

'Raven looks terrifying!' said Robin.

'What about me?' asked Marten.

There was something about Marten's round dimpled face that made it almost impossible for him to look terrifying, however much charcoal he was daubed with. Nevertheless Robin had a go, seizing a stick of charcoal and drawing some more lines on Marten's face.

'There!' he said, stepping back to view the effect, 'you look really frightening now!'

This cheered Marten. The trio picked up their drums and clacksticks and set off down the glen to meet the other boys.

It was always exciting to see what the other apprentices were going to look like. Sometimes it took a while before you recognized someone you'd known all your life. As the small groups of boys from the workshops and farmhouses arrived at the meeting-place, there were gasps of, 'Is that you?' And each 'you' felt a thrill of excitement because, tonight, he wasn't himself, he was someone different, so he could do things that his normal self couldn't or wouldn't do. There was a buzz of strangeness and freedom as the crowd of ragged, stiff-haired, black-cloaked, painted boys set off through the darkness, banging their drums, blowing their whistles and clacking their clacksticks, shouting, 'Night! Night! Beasts of night!' Some of the boys had brought iron cooking pots and iron knives to bang them with.

Their first duty was to visit each farmhouse and disturb the farmer's midwinter feast with demands for food. They stood outside each closed door yelling, 'Food! Food! Food for the beasts of night!'

If any farmer refused them, then the soot-bearer, the smallest boy, took his pot of soot and a stick, and drew a sign upon the closed door. The sign meant that the household would know hunger in the year to come. But nobody refused them. At each farm, the wife had a plate of goodies ready for them. The boys were well fed by the time they reached Hardy's house, the penultimate stop on their journey. Grace and all the servants were honoured guests that night, so Brightleaves herself came to the door to give the boys their plate of meat pasties made with her own hands and baked in the bread oven. Then she brought them beakers of beer.

They ate and drank, then set off again, to a place where, if they were not the beasts of night, they would never dare to go.

The Swan Priestesses' preparations for Midwinter were quiet and solemn. Dainty and her baby were sent over to Brightleaves house to spend the night there, so that the priestesses could concentrate on the festival.

Shortly after sunset, all the Pens put on their white swan-cloaks, even though they might have very few feathers on them as yet, and walked to the temple in a silent procession. They sat down in a circle against the wall and started meditating. The Cygnets came in, wearing their grey cloaks, and were awed to see all the Pens robed in white. They sat down in a smaller circle, inside the Pens' circle.

Then the teachers walked into the temple, wearing their magnificent white feathered swan cloaks. They sat down at the eastern side of the temple, leaving a central seat vacant.

Last of all, Mother Swan came in, wearing her white swan cloak, and sat down in the seat of honour at the centre of the eastern semi-circle.

There were two doors to the temple: an inner door, which was always closed during meditations, and an outer door to the porch, a wide door, more like a gate. This was now shut.

It was going to be a long night, so the girls and women would need to answer the call of nature now and then. For this purpose, two buckets had been installed in the porch, between the inner door and the outer, so that no-one would have to go all the way round the back to the latrine.

The new girls, who had never attended a Midwinter ceremony before, did not understand why this was necessary. As the night progressed, they found out.

Mother Swan led the meditation.

'On this night,' she said, 'the Goddess of the Stars will give birth to the Sun God. We are healers, so we will attend this birth as we would any other. Our job is to invoke our Goddess, the Goddess of healing and childbirth, to come and assist the Goddess of the Stars in her labour. We will all set up the circle of light as usual. Then the teachers and Pens will invoke our Goddess. Cygnets, you will maintain the circle of light, like a silver wall around us, so that nothing can break through. You will keep the circle of light going no matter what happens.'

The circle of light was established. The invocation began. The sacred atmosphere in the temple grew stronger and stronger. All the meditation practice they had put in during the year made sense now; it had been a preparation for this. Some of the girls felt as if they were flying. In this sacred space, time lost all meaning. Apart from the odd stiff joint making itself felt, or a leg gone to sleep, they seemed to be floating in bliss.

Then they heard it, away in the distance at first, so that they were hardly aware of it, until it started to come closer, closer, closer – drums beating, sticks bashing together, rough voices shouting:

'Night! Night! The beasts of night!'

'Maintain the circle of light,' said Mother Swan quietly.

The beasts of night had run into the school precinct, right up to the outer door of the temple. They circled round the temple, banging drums, blowing whistles, clattering knives on pans, clacking sticks and chanting, 'Night! Night! The beasts of night! Night! Night! The beasts of night!'

It was much harder to hold in your mind the image of a circle of light around the whole group in the temple while all the time you were afraid that the beasts of night were about to come through the wall or break down the door.

It was even more difficult when you needed a pee so badly that you had to get up, move round the circle as inconspicuously as you could, tap the doorkeeper on the shoulder so that she would open her eyes and then open the door for you, and go out into the porch, the terrifying porch, where you could hear the chanting, banging, whistling and clattering much more clearly; and you could glimpse, between the woven wicker strands of the outer door, the black raggedy jaggedy shapes of the beasts of night leaping and dancing out there in the darkness.

Even when you were back in your seat, focussing fully again on the circle of light, the noise went on and on and on. Would it never stop? Did the beasts of night never get tired?

No, because they were full of energy from all the food and drink they'd had on the way; and they were high from dancing and chanting and making a noise; and above all, they were high on being someone other than their normal everyday selves, and being in a group, a pack, with others in the same mood.

'Night! Night! The beasts of night!'

As the Cygnets strove to hold the circle of light, one occasionally peeped between her eyelashes at the Pens and the teachers, hoping they might make some signal to show that they had now finished whatever they'd been doing and were ready to help with the circle of light. But they seemed to be utterly absorbed.

After what seemed like hours, at the point where all the Cygnets had resigned themselves to the fact that they would be stuck here holding the circle of light for ever, Mother Swan said, just as if it were an ordinary meditation class,

'Come back into the temple and open your eyes.'

They all opened their eyes. The beasts were still chanting outside. Mother Swan got up and went to the door. The doorkeeper opened it for her, then went ahead of her to open the outer door.

Mother Swan stood in the doorway of the temple and announced, not loudly but in a clear voice that carried:

'The new sun is born.'

The beasts of night nearest to the door had already stopped dancing and drumming when they saw her come out. Gradually, silence spread around the circle of beasts. Then their leader, one of the tanner boys, turned and set off out of the precinct, rebelliously but quietly chanting, 'Night, night, the beasts of night!' The others followed him, also chanting, and still drumming and clacking. The new sun might have been born but dawn had not yet appeared in the eastern sky, so the beasts of night could dance for a few more hours if they wanted.

The three beasts from Brook's house decided to go home. There were was no point in going all the way down the glen with their friends, only to have to come all the way up again. The best of the fun was over now. Nobody was going to give them any more food or beer, not now that the new sun had been born.

How did Mother Swan know when the new sun was born? the Cygnets wondered.

The first time she had led the ceremony, Mother Swan had wondered this herself. How will I know when the midpoint of the night has passed? And as she sat meditating, and trying not to worry, the voice of the Goddess, somewhere in the air above her head, had said, 'You will know.'

And she had. It was nothing mystic that had told her; it was a down-to-earth outside noise, the footsteps or rather pawsteps of some woodland creature running across the thatched roof, a real nightbeast escaping from the acting beasts of night. She heard it and understood it as a signal.

The signal was different every year but there always was one.

Now the beasts of night were dispersing to their homes and turning back into ordinary boys who were going to have trouble getting clean. Many a boy as he crept towards his bed was caught by his mother, who said, 'If you think you're getting under the blankets with all that soot on you, you've got another think coming!' So many a beast of night began the coming day as the unwilling victim of a cold-water scrub.

Meanwhile, the ceremony in the temple was not over. To celebrate the birth of the new sun, the priestesses began to chant; not ominous, threatening chanting as the beasts' had been, but clear, joyful, peaceful chanting to make the heart sing. And it was this sound that greeted the first pale hint of daybreak above the eastern hills.

* * *

Brightleaves had fun weaving the festival: red for the fire glowing in the house; all her colours massed together for the people feasting; angular black shapes for the Beasts of Night; white and grey triangles for the cloaked priestesses; pink and gold for the rising sun.

Then snow fell, and continued to fall for many days. The glen became a world of whiteness. Farmers trudged up to the pastures dragging sledges loaded with bundles of hay for sheep and horses. Willow and Cherry couldn't go to Brook's house but had plenty of opportunities to practise their trade at Hardy's, where Brightleaves kept all the women indoors with her, sitting around the fire spinning or grinding corn by firelight. House doors had to stay shut, to keep the snow out, so it was too dark to do any weaving. Brightleaves sent sledge-loads of food over to Brook and his boys.

At the Temple school, herbalism lessons were confined to studying the dried herbs in the herb-house by rushlight and learning which ones were best for the ailments that people suffered from at this time of the year. Of course a dried herb could 'call' to you in the herb-house, just as a fresh one could out in its natural setting; but the girls were encouraged to acquire a sound knowledge of what each herb could do before developing this special form of intuition. Each herb had its own song, a rhythmic chant that began with its name, followed by a short description of the plant, the kind of places it grew, and whether it liked sunshine or shade; then whether to use the flowers, leaves or roots; and then all the diseases and ailments it could cure and how it was to be administered.

Meanwhile the school's horses were kept busy, trotting through the snow taking priestesses and their students to visit people with sore throats, coughs, and hot skin.

Between snowfalls, children on wooden trays slid down the white hillsides screaming with pleasure; and when there was a long enough gap between one snowfall and the next for the animal-track to be visible, Hardy took his warriors and ghillies to hunt deer, wolf and wild boar.

When at last the snow melted, the farmers went out checking their fields of winter-sown wheat, oats and barley for snow damage. The foresters went coppicing, making new glades in the woods. Brightleaves went to visit Goldie Smith.

At the door, before she had even hung up her fur cloak, she said to Goldie, 'I know you don't like me, but I think the needs of the community override personal differences, and I want to ask your advice about organizing the Festival of Growing Light.'

Goldie stared at her. 'I thought it was you who didn't like me!'

'Whatever gave you that idea?'

Goldie motioned to a slave to hang up Brightleaves' cloak. The house was full of children of various ages and sizes, playing. There were shouts, shrieks, squeaks, scuffles, and sharp words from the ten-year-old girl in charge of them. Goldie, ignoring all this, sat down on a bench by the fire. Brightleaves sat beside her.

'I was told that you didn't like me because I talk about my children all the time. Well, I know I talk about them a lot, of course I do, but then all mothers talk about their children, don't they? It's only natural! And my children are not the only thing I talk about!'

'But I never said that!' Brightleaves managed to interject when Goldie paused for breath.

'Didn't you?'

'No! When I first met you, I felt a sense of kinship with you, because you're the only other woman in the glen who isn't a Hunter by birth; I wanted to get to know you better, and I really hoped we would become friends.'

'Oh! So, do you think Woodrush Tanner's house is smelly?'

Brightleaves stared at her. 'What's that got to do with you and me?'

'Never mind. Just tell me.'

'Woodrush Tanner's house,' said Brightleaves, 'is the most sweet-smelling house in the glen. I expect she keeps it like that because she's worried about the smells from the tannery. But it's sited upwind from the tannery, and she has all those lovely herbs and petals scattered about, and I know she makes her husband and sons wash themselves all over every day after they've finished work.'

'I see!' said Goldie, sounding strangely excited. 'And do you think Daisy Foxwood is a snob?'

'Yes, but I like her anyway. She's got a very good heart.'

'And do you think that Bracken Birchrock is obsessed with her oxen, or that Comfrey Carpenter is always boasting about her husband's work, or that Sunny Waller talks only about cooking?'

'I think we're very lucky to have an expert on oxen in the glen. We rely on them for ploughing – '

'And for pulling things up Festival Hill for the festivals!' Goldie interrupted.

'Well, there you are! And as for Comfrey Carpenter, she's right to be proud of her husband's skills. He's one of the best carpenters I've ever met. And Sunny Waller does talk about cooking a lot, it's true – but I've tried some of her recipes and they're delicious.'

A slave came with two goblets of mead and a plate of oatcakes. The ladies sipped and nibbled.

'Lovely,' said Brightleaves. Goldie looked pleased.

'I'm sorry I've had the wrong impression of you,' she said. 'I shouldn't have listened to hearsay.'

They started discussing arrangements for the next Festival. Then Goldie asked, 'Do you see much of young Vetch Oxhill these days?'

'She's the only woman who's become my friend.'

'Oh dear – '

Then Goldie said something about Vetch Oxhill which Brightleaves couldn't hear properly, because the noise-level of the child-pack rose. Goldie stood up and clapped her hands. There was silence.

'All of you go and play outside,' she said. 'It isn't raining or snowing. Go and run about! Put on your cloaks first!' she added as they all scrambled to the door.

When the house was quiet, Brightleaves said, 'I've got some exciting news.'

Goldie looked at her expectantly.

'I think I'm pregnant,' said Brightleaves. 'I've missed two bleedings. I'm waiting to miss one more before I tell Hardy. But I had to tell someone!'

Goldie nodded. 'I know that feeling,' she said. She took a deep breath, sighed, and went on, 'I think I might be pregnant too.'

'How lovely!' said Brightleaves – then, seeing Goldie's expression, said – 'Or isn't it?'

Goldie shook her head. 'I don't want any more. Fourteen is enough! And I'm still breastfeeding Petal, so I shouldn't be pregnant at all.'

'That doesn't always work,' said Brightleaves.

'Obviously not,' said Goldie. 'Please don't tell anyone. Peak doesn't know yet.'

On her way out, Brightleaves saw Peak walking from the smithy to one of the out-houses. She waved in greeting and he came over to talk to her.

'I've just been to see Goldie,' she told him.

'How did she seem?'

'Fine!' said Brightleaves. 'A bit tired perhaps. But I'm going to organize the next festival, so that's one less thing for her to do.'

'That's good,' said Peak. 'She hasn't been herself lately.'

'I'm sure it's nothing to worry about,' said Brightleaves.

Peak didn't want to think that there was anything to worry about, so he agreed.

Brightleaves went home and wove Goldie and Peak into

her blanket.

Peak realized that he couldn't go on fooling himself that he wasn't worried about Goldie. He went to see Mother Swan. He rode to the school, hitched the reins over a gatepost, and was shown into Mother Swan's house to wait for her.

Mother Swan came in and found him slumped on a bench gazing into the fire.

'What's the matter, Peak?' she asked, sitting down opposite him. 'Is it Goldie?'

He stared at her. 'How did you know?'

'Because if it was one of the children,' said Mother Swan, with a smile, 'Goldie would have sent a runner asking for a healer; and if it was you, you wouldn't ask for my help until you were too ill to move.'

Peak nodded.

'So, what's the matter with Goldie?' Mother Swan asked.

Peak frowned, wondering how to define his worries. 'She's not herself,' he said.

Mother Swan waited for him to say more.

He tried to explain. 'She's pretending to be the same but she isn't. She's like metal that's tired.'

'Oh dear,' said Mother Swan.

Peak looked relieved. He had managed to convey the gravity of the situation.

'Do you want me to come and see her?' Mother Swan asked.

Peak frowned, turning this over in his mind. People were so difficult to deal with! If the situation had been a piece of metal, he would have known exactly what to do with it.

'I know what we'll do,' said Mother Swan. 'If I arrive at your house, Goldie will know you've been to see me, and she might not be too pleased about that. So I'll send one of the younger priestesses. I'll send my assistant, Curly. She and Goldie are quite good friends, aren't they? She can just pop in for a social visit; and perhaps Goldie will talk to her.'

Peak's face cleared. 'Thank you, Mother Swan!' he said. 'I knew you would know what to do.'

Actually, Mother Swan just made it up as she went along, like everyone else. What really helped people was their own belief in her wisdom. Peak, for example, felt much better now. The whole thing was in the hands of the priestesses and he could stop worrying.

A little later that day, Curly dropped in to the Smiths' house for a chat with Goldie. The little blonde woman was sitting listlessly by the fire. Her loom stood neglected against the wall, her spindle and a pile of fleece lay untouched on the bench beside her. Children of various sizes played around her, absorbed in their games. The baby slept in its cradle.

Curly was carrying, as if by chance, a bag containing various herbs. 'Would you like to come out for a walk with me?' she asked. 'It's a fine day.' Going for a walk was a way to get privacy in a household like this.

'Not really,' said Goldie.

Curly then set about psychologically manipulating each child in turn until he or she decided that yes, going to play outside was a brilliant idea. She followed the first one out and made sure there was a servant outside to keep an eye on them.

When all but the baby had gone out, Curly sat down beside Goldie and put her bag down on the floor.

'What's the matter?' she asked.

Goldie bit her lip and whispered, 'I'm pregnant again!'

'Already?'

'Yes and I'm frightened. It's too soon. It doesn't feel right. There's something wrong, I know there is! I don't feel right. I don't feel the way I felt the other times. I'm so frightened, Curly!' She was sobbing by now; Curly put her arms round her and held her until she became calmer.

Goldie sat upright, pushed her hair back from her face and smiled through her tears. 'Thank you,' she said, 'I feel better for that. Perhaps I just needed a good cry.'

'I think you need a check-up,' said Curly. 'Go up to your bedspace and lie down. I'll be with you in a minute.'

'I'm sleeping down here at the moment,' said Goldie. 'I always do that when I'm suckling, it saves having to carry a baby up a ladder.'

'Good,' said Curly. 'That means I won't have to carry my things up a ladder either. Meanwhile, let me carry the baby.'

Curly always told her students, 'Never leave your medicine bag unattended for a moment, even in a really well regulated household where all the children are obedient little darlings and all the slaves are perfectly happy.' Then she would tell a few cautionary tales about children making themselves ill and slaves poisoning their master or mistress, with herbs stolen from a medicine bag.

So now, true to her own teaching, she slung her medicine bag over her shoulder by its strap before she picked up the cradle with the baby in it. She followed Goldie across the house to a curtained section under the platform. Behind the curtain was a double bed with a thick heather mattress and plenty of blankets and furs for covering. Curly put the cradle on the ground near the head of the bed while Goldie lay down. Then Curly drew the thick woollen curtain to screen the bed-space from the rest of the house. She sat down on the bed and started to feel the patient's stomach, palpating it gently. She leaned sideways and lay with her ear close to the stomach, listening. Then she sat up, very still, with her eyes closed, her fingertips laid lightly on the small mound of Goldie's belly.

'What?' asked Goldie.

'Ssh!' said Curly. 'Just relax and let your mind wander.'

Goldie obeyed. Curly sat for quite a long time, sending her mind inside Goldie's body and looking at what was there. Eventually she lifted her fingers away and opened her eyes. Goldie was dosing now. Curly picked up her bag and left the bed-space quietly. Back by the fire, she opened the bag and took out a small bronze cauldron, a horn spoon, and small pouches containing dried herbs. A frequent visitor, she knew where the drinking-water bucket was in Goldie's house. She went over to it, checked that the water was indeed fresh, and filled her cauldron. She added a few spoonfuls of herbs to the water in the little cauldron, then set it carefully on the fire to brew. When she smelled that it was ready, she hooked a stick under the handle of the cauldron, lifted it off the fire and put it on the ground to cool.

Then, holding the little cauldron in a cloth to protect her hand, she tipped the mixture into a cup, which she carried back to Goldie's bed-space. Goldie opened her eyes as Curly came in.

'I must have dosed off,' she said.

'Yes, you did,' said Curly. 'I've brought you some tonic to help you feel better. You drink this now, and have some more later – I'll leave you some herbs so you can brew it up for yourself. You're to drink a cup three times a day.'

Goldie sat up and drank the brew gratefully.

'I feel better already!' she said.

This often happened, Curly noticed. Once the patient had confided in the healer, the illness became the healer's responsibility, so the patient started to feel better at once. And the tonic had a cheering effect. But it would not reach to the core of the problem. Because whatever was growing in Goldie's womb, it wasn't a new life. Sometimes these things went away of their own accord. But mostly they didn't.

Curly rode back to the temple with a heavy heart. She wouldn't tell Goldie or Peak what she suspected until after the Festival of Growing Light. Let them enjoy that first.

Chapter 11. Growing Light

On the day of the festival, children clustered around the door of the building where the timber was stored, waiting for the oxen, and cheered when the great beasts came lumbering along, one pair from Oxhill farm, the others from Birchrock, their drivers walking beside them. All four oxen were harnessed to the timber-cart. A team of men loaded the wood on to the cart. It was to be a huge fire!

The oxen hauled the cart up the hill while the children walked alongside, sometimes running off across the hillside and coming back again, sometimes running round and round the oxcart. When they reached the top of the hill, the men unloaded the timbers and built up the fire.

The fire would not be lit until dusk, so all the food had to be cooked in advance. Housewives arrived carrying pots of herb-flavoured stew, saying things like, 'This needs warming up carefully until it's nice and hot but it mustn't be allowed to boil.' Brightleaves and Hazel Smith were in the outhouse receiving the food and planning the order in which things should be loaded on to the ox-cart for its next trip. Vetch was at the top of the hill, supervising the unloading of the timber.

There was a scream, oxen bellowing, men shouting, sounds of splintering wood... Brightleaves and Hazel ran outside and looked up.

The oxen were standing at a strange angle across the hillside. Behind them lay the cart, overturned, broken.

'I am so sorry!' Vetch wailed, then put her hands over

her face and sobbed, her shoulders shaking.

Nobody knew how it had happened. One pair of oxen lived on Vetch's farm and she was used to handling them. The driver had not tried to stop her when she led them down the hill. Why would he? Nobody had paid much attention; the men were all busy building the fire.

'She made 'em turn too sharp,' said one among the crowd of children. But Brightleaves did not hear, because now she had her arms around the sobbing Vetch and was trying to comfort her.

'You go home and have a rest,' she said.

'Thank you!' said Vetch, dewy-eyed with gratitude.

The men righted the cart – but it was unusable. Everything had to be carried up the hill by hand, which took a long time, even with the bigger children helping. Brightleaves sent Hazel home to get changed.

There was no time for her to go home herself. She, the Chief's wife, would be greeting people at this first public festival she had organized in Wildcat Glen, wearing an old dress, old shoes, no jewellery, and with her hair in a mess.

It was her practicality that saved her. She had brought a messenger with her, just in case she needed anything from home. Now she sent him riding with a long message for Grace, Dawn, and Willow if she was there. Her message was answered in the form of her chariot, driven by Willow, with Dawn as passenger in charge of a large woollen bag.

'I suppose this is Vetch's doing, my lady,' Willow remarked.

'It was an accident,' said Brightleaves.

Willow related everything she had heard about Vetch from Grace and the other women.

'Slaves' gossip!' said Brightleaves dismissively.

As the sun dipped below the horizon Brightleaves emerged from the outhouse with blue ribbons woven into her hair, wearing the blue dress she had worn at her wedding, her doeskin boots, her gold torc, and her cloak of otter fur.

Before she walked up the hill, she checked that the parking attendant was doing his job. Most people walked to the festival but there were a few families with small children and babies who found it easier to load everyone into a cart and drive there. The parking attendant had to arrange the carts so that each could be driven away without any of the others having to be moved and therefore without any effort on his part. Once this had been achieved, he could go up the hill and get drunk.

Groups of people were flowing up the hill under the fading sky. There was a continuous hum of quiet chatter, accompanied occasionally by the cry of a baby or a toddler's howl of protest at not being carried; at the same time there was a sense of excitement, expectancy.

Everyone gathered on the hilltop around the unlit fire. The wise elders, including Farmer Oxhill, worked out which way the wind was blowing before they chose a place to stand. Vetch, beside him, gave a little start when she saw Brightleaves.

'Oh, Lady Brightleaves! You're in all your finery!'

'As are you,' said Brightleaves, smiling.

The housewives moved about finding the dishes they'd prepared and positioning them near the fire so that they could be popped onto it once it got hot. The pale light in the western sky darkened. Now little red lights could be seen coming up the hill in the dusk; the torchbearers, bringing the flame to light the fire.

'Who will light the fire?' Mother Swan asked the crowd.

This fire had to be lit by a young girl, representing the young Goddess.

People called out the names of various girls.

'Willow!' called Marten, who had been bribed by Raven. Raven wasn't allowed to vote on this occasion but had his own reasons for wanting Willow to light the fire.

'Cherry!' called Robin, who liked things to be fair.

Then someone shouted, 'Hazel Smith!' and more people echoed it, 'Yes, Hazel!' 'Hazel to light the fire!'

The two torchbearers arrived on the hilltop. It usually took just one torch to light the fire but Mother Swan knew the practical value of having an extra torch, just in case. The success of most rituals depends on attention to practical detail.

The torchbearers were Lofty and Dawdle, the warriors who had done best in the various military exercises that Hardy had put them through since last summer's end. To show how tough they were and to let the girls see their muscles, they were naked except for loincloths, knife-belts and jewellery. They had ground up sandstone and painted each other with intricate red patterns to emphasize their biceps, pectorals and thigh muscles. The girls were struck dumb with admiration.

Hazel took the torch from the warrior nearest to her, carried it over to the fire and thrust it in. Everyone waited. The flames licked upward, catching the kindling. The fire was lit.

The housewives moved their pots on to the fire. Everyone else stood back, looking upwards for the moment when the flames would leap out at the top of the pile of wood. The flames leaped; the people cheered. Then they looked around them, north, south, east and west, to see if the flames were lit on the beacons of other glens, and cheered again when they saw anyone else's beacon, a little red tip of flame in the dark distance.

Now that Hazel had lit the fire, it was time for the part of the ceremony that everyone looked forward to: the wrestling match between the young Goddess of Light and the Black Hag of Winter.

A large black dress was passed around each year to the next performer of the Black Hag role, along with a black hooded cloak. This was the costume Raven wore. The hood failed to conceal his young moustache.

The Black Hag carried a wooden staff with a strip of black wool wound tightly around it, all along its length, completely concealing the wood beneath. The young Goddess had to snatch this staff away from the Hag.

Now the people made a circle round the Hag, who stood looking defiant, clutching the staff with both black-painted hands. The young Goddess stepped into the circle. The firelight glowed on her blonde hair. She went up to the Hag, grabbed the staff and started trying to wrestle it away. The people cheered and shouted encouragement.

Raven had wanted to wrestle with Willow, which was why he had bribed Marten to vote for her. He didn't fancy Hazel at all. So he was surprised to find that wresting with her was such an erotic experience. He didn't want her to stop. The Black Hag was supposed to yield after a short time and allow the young Goddess to take the staff, but Raven wouldn't let go.

Hazel was a big strong girl, so she just kept on wrestling and eventually she managed to twist the staff out of Raven's hands. The two stepped away from each other, panting and wondering, What happened there?

The spectators clapped and cheered.

Hazel recited the traditional words:

'Lo, I take this wand of night,

In my hands it turns to light!'

She thrust the tip of the staff into the fire for a moment, so that the black wool cover was singed off its tip. Then she unwound the rest of the wool, while the spectators chorused,

'See, she takes the wand of night,

In her hands it turns to light!'

While the Goddess was unwinding the wool, the Black Hag had to fade away into the crowd, which Raven duly did. When the black wool was all unwound, Hazel held up the naked staff. It was made of holly, whitest of woods, with the bark peeled off to show the wood's whiteness, pale gold in the firelight.

'The wand of light!' she said.

'The wand of light!' echoed the spectators.

That was the end of the ceremony. Then the feasting began.

The feasts were always an opportunity for boys and girls to meet. All the young priestesses were there and the apprentices looked at them with great interest. Imagine having a girlfriend who could fly!

The Black Hag removed both cloak and dress as quickly as possible, to become Raven again and go and chat to Hazel. But Hazel was talking to some of her friends; Raven didn't want to go up to her and say anything with all those girls watching. And perhaps the feeling he'd had was just the effect of being in the ceremony – although he was pretty sure the Black Hag of Winter wasn't supposed to feel like that about the young Goddess who had supplanted her.

Brook said the Black Hag and the young Goddess were aspects of the same being. Raven had not made up his mind about this idea; he was examining it, cautiously and rather suspiciously, before he decided whether to accept it or not, as if it were a mushroom that might be poisonous or might be good to eat.

'Aren't you going to eat anything?' said Marten, suddenly appearing at Raven's elbow. 'I can tell you which stews are good.'

'Oh – yes – I'll have something soon.' Raven was watching Hazel, wondering when he'd have an opportunity to speak to her on her own. Then, remembering how inquisitive Marten was, and how observant, Raven turned away and went over to the fire, where the women were serving food. He accepted their congratulations on his performance with a distracted smile, took his plate of food and wandered away, looking for somewhere to sit. People had brought blankets to spread on the grass and were sitting on these, groups of cloaked figures lit red by the firelight. The Smith family was spread over several blankets. Hazel was sitting with them now. Raven wanted to find a spot where he could sit and watch her without anyone noticing. But next to the Smiths were the Chief and Lady Brightleaves; and next to them his bardic 'family', Brook, Marten, Robin, Cherry and Willow.

'Over here, lad!' Brook waved at him. 'Come and join us!'

Raven sat down with them to eat his meal.

'Are you going to play later?' asked Willow with her winsome smile.

'I don't know if I will,' said Raven. 'I thought I might do some dancing tonight.'

'Yes, musicians don't get to dance much,' said Cherry. 'Perhaps we could take turns?'

'Maybe,' said Raven. He wished they would all shut up and leave him in peace.

'Raven keeps looking at you,' Hardy said to Brightleaves.

'He's not looking at me! He's looking past us. He's looking at Hazel.'

'Peak won't like that.'

'Why not? It's an honour for a girl to marry a bard.'

'Marry, yes. But you know what they say about bards. Better at wooing than wedding.'

Hazel – while making sure that all her brothers and sisters were behaving properly and eating up their food without making a mess, and that her mother was comfortable and had enough to eat, and that her father had a full plate and a full beaker – was thinking: But he's a bard! How would I talk to him?

When the eating phase of the evening seemed to be coming to an end, Marten and Robin started beating their drums, slowly at first, then faster; Cherry and Willow joined in, playing tunes on their pipes; and as the rhythm caught the crowd, the dancing began.

The first dance was one where the men danced in a long line and the women in another. The two lines went weaving about, to and fro across the hilltop, and around the fire, until they formed two concentric circles, the men on the outside and the women on the inside. Then they danced round and round in opposite directions. When the music stopped, you held crossed hands with the person opposite you. The music started again and you danced with that person until the music stopped again. Then you went back into your line and danced round in a circle once more. So it went on. Raven kept trying to push the men's line to dance faster or pull it to slow it down, so that he would be opposite Hazel the next time the music stopped. But this didn't work. In the end he gave up. He would just have to wait until the next dance. And suddenly, when the music stopped, there was Hazel in front of him. They held crossed hands and danced, round and round, each with their eyes fixed on the other's eyes. Suddenly Raven glanced over his shoulder at the musicians. He could tell, from the rhythms they were playing, from the way they were nodding at each other over their instruments, that they were about to stop the music again. So he whirled Hazel away, out of the dance, round to the other side of the fire.

This wasn't exactly private. There were still people, people who didn't want to dance at the moment, standing in groups, drinking, chatting.

Raven and Hazel stopped whirling and just looked at each other. He hadn't let go of her hands. She looked down at their joined hands and then questioningly up at Raven.

'Sorry!' he said, and let go.

Hazel burst out laughing.

'What?' asked the confused young man.

'I was wondering what you might say to me.'

Hazel was smiling. What dimples she had! He'd never noticed before.

'I just didn't think it would be "sorry", that's all,' she continued.

'What did you think it would be?'

Hazel frowned slightly, wondering how to express it.

Even her frown was charming!

'I thought it would be something more...more bardic,' she said.

'I can do bardic!'

'I should hope so!'

'I can compose a song for you, if you like.'

'What, now?'

'Well – no...' Raven felt that he was losing control of the situation. He couldn't think of anything to say. He, a bard, could not think of anything to say. And he felt that she was waiting for him to say something.

Inspiration came from the musicians, who stopped playing the first dance and almost immediately started on another one. It was a familiar tune; everyone knew this dance. You had to dance it with a partner.

'Shall we dance again?' said Raven.

'Yes please,' said Hazel, with that smile.

They joined the other dancers. Now that he was her accepted partner, for this dance at least, Raven felt as if he had climbed some kind of mountain. When they were separated by the patterns of the dance and danced temporarily with other people, he could smile at her across the heads of the other dancers. He couldn't stop smiling. He was happy to smile at the various girls he danced with. After the dance, some of them were weak at the knees because Raven, tall, dark, handsome Raven with the dangerous eyes, had smiled at them so gloriously.

The dance ended with the original partners dancing together. When the music stopped, Raven didn't let go of Hazel straight away – but he didn't hold on too long either. He said,

'I'd like to dance with you again but I think I should go and play some music now.'

'All right!' said Hazel, with a little shrug.

She didn't seem to care!

Raven went back to the other musicians feeling dejected. Cherry got up to dance, making room for Raven on the blankets. He sat down and picked up his lyre. He glanced across at the Smiths. Hazel was watching him! She smiled! She raised her hand and waved the tips of her fingers at him!

Raven played and sang wonderfully. People cheered and shouted for more. Then he played along with the other musicians. People danced like wild things.

'What's that boy like to talk to?' Peak asked his eldest daughter. 'Honey-tongued, is he?'

'No,' said Hazel, 'quite the reverse. He hardly said a word. I think he's quite shy, really.'

'Just as well,' said Peak, feeling relieved, as his daughter had intended.

She looked across at Raven again. He wasn't playing at that moment, he was tuning his lyre. As if he sensed her looking at him, he looked up from his lyre and turned to smile at her. Hazel didn't try to pretend she hadn't been watching him. She just smiled back. She liked him, she decided, much better than she had expected. Perhaps her smile conveyed this. Raven, smiling back at her, felt almost faint with rapture.

I will never forget this evening, he thought.

* * *

Brightleaves wove the Festival of Growing Light: the points of fire on the hilltops, the Goddess wrestling with the Hag, the lines of dancers, dark Raven and fair Hazel dancing together. Willow looked at the weaving and commented,

'You haven't put in Vetch making the cart fall over!'

'I have put in the *accident*,' Brightleaves said. 'This brown bit here is the cart.'

* * *

The days were growing longer, but on most of them people opened their doors to see the thatch of their outhouse roofs white with frost.

Raven was focussed entirely on how to see Hazel again.

'We must be due for a visit to Peak Smith's house,' he said to Brook.

Brook shrugged. 'He hasn't invited us.'

'Well, it's about time he did! Couldn't you drop a hint?'

'Certainly not. It's an honour to have a bard in one's house. This bard isn't going to stoop to dropping hints.'

Raven decided that he, like his teacher, would go out 'composing' in the afternoons. He tried to compose something while he was tramping down the glen to the Smiths' house; and he tried to compose something else while he was tramping back up the glen to Brook's house.

At the Smiths' house he loitered outside the gate, hoping to catch a glimpse of Hazel without having to go into the house and sit there being watched by all Hazel's brothers and sisters. Sometimes he would be spotted by one of these vile children, who shouted at the top of its voice, 'Hazel! Your boyfriend's here!' Then all the other children would come out to stare at him.

Sometimes Hazel would see him before any of the others, and she would come to the gate and say, 'I'm sorry, I can't come out just now, Mother's resting and I have to look after the children.'

But sometimes Mother wasn't resting; Hazel would be

crossing the yard on some errand, wearing her cloak – and she'd come to the gate and say, 'I've just got to finish…' whatever it was; and then she would come out for a walk with him.

So the songs he composed on the way to the Smiths' house were hopeful songs, while the ones he composed on the way back varied from angry to ecstatic. It was a two-hour walk each way. His leg muscles were getting bigger.

As the days passed, he noticed that Hazel was becoming worried and preoccupied. When he asked her about it – fearful that she was going off him – she told him she was concerned about her mother.

'She seems to be getting weaker. One of the healers came to see her before the festival –'

The Festival! Raven heard the word with a quiver of memory. Our Festival! That was how he thought of it.

'–and gave her some herbal remedies,' continued Hazel, unaware that there had been any interruption, 'which seem to be keeping her calm, but they're not making her stronger.'

Then Raven rebuked himself for being so self-centred.

'Perhaps you should ask the healer to come and see her again. I can call in and ask them on my way back, if you like. The temple isn't far out of my way.'

'Oh, would you? That would be so kind. It was Curly who came to see her, so if you can ask for Curly – I know Mother likes her.'

'I'll go at once.'

'Thank you!' She smiled at him.

Raven hugged her in a manner that was intended to be comforting, as far as possible, considering he spent most of his time around Hazel in a daze of lust. Then he set off back up the glen.

In the fringes of the loch beside the temple, men were standing in the cold water cutting reeds. Raven, thinking that such work might have been his fate, thanked the goddess of bards for finding him.

When he arrived at the temple, he thought of the last time he'd been there, as a beast of night, in midwinter. Everything had changed since then. He was a different person now.

The Cygnet on gate-duty went to get a senior priestess. He told her he needed to speak to Curly and she took him to Mother Swan's house to wait. He sat on the bench by the fire, running possible lines of songs through his mind, until Curly arrived. Raven stood up.

'I've come on behalf of Hazel. She's really worried about her mother and she knows you came to see her before and gave her some herbs, so she, Hazel, wondered if you would come again. She says her mother is getting weaker and she thought you might have something that would help.'

'Thank you for coming to tell me.' Curly had seen, by the way the colours in his aura flared when he spoke the name, that he was in love with Hazel; and that was good, because the girl was going to need love and support in the weeks to come. 'I'll go and see Goldie straight away.' She went back to the door. Before she went out, she looked over her shoulder at him. 'Don't stop going to see Hazel, whatever happens.'

Curly rode to the Smiths' again, with a fresh supply of herbs. When she reached the house, Peak had just got in from the smithy, changed out of his work clothes and was sitting down to relax for the evening. Curly introduced herself. Peak looked alarmed.

'Did Goldie send for you? I thought she was getting better.'

'I've just come to check on her. Where is she?'

'She's resting. She often likes to have a little rest at this time of the day.'

A little rest at this time of the day, thought Curly as she went over to the curtained bedspace. That's what Goldie's telling Peak. But she probably rests for most of the day, or Hazel wouldn't be so worried.

As soon as she drew back the curtain and saw Goldie, her worst fears were confirmed. She sat down on the edge of the bed and took Goldie's hand.

'You're not pregnant, Goldie, you are ill. And you must wean the baby. Start today.'

'Oh no, not yet! Petal is only six months old!'

'Old enough to be fed with a spoon. It will be much kinder to her if you start now. Give her time to get used to it.'

Goldie and Curly looked at each other. They exchanged silent knowledge.

'Can't you do anything?' Goldie asked.

Curly shook her head. 'I'm sorry. All I can do is help to ease the pain. I've brought some herbs for that. But you mustn't take them while you're breast-feeding. So that's another reason to wean Petal.'

'How long have I got?' They were speaking in whispers now.

'I'm not sure. But I doubt you'll be here for Brightfire Day. You may not even be here for the Spring Festival. That's why it's important you wean Petal now.'

Goldie lay back in her nest of blankets and furs, shaking her head as if to shake off what Curly had just said. Yet

223

something deep down in her knew it was true, had known for some time.

'You must tell Peak and Hazel,' said Curly.

'Yes.'

'Shall I call them now? Or do you want to wait until I've gone?'

Goldie gripped Curly's hand tightly. 'Call them now.'

She felt as if she was taking the first steps into some fearful new land on her own; and although she hated to distress her family, she wanted them to be with her on this journey.

They took it much as Curly expected they would, because it was the way most people took such news. She always hated giving a family news like this, could never get used to it, but was familiar with the way they reacted. They didn't want to believe it, of course, so first they didn't believe it. They said things like, 'But there must be something you can do!' Then they hoped she might have made a mistake. 'We all make mistakes, don't we? I make mistakes in my craft, so healers must make mistakes too.' Oh yes, Curly agreed, healers make mistakes like anyone else; and then she and the family looked down at the patient lying pale and feeble in bed; and a second opinion was suggested. 'Perhaps we could get someone else to look at her? Would Mother Swan come?' Yes, Mother Swan would come.

It was a ritual they had to go through on their journey from denial to acceptance.

Next day, when Raven was on his way to see Hazel, he had just reached the place where the track divided, one way carrying on down the glen and the other going to the temple, when he was stopped by a Cygnet who told him that Curly wanted to see him. He went with the child to the temple. Curly met him at the gate, leading a horse.

'We've decided that you can borrow a horse, for visiting Hazel. Bring it back here every evening, because Brook hasn't got a stable, has he? Come here every afternoon to collect the horse. The stable boys know about the arrangement. You may not get the same horse every day – and if there's an epidemic, we'll need all the horses, so you'll have to go back to walking.'

Raven thanked her sincerely, mounted the horse and rode off along the track. Curly watched for a moment as he rode away and wondered at the strange fate he had attracted, falling in love so suddenly with a girl quite different from the sort of girl he had expected to fall in love with, only to have her plunged into a grief that he could do nothing to assuage.

Raven arrived at the Smiths' place, dismounted, led his horse up the hill and in through the gate, and hitched its reins over a fence post. Hazel, who had come out of the house to see who was arriving, ran across the yard to him. She flung her arms round him and clung to him like a drowning woman clinging to a rock. Raven put his arms round her and held her while allowing himself to be clung to.

'Curly's lent me this horse,' he told her cheerfully when she stepped back.

'Oh. Has she?'

'Specially for coming to see you.'

'Oh – so she's told you, then?'

'No, she hasn't told me anything. Except that I should keep on coming to see you no matter what.'

'Is that what she said?'

Raven nodded.

'My mother's dying,' said Hazel.

Raven didn't know what to say, so he just said, 'I'm sorry.'

'That's the first time I've actually said it. We couldn't believe it at first, when Curly told us. Father still can't believe it. Doesn't want to believe it. Mother Swan's going to come and see Mother, because Father hopes Curly might have made a mistake. But Curly's a very experienced healer.' She sighed.

'D'you want to come for a walk?'

She shook her head. 'With Mother in bed all day, I've got too much to do. And when she's not asleep, I like to sit with her.'

'Can I do anything to help?'

'I don't think so.'

Raven was about to unhitch the horse and ride away again, when it occurred to him that Curly must have lent him the animal for a purpose. He could get to the Smiths' house and back so much more quickly now, he could spend more time there. So there must be something he could do.

'Can I come in for a while? I won't get in your way.'

Hazel shrugged. 'If you like.' She looked up at the sky. 'You'd better stable your horse, it might snow.'

After Raven had taken the horse to the stable and made sure there was some water and food for it, he went into the house and sat down by the fire. He could hear low voices, Hazel's and her mother's, coming from behind a curtain. A baby started crying; Hazel came out, went to another part of the house and came back with a little pot and a spoon. There was silence again.

After a while Hazel came out and bustled about doing

housewifely things. Raven sat there trying to look helpful in case she suddenly realized she needed him. But in this household of many slaves, she didn't even need him to bring in wood for the fire.

He was just beginning to wonder if he should go home after all, when the children started arriving. 'It's snowing,' said one, 'so we've come to play inside.'

'All right,' said Hazel, 'but play quietly! Mother and Petal are asleep.'

There were only nine children there; the other three were boys old enough to help their father in the smithy. Nine was quite enough for now. The noise volume rose. Tussles broke out. The slavegirl was very sweet with the toddler but incapable of controlling the others. A ten-year-old girl was trying to entertain a three-year old while her brother was pulling her hair...

'Once upon a time...' said Raven in a clear voice.

Silence spread out around him like ripples from a stone cast into a pool. One by one the children came to sit beside him on the bench or on the floor at his feet, gazing up at him, waiting for the story to begin.

Raven told a story. When it was finished he told another. Hazel went to and fro in her various tasks, and smiled at him.

So he was useful, after all.

The next day, Raven took his lyre with him, slung across his back under his cloak, which gave him a strange lumpy appearance but kept the lyre protected in case of snowfalls. The children were all out when he arrived, except for the toddler and the baby who were being minded by the slavegirl. So he sat by the fire, playing and singing softly.

Hazel came out from behind the curtain.

'Mother wants to see you.'

Raven put down his lyre on the bench and stood up.

'No, bring that with you,' said Hazel. She led him into the room behind the curtain. Her mother was sitting up in bed, leaning back against a pile of heather-stuffed pillows, with her eyes closed.

'Mother, Raven Brook's is here,' said Hazel. Raven would be called Brook's until he graduated; then his name would be Raven Bard.

Goldie opened her eyes. Raven bowed to her.

'A pleasure to see you, as always, Ma'am.'

Goldie pointed to a stool at the foot of the bed. 'Please sit down.'

Raven sat.

Goldie looked up at her daughter and waved her away. 'Please leave us.'

Hazel went round the edge of the curtain and, out of sight of her mother but still within sight of Raven on the stool, shrugged with outspread hands, to signal that she had no idea what her mother wanted. Then she drew the curtain closed.

'Sing me a song,' said Goldie.

Raven played and sang, an old and well-loved song that he thought she might like.

'Thank you,' she said when he had finished. 'Now, bring the stool closer, so I can speak quietly.'

Raven picked up the stool and edged it further along the side of the bed. Goldie nodded, satisfied.

'Do you know the history of the Hunters from the time of the Great Darkness?'

'Yes. Do you want me to recite it to you?'

'No, no. I want you to listen to my story and make a song

about it. Can you do that?

'Yes, I can do that.'

Goldie nodded, satisfied. 'Then I will tell you my story. Listen.'

Raven sat up straight and looked attentive, to show that he was in listening mode.

'Before Peak married me, the Hunters were not my people. My people were the Sky's-eye people. "Sky's Eye" was our name for the sun. We were a poetic people. And musical too – you should have heard the men sing in the valleys! And we were an ironic people. It rained more in our country than it rains anywhere else, so we hardly ever saw the Sky's Eye. No wonder we worshipped it!' She smiled. Raven smiled in response.

'Above all,' she continued, 'we were a defiant people. I was only seven years old when the Romans invaded us. We fought them. We fought them for years. We never gave in. All my life, as I grew up, we were fighting the Romans. The Romans don't like people with spirit, they don't like people who fight back. So they punished us. They seized our crops and our animals, they robbed our homesteads. That just made us fight them all the more. They threatened that if we didn't stop fighting them, they would kill us all, even children and babies, or sell us all as slaves. But we went on fighting them. We defeated a legion! We sent raiding parties over our borders into other countries that were under Roman rule!'

Then she sighed. 'Of course the Romans sent raiding parties back again. I was caught in raid and sold to a trader, who put me on a ship bound for Muddycreeks, in the Coastlanders' country. But the trader was too mean to pay for a pilot – and the tides around my country sometimes run in opposite directions at the same time! The oarsmen were thrown from their seats and injured, including the skilled ones, and some of the oars were broken, so we had to rely on our sails. And the wind was blowing north. The captain could not sail against it. We ended up in the Seagod's Island. That's where Peak found me, standing in the market with chains on me. He'd gone there to collect a shipment of raw glass. He said he fell in love with me the moment he saw me. He bought me, knocked my chains off – he actually had his toolbag with him! – and married me. I was fourteen years old.'

'That's quite a story,' said Raven.

'It's not such an unusual story, not these days. But it's mine. And I want you to make it into a song and sing it at my burial. Because my ancestors are buried far away and Peak can't bury me with them. He'll bury me here, up on Ancestors' Hill, with all the Hunter ancestors. And they're not my ancestors, so they won't know who I am or what I'm doing there. That's why I want you to sing my story. The Hunter ancestors will hear it and they'll know why I've come to join them. Will you do it?'

'Of course I will. I'm honoured that you've asked me.' He stood up. 'If you'll excuse me, I'll go now, while the story's fresh in my mind, and start making it into a song.'

Hazel, sitting by the fire feeding the baby with a spoon, was surprised when Raven strode out of her mother's room and through the house, carrying his lute, just waving to her as he collected his cloak and left. As soon as she could hand the baby over to the maidservant, she went into her mother's bedspace.

'What did you say to Raven? He left in such a hurry!'

He didn't even stop to kiss me goodbye, she thought.

'I gave him a job to do, He'll be back tomorrow.' Goldie closed her eyes and drifted off to sleep.

The next day, Raven apologized to Hazel for having left without saying goodbye properly the day before.

'I'm like that sometimes, when I'm composing. I have to concentrate on it, I can't let myself be distracted by anything else.' He smiled at her, that smile of his that made her melt inside, especially when he was holding her in his arms and looking down at her at the same time.

Hazel wondered how it was possible for her to feel such delicious feelings while her mother was dying.

They could all see that Goldie was getting weaker. Mother Swan visited a few days after Curly and, as they'd known deep down that she would, she confirmed Curly's diagnoses. The baby was weaned. Curly's painkillers started to take effect. Goldie was becoming more absent, drifting away more often.

Raven came every day and sat telling stories to the children, or singing and playing to Goldie.

'You're a good man,' she said to him one day. 'I shall tell Peak not to stand in your way.'

'I've composed your song. I sing it to myself most days when I'm on my way here. Would you like to hear it?'

'Not yet. I'll tell you when.'

But as her pain grew stronger, so did the herbal mixtures that Curly prescribed, until they reached that borderline between making the patient's life bearable and easing her passage into death.

Peak gave up going to the smithy, leaving the work to his apprentices, and sat almost all day at Goldie's bedside, wishing that she would chatter as she used to do. The children, now, all knew that their mother was ill. They were allowed to come and see her, not all at once but in twos and threes, twice a day. They would each kiss her and whisper, 'Get well soon, Mother,' then creep away and cry, or sit in silence, or fight each other, or play a game with a doll ill in bed and a priestess doll bringing it herbs.

Now that Peak was spending so much of the day sitting with Goldie, Raven sat with Hazel and the children during his afternoon visits, or sometimes insisted on taking Hazel out for a walk, even just a short walk, through the bare-branched woods or over the frosty fields in the clear sunshine of the time between winter and spring. He felt it was good to get her out of the house with its atmosphere of grief and suspense. Yet she was part of that and could not stay away for long – 'in case Mother needs something,' she said; but really it was because she needed to be there, to be part of the process that was unfolding within the family.

One evening, when Hazel was bringing her mother a mug of the latest herbal brew, Goldie opened her eyes and said very clearly, 'Tell Raven I want to hear my song in four days.'

'Four days,' repeated Hazel, with a little smile, because she thought it was such a funny number to choose, so strange of her mother to be precise about something like this.

'She wants to hear her song in four days,' she told Raven and he too smiled.

The next morning she couldn't wake her mother. Goldie's spirit had slipped away in the night.

Chapter 12. Spring

Word was sent around the glen. Hazel and two slaves dressed Goldie in her festival dress and all her best jewellery. Peak came and lifted Goldie off the bed, which Hazel and the women covered with the skins of golden lynx. Then Goldie was laid down again upon the soft pale gold fur. The curtain that had concealed her bed was tied back so that everyone in the house could see her.

People started arriving, with food and drink and musical instruments. Goldie's farewell party began.

The first phase of the party was the time of Nay-saying. Each guest who came into the house would say something like, 'Surely it can't be true!' or 'I can't believe Goldie's dead.'

And a member of the family would reply,' No! She's not dead! There's been a mistake!'

So the guests smiled, handed over their offerings of food or beer, had their cloaks hung up, and all sat around the fire, eating, drinking and chatting, pretending Goldie wasn't dead.

Raven was one of the first to arrive; and he said, quite genuinely, 'I can't believe she's gone without hearing her song!'

'Oh, you'll still be able to sing it to her,' said Peak gruffly.

'No, she can't be dead,' said Dainty, 'because I was only just getting to know her.' Such an act of rudeness to Dainty was obviously impossible.

There was no set period for the Nay-saying phase of the farewell party. Its purpose was to let people adjust to the idea that one of them was dead; and it went on until some member of the bereaved family changed the mood.

On this occasion, in this family, it was Hazel. She had spent weeks nursing her mother, watching her grow weaker every day; and during these weeks she had passed through her own time of nay-saying and grown used to the idea that her mother was going to die. So she soon became impatient with all these stupid people sitting around chatting as if nothing had happened. Some of them even went so far as to address remarks to her mother – 'Isn't that right, Goldie?' they would say, turning where they sat to look over their shoulder at the body lying on the golden furs. Bracken Birchrock approached Goldie's bed with a plate of biscuits, saying, 'I've brought you some of my hazelnut and honey biscuits, Goldie, because I know how much you like them.'

Hazel jumped up off the bench where she'd been sitting and shouted at Bracken, 'Stop it!' She stamped on the floor and went on stamping, stamping, and shouting, 'Stop it, stop it, stop it!'

'Now Hazel,' said Peak warningly, 'don't be rude to our guests.'

'And you can shut up!' said Hazel. 'It's your fault she's dead! You should have noticed she was ill! If you'd noticed sooner, Curly might have been able to cure her and she might still be alive!'

Peak lifted up his head and roared like a wounded bull.

This was the sign they'd all been waiting for, although they only knew that when they heard it. Everybody stood up and roared and stamped. This went on as long as people had energy for it. The younger visitors enjoyed this licence

234

to roar and stamp and did it with great gusto. It was the best bit of the party as far as they were concerned.

People slowed down one by one, the older ones before the younger. The noisy stamping became a shuffling walk, the roaring faded into grumbles. Some people wandered about looking dazed, others slumped down on the benches. Bewildered children began to cry. This phase of the party was the time of Grieving.

Hazel sat on her bench weeping uncontrollably. It was the first time she had cried since Goldie became ill. Her brothers and sisters gathered round her, first trying to comfort her with their hugs, then joining in her grief. Peak came and sat beside them and put his big arms round them all. Everyone else in the house began to cry in sympathy. The musicians played slow, sad music and sang slow, sad songs.

After that, everyone had some more to eat and drink. Then those who were going home went home and those who were staying in the Smiths' house went to bed. Before Hazel went to bed, she drew the curtain across her mother's bedroom. As she did this, she looked at the body on the bed and felt confused, because it was her mother and yet it wasn't.

Thus the first day of Goldie's farewell party came to an end.

The second day followed the same three phases as the first; but the Nay-saying phase was much shorter, the Raging phase was louder, if that was possible, and the Grieving phase was longer. It developed its own sub-phases and rhythms, with people weeping or blaming themselves – I should have noticed she wasn't well – or telling little stories about things Goldie had said or done: D'you remember that time she...?

It was the Grieving phases of the party that Peak hated the most. Nay-saying and Raging were shields against sorrow but Grieving trapped him in it.

'What am I going to do?' he kept asking. 'What am I going to do without her?' He looked with new respect at his friends in the glen who had lost people they loved. How had they managed to go on?

Marten and Robin didn't like the Grieving phases either. The third day of the farewell party would be all Grieving and they were dreading it. Being sad all day! How could anyone do it?

The Grieving day was the quietest of the three. Raven and the other musicians played soft music or sang quiet, mournful songs. There was also remembering. People sat remembering their own lost loved ones.

Brook remembered his teacher. Cherry and Willow remembered their father and wondered about their mother's fate. Hardy remembered his first wife, Linnet, and their little baby who had never drawn breath. Brightleaves sat with her head bowed, remembering her lost baby. Many people lost children. That did not make a loss any easier to bear. Hardy moved closer to Brightleaves and put his arm around her shoulders. They sat grieving together.

Raven wondered about the father he had never known. Had he been a fisherman drowned at sea, as Raven's coast-dwelling mother claimed? Raven was not convinced by this story. He suspected that his father might be a wandering bard who had charmed a young woman with his songs and then wandered on; or a sailor from foreign parts, still hauling a rope or swinging a steering oar somewhere, not knowing that he had a son in the land of the Hunters.

Raven also wondered about what was to happen next. He could not, now, imagine his life without Hazel in it. But after the funeral was over, Peak would need Hazel to run his house for him. He would never want to let her go. And even if he did, where would they live? They couldn't live in Brook's house. If he took Hazel to live there, she would just end up being Brook's housekeeper. Perhaps he could go off to seek his fortune somewhere else – but then he wouldn't be able to take Hazel with him, he couldn't subject her to a life of sleeping in barns and uncertain meals; and how long would it take to find his fortune, whatever it might be? And if he stayed in Wildcat Glen, when would he have his own house? Not until he was as old as Brook, probably. He couldn't wait that long, he would go mad.

So Raven did not mourn for past losses; he fretted about his hopeless future.

On the morning of the fourth day, Cliff Carpenter and his boys arrived at the Smiths' house with a square bier whose wooden carrying-poles were carved with oakleaves. They laid this beside Goldie's bed. Peak lifted her body off the bed, still in its blanket, and laid it on the bier, curled like a baby in the womb. Hazel spread a golden lynx fur over the body.

Four men carried Goldie on her bier, although she was so small and slight that one man could have carried it. Peak led the procession up Ancestors' Hill. Hazel carried a bag of small things her mother had owned and used. Following them in the procession were all the people who had been at Goldie's farewell party

Mother Swan was waiting for them at the top of the hill by a freshly dug grave-pit with a mound of earth beside it. The bearers laid down the bier next to the pit.

Raven unslung his lyre from his back and tuned it quietly while the people arranged themselves in a semicircle around the grave.

'We have said farewell to Goldie Smith,' said Mother Swan. 'She will now become one of the ancestors.'

Raven stepped forward and sang Goldie's story.

When he had finished, Mother Swan nodded. Peak lifted the blanketed body off the bier.

'Goldie is going into the earth,' said Mother Swan. 'She is joining the ancestors.'

Peak lowered the body into the grave-pit.

Hazel stepped forward with her bag and beckoned the other children to join her. She took things out of the bag and gave one to each child – a cloak pin, a hair-clip, a comb, a spindle, a needle, a loom-weight. She knelt down and took from the bag a small cup, which she carefully dropped into the pit beside the fur-covered mound of her mother's body. One by one the other children dropped their tokens into the pit. Last of all, Peak knelt beside the grave and dropped something in. It was an iron collar and a short chain.

The gravediggers shovelled earth into the pit.

'Goldie is with the ancestors now,' said Mother Swan. 'When we look up at the hills, we can remember her life with us here and all that she meant to us. Her soul is in the keeping of the Goddess of the Stars. Next time we look up at the stars, we can wish her well on her journey.'

They all stood in silence on the hilltop, heads bowed, remembering Goldie and wishing her well.

It was a very cold day.

I'm sure Mother wouldn't have wanted us all to get cold standing out here remembering her, thought Hazel.

'I don't think Goldie would have wanted us to get cold,' said Mother Swan. 'She was a home-lover and like to be comfortable. So let's return to our homes now and remember her there.'

As they walked back down the hill, Hazel's little brother Torrent asked her, 'How can Mother be in the earth with the ancestors and with the Goddess of the Stars at the same time?'

'I don't know. Let's ask Raven. Raven? Did you hear the question?'

'I did,' Raven was walking on Hazel's other side. Help! he thought. What would Brook say? The answer came immediately. Brook would say, 'It's you who've been asked the question, not I.'

'Well,' Raven began, 'Goldie will always be your ancestor. And she'll be your children's ancestor and your children's children's ancestor. And you'll remember her, and you'll tell your children stories about her. But Goldie's spirit will go up to travel in the silver ship among the stars, until she gets reborn as a new person. That new person won't be Goldie. But Goldie will still be your ancestor.'

And he thought about how the new person would in time become an ancestor, and so it would go on, again and again, with the spirit like a growing tree shedding lives like leaves, each leaf in its season so precious, unique and irreplaceable to the other leaves who loved it.

* * *

Brightleaves wove Goldie's funeral; the stiff fence of denial, the fire of raging, the rain of grieving. Heather Dyer had a batch of particularly deep blue, some of which Brightleaves used to weave a stripe of night sky – 'but I can't get a silver dye,' Heather told her. 'You'll have to use white for the Goddess's ship. Or you could get a very thin chain of real silver from the Smiths and weave that in.'

'From the Smiths?' echoed Brightleaves. 'I don't want to bother them.'

'Business must go on,' said Heather. 'If I had a loss in the family, I'd rather be bothered than brooding.'

So Brightleaves went to the smithy, where the sound of the bellows told her that work had started again. Peak's oldest son, Hawk, aged 14, brought out a selection of silver chains to show her.

'These are so fine!' she said admiringly. Hawk blushed.

'I made that one.'

'Then I will use it,' she said, 'to weave a symbol of the silver ship carrying your mother's spirit. I think she would like that, don't you?'

* * *

The earth that had swallowed Goldie was pulsing with new life. In underground burrows, vixens and badger sows nursed their cubs. Otter bitches suckled their blind pups in river-bank holts. Woodpeckers drummed messages on treetrunks with the same rippling spring rhythm that the male frogs were burbling in the mating pools until the water was thick with frogspawn. Birds defended their nesting sites with choruses of rippling notes and mother squirrels in twiggy dreys suckled their naked kits. In the she-bear's den, her cubs sucked milk from their mother while she slept; and the wolf pack in the hills was digging out a site for its queen to whelp in. On the farms, the little brown ewes were pregnant and the nanny-goats were giving birth. The ash trees had put forth their mole-black buds; and pale gold catkins dangled from the boughs of the hazel trees. The winds came from the west and sometimes blew gales that sent packs of clouds scudding across blue skies; on other days the sky was a soft grey-white blur, as if the whole glen was inside a cloud, and the air was filled with continuous small pattering raindrops. The birds sang loudly; and the streams sang as they grew.

The farmers sowed beans and spring barley. The next charming pastoral task was the digging-out of all the shit pits in the glen so that their fertilizing contents could be spread on the fields. Anyone who had indoor jobs to do chose this day to do them. People who had to be outside wore cloths over their mouths and noses, so that for a few days, until the smell wore off, the glen looked as if it were inhabited by a tribe of bandits.

The birch-trees were tapped for their sweet sap, to make birch wine, which was put in pottery jars with wooden bungs and stored for next year.

The women went out to the pastures collecting moss, the bright yellowy-green new moss that had been miraculously growing beneath the snow. The moss was wet, of course, but it could easily be dried in nets hung from the rafters. All the women in the glen, including Brightleaves, gathered moss, combing it from the grass with their fingers as they would later comb the wool from the coats of the little brown sheep; for you could never have enough moss; you needed a basketful always by the latrine, mothers of babies needed it to line nappies, and grown women needed a large extra supply once a month.

Brightleaves had missed her third bleeding-time.

Walking home with a netful of moss, she met Hardy coming from the practice ground.

'I've got something to tell you,' she said.

He turned to go to the house with her; but she stood still.

'No, here.' Out in the open was the best place for secrets.

He looked at her enquiringly.

'We're going to have a baby,' said Brightleaves.

Hardy heart swelled with joy for an instant before terror gripped it. Childbirth was more dangerous than war.

He took the net of moss from her. 'Come and sit down! You should rest!'

Brightleaves laughed. 'If I sit down for the next six months I'll be too weak to give birth!'

'Is there anything you want? You can have anything!'

'Just give me a kiss.'

They stood there in the middle of the compound, kissing, with Hardy holding the net of moss and the servants coming and going all around them. Vetch, coming for a visit, opened the gate, saw them, shut the gate and went away again.

Then there was the Spring Festival to organize. It was too chilly for sitting outside to spin; Brightleaves sat by the fire making plans with Hazel, and with Vetch; for Brightleaves refused to believe that her friend had deliberately tipped up the oxcart at the last festival.

'Any suggestions for someone to be the Plant Goddess?' Brightleaves asked.

'My friend Ripple Burner,' Hazel suggested.

'Good idea!' said Brightleaves. 'She'd be just right. And we need a fair-haired boy to be the young Sun God.'

'Crag Tanner has a boy about the right age,' said Vetch quickly, before Hazel could suggest anyone. 'He's called Lightening, which must have been a joke because he moves more slowly than anyone I know.'

'I was the Sun God at a Spring Festival when I was young,' Hardy told Brightleaves that evening.

'Were you? I'm jealous of the girl who was the Plant Goddess, whoever she was. And if you carry on smiling in that fondly reminiscent way I shall tickle you until you beg for mercy.'

'I'm not smiling!' Hardy kept the muscles of his face completely still while Brightleaves stared at him sternly.

'I was the Plant Goddess once, as a matter of fact,' she remembered. 'I didn't like the boy who was the Sun God – he was an arrogant lout. I went to see him before the festival and told him, "If you stick your tongue in my mouth while you're kissing me, I'll grab your balls and twist them so hard that you'll never have children." It worked, I'm glad to say.'

'So he's never had children, then?'

'That's not what I meant! He was so nervous, his lips barely touched mine.'

'A nervous Sun God! What was the weather like that year?'

'I don't remember, so obviously there was nothing unusual about it. We didn't have a Great Darkness over our part of the country, not even a Slight Dimness.'

From outside came the gentle sound of rain dripping off the thatch. Brightleaves sighed. 'I hope it doesn't rain for the festival! It's so dreary trying to rejoice in the pouring rain, with everyone wanting it to be over so they can go home and get dry.'

But the day of the Spring Festival was clear and sunny. Most of the people who assembled on Festival Hill were smiling, partly with relief and partly from the simple joy of springtime.

The summit of Festival Hill dipped slightly, like a wide shallow bowl. A small flat-topped hummock rose, towards the western edge of the bowl, creating a natural performance or ceremonial area. Around the rim of the bowl, to the north, east and south, there were different sized hummocks that made ideal viewing points.

The firewood, food and drink were brought up to the hilltop in advance, as usual. Vetch was not allowed to help with this, although she protested that she would never make a mistake with the oxen again.

The actors followed the supplies. When the spectators arrived, led by the torchbearers who would light the fire, the Green Girls were already standing in a circle on the ceremonial area. Each one was wearing a green cloak and a green ribbon in her hair. Each carried a basket of some fresh green vegetable – cleavers, hedge-mustard, wood sorrel, hawthorn leaves. Within the circle, hidden from view by the Green Girls, Ripple Burner lay on a blanket spread on the ground. Another blanket, a large white one, was spread over her. Around her sat seven children, representing the Earth Spirits who had nurtured and protected the Plant Goddess under the ground during the winter months. The children were dressed in dark brown clothes and had mud smeared on their faces.

The fire was lit. At a pre-arranged signal from the musicians, Ripple pulled the blanket up over her face while the children cuddled closer to her and pulled the edges of the white blanket over themselves.

One of the Green Girls checked that the children were all concealed and nodded to the leader. Sad music began to play as the Green Girls moved away in procession from the little hummock, revealing the white blanket, which represented winter.

This part of the ceremony had to be sad and solemn but could not last for too long, because a group of children hiding under a blanket together would soon find it difficult not to giggle, tickle and pinch, despite their mothers' dire warnings.

Ripple, aware of the tension in the small bodies around her trying to be quiet and good, was relieved to hear Raven blowing a horn.

At the sound, Lightening Tanner appeared over the eastern edge of the summit. He was dressed in the special Sun God costume; bright yellow shirt and trousers, a gold torc, and a yellow cloak fastened with a large round gold brooch. In his right hand he carried a spear, a bronze spear, not an iron one; the bronze spear was kept for ritual occasions, its head scoured and polished until it mirrored the sun. The brooch and the spear were two of the community's treasures; when not in use for rituals, they were kept stored in a special place known only to Mother Swan and her two senior priestesses. The torc had been lent by Hardy.

When this glorious golden figure with his gleaming torc, brooch and spear appeared over the rim of the eastern hill, everyone burst out cheering.

Vetch had suggested Lightening because he was slow, so she thought he was stupid and would probably make a mistake. But Lightening was conscientious, careful and thorough. When he was making a shoe, a belt, or a harness, he made it slowly and well. He was acting his part just as carefully as he might work on a piece of leather. He had paced the ground out in advance and worked out the sequence of his movements. Now, as the Sun God, he walked across the hilltop until he reached the little western hummock and the white blanket spread over Ripple.

Brightleaves wondered if the Smith family was being reminded — as she was — of Goldie lying under her covering of furs. But the Sun God could do for the Plant Goddess what he could not have done for Goldie.

The Sun God laid down the spear and pulled back the white blanket, revealing the beautiful young Goddess with the Earth Spirits clustered protectively round her. He knelt down beside her and kissed her gently on the lips.

The Goddess opened her eyes, smiled and sat up. The Sun God stood up, held out his hand, and helped the Goddess to her feet while the Earth Spirits clapped and cheered. The Goddess wore a green dress embroidered with the white star-shapes of windflowers and the yellow star-shapes of celandines. The musicians played joyful music. The Sun God and the Plant Goddess danced. The Green Girls danced. Everyone danced. The Earth Spirits ran about wildly, as if they had been made to keep still for hours and not just for a matter of minutes.

Then everybody had something to drink and something to eat; and the festival turned into a party.

'I do hope you'll let me come and stay with you now!' Dainty said to Brightleaves in front of several other people — Daisy Foxwood, Sunny Waller, Bracken Birchrock — in the hope that by making this a public request she would shame Brightleaves into saying Yes.

Goldie had become ill and then died before she could

correct the false impression of Brightleaves that Vetch had managed to create among the senior women in the glen. Now they waited to hear Brightleaves' reply to Dainty.

'As soon as you've seen Druid Northway,' Brightleaves said. 'Surely you're fit to ride by now?'

That confirmed the women's worst opinions. Refusing hospitality to a lady with a baby! Everything Vetch had said about Brightleaves must be true.

Vetch had not managed to disrupt the ceremony a way that would direct the blame at Brightleaves. But during the feast she found an opportunity to talk to Hardy on his own.

'I hope you're not going to mind me mentioning this,' she said, 'but I wonder if you know that, whenever you go hunting, Lady Brightleaves always sends for Brook.'

Hardy nodded. 'She gets worried when I go hunting. Brook cheers her up.'

'So you're not worried that there's anything...'

'Anything what?'

'Between them?'

Hardy burst out laughing. He looked at the child – for that was how he thought of her – and shook his head, still laughing.

Laughing at her. Now Vetch didn't only want to discredit Brightleaves. She wanted to kill her. But she smiled at her hero and said, 'I am so sorry! I misunderstood. Please don't tell Lady Brightleaves, I wouldn't want to upset her.'

Hardy shook his head. 'I'm sorry, my dear,' he said. 'Lady Brightleaves and I tell each other everything.'

Brightleaves was confused when Hardy told her. Surely a real friend would have asked her about it first? She could imagine Pearlywaves teasing her – Do you fancy that skinny bard, then? Of course Vetch was very young. Still, there was something sneaky about her going to Hardy like that.

Meanwhile, Dainty went riding to see Druid Northway. She came to visit Brightleaves first.

'I thought you'd like to know that I've finally plucked up the courage!' she said, smiling, pleased with herself.

You mean now that it's officially spring, you've run out of excuses, Brightleaves thought; but she said, 'I'm so pleased that you're going. You'll feel much easier in your mind once you've seen him.'

'Yes, and I'll be able to come and stay with you afterwards! I'm so looking forward to that! I asked Mother Swan if I could take a healer with me on the journey, just in case, but she said that wasn't necessary, which I thought was a bit mean. So I asked for a Pen instead. She said I could take a Cygnet. A Cygnet!'

'A Cygnet probably knows more about healing than that fake healer you had at home,' said Brightleaves.

'But a Cygnet won't be able to carry Traveller, will she? He's five months old now.'

'You can carry him yourself, tied to your front,' said Brightleaves. 'That way he'll get the feeling of riding a horse and he'll feel safe with you at the same time – it'll be a wonderful start for him.'

'Actually, I came to ask you if I could borrow a woman or girl to go with me. Then she can carry him.'

'Hasn't Mother Swan got a woman or girl she could lend you?'

Dainty blushed. 'I asked her but she said No.'

'Then I'm going to say No too. Sorry, Dainty. You're quite capable of carrying your own baby. You're a mother now, you can't pretend to be a little girl any more.'

Dainty gasped. 'Oh! Vetch is right! You are a nasty person!'

She tossed her head and strode away.

* * *

Brightleaves wove the Spring festival, the Green Girls, the brown earth-spirits, the yellow Sun God. She did not weave Vetch. She did weave Dainty, though, flouncing off to see Druid Northway.

While she was weaving, Brook came to visit her. She was always pleased to see him. It was good to spend time with someone who liked her.

She told him what Vetch had said to Hardy, and what Dainty had said about Vetch.

'Vetch must resent you,' said Brook. 'Everyone knows she wanted to marry Hardy.'

'I thought that was just slaves' gossip?'

'There are some,' said Brook, 'who think that slaves aren't really people, so they talk in front of them the way they wouldn't talk in front of a "real" person. As a result, slaves know everything.'

Brightleaves felt chided and changed the subject. 'How are Willow and Cherry getting on?'

'Fine. It's Raven who's causing me problems.'

'Raven? Your star pupil?'

'My senior apprentice. He goes on a so-called composing walk, which means traipsing down the glen to see Hazel. Every day!'

'Such devotion is impressive.'

'Yes, if he had no duties! It started when Goldie was ill; it felt right then but it doesn't now. The others see I'm

249

being too lax with him, so they're starting to push their boundaries.'

'Tell Raven it's got to stop.'

'He's talking about going off to become a wandering bard.'

'No!'

'He feels trapped. He wants to marry Hazel but he hasn't got a home to offer her. He can't bring her to my house, because she would just become my housekeeper. Hence this talk about going away. It's desperation.'

'Perhaps he wants to go wandering and this is a useful excuse?'

Brook shook his head. 'I think he genuinely loves Hazel. And he's already been a wanderer, as a small boy, when he worked for that salt pedlar, before he came to live here. I don't think it holds any romance for him.'

'But going off to seek his fortune is no solution! Throwing away the perfectly good fortune he's got here, breaking Hazel's heart as well as his own and leaving you with no teaching assistant!'

'It's the idea of moving out of stuckness that appeals to him. The situation won't change, so he must change. The only way he can see to do that is by going away.'

Brightleaves looked across the fire at Brook's face. He really cares about his pupils, she thought. It's a shame he never had children.

'The solution is obvious,' she said. 'Raven must live in Peak's house.'

'Peak would never agree!'

'Leave it to me.'

The next day, Brightleaves drove to see Peak Smith, parked her chariot in the parking area that Peak had created for delivery carts, and walked up the path to the smithy. Hearing the rhythmic wmph-wmph-wmph-wmph of the bellows and the donk-donk-donk of iron on iron, she waited for a break in the rhythm to tell her that a phase of work was over. At last the metallic donking stopped, although the wmphing went on. She stepped in through the smithy doorway. In doing so, she blocked the light for a moment, so that everyone looked round to see who had come in. Brightleaves moved quickly away from the doorway and went further inside.

The fire glowed in the centre. Beside it knelt one of the Smith boys pumping the goatskin bellows. Next to the fire was the forge, with a metallic work-in-progress lying on top of it. Beside the forge towered the firelit figure of Peak Smith, hammer in hand. Elsewhere in the smithy were boys working by rushlight at various smithcraft mysteries.

'Brightleaves!' said Peak.

He laid the hammer down on the forge and nodded to the bellows boy, who paused in his labours.

'What can I do for you?' Peak asked.

'Could I have a quick word with you, in private?'

'Of course.' Peak turned to one of the boys. 'You carry on with this.' He nodded to the bellows-boy, who started up again, wmph-wmph-wmph-wmph. Another boy took up the hammer and started hitting the metal while Peak, rubbing charcoal dust off his hands with a rag, ushered Brightleaves back to the door. They stepped out into the cool daylight and moved far enough away from the smithy to be able to speak without raising their voices.

'I am sorry to bother you at work,' said Brightleaves, 'but there is something I want to talk to you about, without Hazel or any of the children overhearing.'

'Oh?' said Peak, and waited.

'It's about Hazel,' said Brightleaves. 'Or, rather, it's about Raven.'

Peak made a sort of humphing noise.

'What do you think of Raven?' Brightleaves asked.

'Well.' Peak paused. Brightleaves waited. 'I have to admit,' Peak said eventually, 'he's better than I expected. He was helpful to Hazel while Goldie was ill. And he was kind to Goldie. She thought well of him.'

This was a long speech, for Peak, so Brightleaves was not surprised when he paused again. She waited.

'In fact,' Peak went on, 'she asked me not to stand in his way.'

'Goldie did?'

'Yes.'

'So, what's the problem?'

'His intentions! I thought he wanted to marry Hazel. But he's never asked me. He's never asked her. What's he playing at?'

'I think I can answer that.'

'I hope so. Poor Hazel's getting very confused.'

'Oh dear, young people do get themselves in a muddle, don't they? The reason he hasn't asked Hazel yet is that he doesn't want her to feel torn. You see, once they're married and living in Brook's house, you'll need to get a housekeeper. And Hazel probably feels it's too soon after Goldie's death for you to do that. I think that's why Raven is putting off asking her. It's out of consideration for her feelings, and yours. I'm sure the last thing he wanted to do was confuse her.'

'Living in Brook's house?' echoed Peak, as if that was the only thing he'd heard. 'Why on earth would they want to do that?'

'Well, because normally when a girl marries she leaves her father's house and goes to live with her husband. That usually means with her in-laws, if her husband is young. Brook's the nearest thing Raven has to a father, so Raven and his wife would naturally live in Brook's house.'

'But it's a hovel!'

'Oh, it's had a few home improvements. Nice new curtains, for instance.'

'New curtains!' Peak snorted. 'It's not a proper home, it's just a school with beds in it!'

'Well, where do you suggest?'

He stared at her. 'It's obvious! Hazel stays with me and Raven moves in. Simple!'

'Oh, that's a wonderful idea! But Raven would never dare to suggest it or even think of it. He wouldn't presume.'

Peak nodded, pleased to think that his prospective son-in-law would not presume.

'So are you implying,' said Brightleaves, 'that if Raven proposes to Hazel, you'll allow her to accept on condition they live with you?'

'Yes. She seems to like him. There's no point in making her unhappy. He's decent enough. And Goldie approved of him.'

'Well, I'll mention it to Brook. He's been a bit worried about Raven recently. Thank you, Peak! You've taken a weight off my mind.'

Raven's visit to Hazel that day had not been a success. The children were noisy and difficult. Raven was grumpy and in no mood for story-telling, so Hazel accused him of being unprofessional. She was right. A bard ought to be able to tell a story no matter how he felt. So he'd failed there. And it was her birthday tomorrow. He knew what she wanted. She wanted him to ask her to marry him. But he couldn't, because of not being able to provide a home for her. So he'd failed there too. Instead, he was going to compose a poem or a song for her. Better than nothing. But he had no inspiration at all: everything he thought of, every image and rhyme, seemed dull and flat, every tune trite. Because he didn't want to write a poem or a song to her. He wanted to make love to her, repeatedly, as soon as possible. What was a song compared with that?

He left early, muttering some excuse about Brook needing him, and turning away, not quite soon enough, to avoid seeing the disappointment on Hazel's face. She adjusted her expression, shrugged, laughed; but when she kissed him goodbye, her kiss was not as warm as it might have been. If anything, it was polite.

Raven wanted to curse, swear and stamp about. Instead he plodded away wondering what, in the name of the Black Hag, he was going to do. He had hoped that the energy of the Spring Festival would change something and make his way clear. When he had sounded the horn to announce the Sun God's arrival, he'd felt the future was opening up before him. But now...

Hearing hooves and wheels on the track, he looked over his shoulder. Oh no! It was Lady Brightleaves! He would have to be polite!

She reined in her horses to stop the chariot beside him.

'Hello, Raven!'

'Hello, my lady.'

'Going back to help Brook, are you?'

'Yes,'

'Good! Just between ourselves, I've been rather worried

about Brook.'

'Oh,' said Raven, with a gloomy and despairing young man's total lack of interest in anyone else's emotional state.

'I think he's been finding it very difficult to cope, with you being away every afternoon.'

'Oh.' Raven knew he was supposed to feel guilty about this but couldn't fit in guilt beside everything else he was feeling.

'But of course he wouldn't dream of saying so.'

'No,' said Raven, as some response seemed to be expected.

'It's the others, you see, they're the problem.'

'Others?'

'Marten and Robin and the girls. They see you having every afternoon off, so they think, "Why shouldn't we?" and they become more difficult to control. The little ones, anyway. And you're so good with children.'

'Mm,' said Raven, thinking, *please go away and leave me alone, please go away and leave me alone, please go away and leave me alone.*

'Would you like a lift?'

Raven took a deep breath and summoned a few tattered scraps of manners. 'No thank you. I'm trying to compose a poem, and walking gives me the right rhythm.'

'Ah! Well, I won't interfere with your bardic processes. But would you be very kind and give Brook a message? Tell him he's invited to dinner at our house today. All of you are. The little boys as well.'

'I'll tell him.'

'Thank you!' Brightleaves gave him one of her glorious smiles, which did nothing to cheer him. She gathered up the reins, then paused.

'Don't despair, Raven,' she said, which gave him a shock – had she known what he was feeling all the time? 'I'm sure it will work out. I know it seems difficult at the moment. Waiting to be with the one you love is very hard, I know.'

She clicked her tongue and flicked the reins. The chariot moved away. Raven watched it go with some confusion. Lady Brightleaves had been trying to tell him something. How long had she waited to be with Chief Hardy? A few months, that was all! And she was old! She was twenty-something! It was all very well for her to talk about waiting. He couldn't go on feeling like this for much longer. He would die.

Vetch, riding down the track from Oxhill Farm, saw Brightleaves and Raven talking, then Brightleaves driving away. She rode to the main track and caught up with Raven.

'Hello, Raven!'

He just glared at her.

'What has Lady Brightleaves said to upset you?'

'Mind your own business.'

'Perhaps you should compose a rude song about her.'

Vetch carried on to visit a friend at a farm further along the glen, where she started a rumour that Brightleaves had upset Raven and made him very angry.

* * *

When Brightleaves came home, Dawn darted into the porch to intercept her.

'Grace asked me to tell you, milady, you have a visitor.'

'Oh? Who is it?'

'Lady Dainty,' Dawn whispered.

Dainty was sitting by the fire, holding Traveller beside her on the bench and talking baby-talk to him. She glanced up when Brightleaves came in. Several different expressions passed across her face – fear, annoyance, embarrassment.

Brightleaves stood unfastening her cloak-brooch. Dainty made as if to stand up, but could not let go of Traveller, so let her bottom sink back onto the bench.

Dawn, who had come in behind Brightleaves, took her cloak and hung it up.

'Dainty,' said Brightleaves. '

'I came to tell you I'm sorry,' said Dainty.

Traveller blew a raspberry and chuckled.

'Would you care for some refreshment?' Brightleaves asked as she sat down.

'Oh – yes – thank you,' said Dainty.

'Dawn,' said Brightleaves, 'do you know where Grace keeps the mead?'

'Yes milady.'

'Please bring us some mead from the second flagon to the left.' That was not the best mead, as Dawn knew, although Dainty did not.

'Yes milady.'

'And some oatcakes and goat's cheese?' She looked enquiringly at Dainty.

'That would be nice, thank you.'

Dawn went to get the refreshments.

'I hope you haven't been waiting too long,' said Brightleaves.

'Well, as a matter of fact–' Dainty began.

'I've had business to attend to,' said Brightleaves. 'Problems to solve. I'm sure you understand. You must have had business to attend to, and problems to solve, in

Rushglen.'

'Er, no, not really.'

'No?' said Brightleaves. 'How extraordinary. Didn't anybody have problems in Rushglen?'

'Yes but – it was my mother-in-law who dealt with all that kind of thing.'

'I see.'

'Druid Northway said I had a lot to learn from you!' said Dainty.

'Did he?' Brightleaves tried not to show that this pleased her.

'He said that little girls are very sweet but grown women pretending to be little girls are just nauseating. He said that Traveller had been sent to teach me to be a grown woman. He said you were right to tell me to grow up and that I had a lot to learn from you, and that I should spend as much time with you as you would let me, and that while I'm with you I must never ever talk about myself – and then, when I'm strong enough, I'll be able to deal with my mother-in-law. And he also said that my mother-in-law's attempts to poison me were grounds for divorce, if I wanted that.'

Dawn arrived with the refreshments. While they sipped and nibbled, Brightleaves told Dainty about Brook's problems, Raven's problems, Hazel's problems, and Peak's problems, and what she had done that morning to try to solve them.

* * *

Brook arrived for dinner at Hardy's house to find his girl pupils in their best dresses, sitting by the fire on the carved benches with Brightleaves, Hardy and the warriors, and

Lady Dainty. Brightleaves jumped up to give Brook a kiss of greeting and whispered, 'Peak agrees! He suggested it!'

'Well done!' whispered Brook.

The two little boys came in, closed the door behind them and took their cloaks off.

'Where's Raven?' Brightleaves asked.

'He sends his apologies,' said Brook. 'He's composing a poem for Hazel's birthday, which is tomorrow, and he hasn't finished it yet.'

'That's a shame,' said Brightleaves. 'He'll have to wait to hear his good news.'

They all enjoyed a good dinner anyway, with much talk and laughter, songs and stories. Robin was praised for his progress in history, Marten for his wit and imagination.

Raven, alone at Brook's house, had not composed a poem. He waited until Brook and the boys were out of sight. Then he packed a leather bag with things that he might need: spare clothes, a comb, some bread and cheese wrapped in linen. He made his bed, drew the curtain closed across his bedspace, put a few logs on the fire to keep it going, slung his lyre over his back, put on his cloak, shut the door of Brook's house behind him and strode away over the hills, out of the glen.

END OF BOOK ONE

Book II of THE BRITLINGS is

TRIALS AND TRIUMPHS

About the author

Susan Palmer-Jones was born in Edinburgh and lives in Dumfries & Galloway, whose landscapes and people inspired her to write The Britlings series.